HAWK'S FLIGHT

Books by Helen Hull

THE ASKING PRICE

CANDLE INDOORS

A CIRCLE IN THE WATER

EXPERIMENT

FROST FLOWER

HARDY PERENNIAL

HAWK'S FLIGHT

HEAT LIGHTNING

MAYLING SOONG CHIANG

MORNING SHOWS THE DAY

THROUGH THE HOUSE DOOR

UNCOMMON PEOPLE

LABYRINTH

THE THIRD FAMILY

ISLANDERS

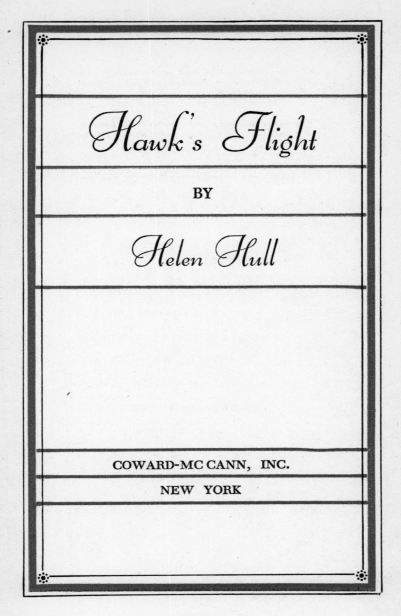

Hawk's Flight

BY

Helen Hull

COWARD-MCCANN, INC.

NEW YORK

For M. L. R.

Whose heart is in the book.

Contents

Contents

Book One

FIRST HOVERING SPIRAL

I'VE BEEN BACK here on the Ridge in the small house Gilbert and I built a quarter of a century ago for almost a month now. A complete rest, the doctors said. No work, no social life, nothing but rest. You've driven yourself too hard for years, you've worn out parts of your excellent machine, and now you've had a bad shock. Time will do wonders for you, if you give it a chance.

Time? Time is an old man playing on an accordion, all shiny metal and strips of polished wood. He draws it out, out, the fluted leather stretching, and not a note comes out for my strained ears to catch. It will stay thus for all eternity, time stretched to emptiness, taut, not a note for my human ear to capture, blank, dreadful. Then suddenly, in the thin ashy hours before dawn, those bony, swollen knuckled hands fly, the folds in the leather deepen, the accordion sways, contracts, in a shrill, jarring cacophony of noise without meaning.

In past days I should have taken to movement to escape myself and Time, driving swiftly along unfamiliar roads with mountains, lakes, flat disks of prairies wheeling past, or lying at night with the vibration of engines louder than my own heart, the sound of deep water thrust aside by the ship's bow louder than blood in my ears, and change of scene might have seemed change of self, movement through space might have

3

seemed a movement away from myself. But today only the young and strong take ship or plane, the old and useless move only as harried fugitives, seeking shelter and safety.

I suppose I am a fugitive, stumbling in the darkness to elude pain and loss and bitter suffering. This house is the kind of shelter all those harried refugees would seize with gratitude, quiet, unmolested, keeping out storms and summer sun. And I am numb to the marrow of my bones. If I could die before I wake! But I won't. "There's nothing the matter with you," the doctors said. "Give yourself a little time."

I've tried to read, all the books I've been too busy to read for years, and the words on the pages have no meaning. They might be in some language I have never learned. Something has broken the shadow which a word should cast, the page is nothing but ridiculous small black marks.

Last night when twilight had deepened until I thought no one else would be likely to be abroad, or if someone happened to be late in his home-going he could not see me clearly enough for recognition, for greeting, I set out for a walk over the Ridge, venturing into driveways, seeing lighted windows and seeing where dark, unlighted houses blacked out the stars. I felt my mind begin to move sluggishly, picking out of the past random images of people Gilbert and I had known, men and women who had lived in these houses, friends, neighbors, in the old days.

We knew them fairly well. In some ways the Ridge had no more privacy than any small New England village, for all the greater diversity of the members of the community. Temperament, personal idiosyncrasies, the behavior of each of them under pressure of some crisis whether personal or world-wide, such things were general knowledge. Women from the neighboring village came out to work by the day, moving from one kitchen to another, letting fall casual bits of gossiping appraisal, terse and simple comment. Mrs. Willetts was the kind who'd get down on her knees to see if you'd scrubbed behind the bath-tub, and when she bought chops for luncheon, the paper-thin one was thumb-marked for the cleaning woman. The Ridge residents exchanged similar tittle-tattle, a little more subtly, perhaps. No use asking Lawrence to serve on that committee for the library fund or for the Community Center, he's too anti-social, too lazy. Or, I see John Burchall's taking his Sunday exercise chopping down trees in that piece of woods he bought. He'll cut down half a dozen, and then let them lie there until someone else clears up the brush.

I never thought before that they must all have had some such succinct summary of me! And of Gilbert, too. Why, it's appalling! Like boiling each of us down in a laboratory retort, until nothing is left but a single drop, with a single flavor to which a label can be put. All of the struggle, the intricate texture of daily life, the secret guilt, the secret hope, the shifting light and darkness of love, of ambition, the inner weakness and despair, the reaching out for strength, the moment of failure, the moment of high triumph, all of these reduced to a figure as simple as a child's line drawing which he calls a man! When I am so unsure as to what I myself add up to, when I have these tremors of doubt about my understanding of Gilbert, how can I believe that whatever through the years these neighbors have boiled me down to can be the truth about me? And yet as I walked in the night looking at the yellow rectangle of a lighted window, or at the slope of a roof over a dark and empty house, as I set myself to remember who lived there or who had gone away, random visual images slid across my mind, unimportant moments— why these rather than some others should exist in my memory I can not see—a woman knitting in a corner of a room, a man bending in sunlight over yellow soil, an old woman with her scalp pink through thin white hair, a boy in blue jersey, school-books in a strap, stoning a squirrel in a hemlock, running when he sees me standing in the lane, and for each of them this simple, total impression, like a single thin note struck on a tuning fork.

Most of us make sturdy efforts to conceal ourselves from public view. We resort to artifice and deceit, we build up a figure for inspection, call it a mask, a social front, a persona, whatever you like. For the most part we are sure we have succeeded, we think the face we carry abroad is more impressive, more enviable, more praise-worthy than the self which hides behind it. Why, we begin in childhood to construct our mask! Perhaps our very consciousness of self begins with the notion we can fool the world. It is disconcerting and ironic to consider that all our efforts have been no more than so much cellophane! Which is real, the self we spend our lives trying to create and trying at the same time to disguise and hide, or the kernel, the line sketch, the single note on a tuning fork which stands for each of us? Would I even recognize myself if I could catch this simple impression which stands for me to any of these people who have known me, thought they knew me? Would I ruefully admit, there's the gist of me? Would I resent the image as a crude caricature?

Luckily for me, I can't see this image. I don't have to reckon with it. It might disturb this numbness which dulls my senses and slows down my heart-beat. Shades drawn, doors fast shut, sh! do not wake the sleeper, for he wakes only to pain!

I shall think instead of these other men and women I have known. Perhaps if I should reconstruct their lives, filling out the whole picture, I should discover how far this imprint left by each of them, this single note had any truth. This would be a journey of a sort, a way of escape, postponing the day when I must come home, must wake, must look at my own past and future. I can even think of Gilbert in connection with these others, remembering his occasional tolerant comment on some neighborhood affair, the friendly impersonality with which he treated everyone. He held people at a distance, so much so that I was sometimes embarrassed, for all I knew he retreated behind that manner as a defense. He didn't want his neighbors for patients, nor did he wish to spend his brief hours of the weekend going right on practicing psychiatry. People have a compulsion to turn up a symptom or two the moment they know the man next to them at a tea or the partner at bridge is a doctor. A free sample, something for nothing, and a chance to talk about one's self at the same time! So Gilbert built up a reputation for shyness, for taciturnity, until. . . . But I will not think of Gilbert except as he turns up in the stories of these other people, perhaps with a phrase which lights a corner dark to my less perceptive eyes. Gilbert knew much more about his neighbors than they guessed, much more than he ever told me. Why, I found out only accidentally that Ellen Hunter had gone into his city office to consult him about her husband, and if she had gone earlier, Gilbert might have prevented that tragedy!

I might begin with the story of Ellen and Lawrence Hunter. Since that goes back to the early days of my acquaintance with the Ridge, perhaps I should begin with the place itself. Ellen's father, Dr. Randall, was connected with the hospital where Gilbert had put in his years as interne, and had always been friendly. I think Mrs. Randall planned to nab Gilbert as a match for Ellen; she didn't know I was just marking time in Michigan until Gilbert was through with all his training and we could marry. Dr. Randall had talked about his farm in Connecticut, and had said that one day we must spend a weekend there.

But with Gilbert's study abroad and then the concentrated

grind of getting started in New York after I came east to marry Gilbert, to say nothing of my own work, we hadn't had weekends for play. Weekend and week-beginning were all of a piece, and the piece was hard work. Gilbert was teaching a course in evening school, he was working long hours in a clinic at a city hospital for experience, he was earning not much more than a thousand a year. On that we managed to live and to pay my tuition for classes at the University. Gilbert helped me with the family washing on Sunday, and I learned how to bake pies and bread with a text-book on bacteriology or chemistry propped beside the cook-book. Gilbert was as eager as I was that both of us should get ahead, and as I hadn't liked teaching (that was what I had done while I waited for Gilbert to finish his training) I was to work for a degree and then get into some kind of research. We had talked it all over in the days when we were falling in love—Gilbert was already in his last year as medical student and I was just a freshman at the State University—and had agreed we would make our marriage a real partnership and not the end-all, be-all trap of flesh and instinct in which my mother, and Gilbert's, too, had been imprisoned and tortured to death.

Queer how I can look back at that young pair, Carey and Gilbert Moore, thirty years ago, as if they were distinct identities, no connection existing with this tired, ageing woman who writes down words about them, much less connection than children (whom I never had) might have had. And yet they are clear to the very rhythm of the sanguine expectation, the energy, the dauntless elation which quickened their warm blood. The world was theirs for the taking; nothing was impossible. All they had to do was to work and plan and drive ahead. They are like flies imbedded in the amber of time, perfect, unaltered. I had forgotten how they felt, how they planned, until I turned back to those early days of the Ridge. But they

are so separate from me that I can write of them as easily as I
write of the other residents, with no disturbance of the present.

Gilbert had said that when I came to New York I must meet
Ellen Randall. "You girls ought to be good friends. She's
another smart one. She can show you the ropes." He had sent
me clippings about her wedding, half a column and a photograph of Ellen all white satin and veil in the Sunday rotogra-
vure section. The bride, Ellen Randall, only daughter of Mrs.
George Fletcher Randall and Dr. George Randall, is a graduate
of the Brearley School and Radcliffe College. She has been
connected with the Haxton Advertising Agency. The groom,
Mr. Lawrence Hunter, is a graduate of Harvard, a member
of . . . a long list of clubs. He is a member of the brokerage
firm Puller, Welseet and Puller. I thought well, she didn't
catch my Gilbert! I was curious about her because Gilbert had
liked her and because she was going on with her advertising
work in spite of her elaborate wedding. Gilbert said probably
the wedding was Ellen's mother's idea. "She's one of those
ritzy old dames." But after I met Ellen I was sure she'd
planned it herself.

For I did meet Ellen earlier than the weekend on the Ridge,
although we failed to establish the friendship Gilbert had
planned. Ellen never really saw me until years later. At our
first meeting I was a provincial little middle-westerner, over-
eager about everything in my new life, badly dressed, a gauche
nobody with whom Gilbert had unfortunately become involved
in his youth and from whom he had not broken. Ellen took me
to a luncheon of a business women's club, she was hard and
sleek and smart, not a bit pretty but interesting looking, she
talked about lay-outs and selling points and gripping the public,
and she brushed me off very fast once luncheon was over. I
didn't admit to Gilbert than Ellen had—well, call it a diminishing effect upon me. Like most folks, I prefer people who have

an expanding effect. I was afraid Gilbert would think me silly, for even then he had a detachment from casual encounters. He was more observer than participator. Perhaps his hard youth, the way he'd lifted himself by his own boot-straps out of poverty and lack of opportunity, had developed a thick insulating surface within which his urgent ambition, his clear intention would drive ahead, unhindered.

When Ellen's mother died, I wrote her a proper note. And when, in early summer twenty-five years ago, Gilbert suggested that we take a holiday of a week (he could get away from the clinic, the University was being swept out for the summer session, Dr. Randall had written that Ellen was at the Ridge, that young guests would do them all good) I couldn't very well say, "Ellen makes me feel like a backward child." I did ask how Ellen could get away from her advertising agency, and Gilbert said, "Hadn't I told you? She's going to have a baby."

So we took a dusty local New Haven train for the Ridge, and in the week we spent there we met the people who were to become our friends and neighbors during all the active, out-going years when life makes its ultimate shape.

Dr. Randall met us at the station. He was bare-headed, his high forehead sunburned, and he wore a baggy gray sweater and golf trousers that drooped around his spindly shanks. I wasn't sure it was Dr. Randall at first, until he spoke to Gilbert, he looked so unlike the city doctor I had met. Not just his clothes; he'd lost the tense, concentrated manner of town, his face and manner had a kind of vagueness, as if something had come untied. He was glad to see us, his car was right around here, behind the station. I remember the way I braced my feet against our wicker suit-case on the rear seat of the Maxwell touring car, as we bumped along a dirt road at what seemed alarming speed. Gilbert's ears were bright red, and the back of his neck, along the clean-shaven edge of his fresh hair-cut, was red, too; he was concentrating on the way Dr. Randall managed the car, and I knew he was thinking one of these days we'll have one! I noticed that the collar of his blue serge suit was shiny, and thought, oh, dear, we haven't any real country clothes, we haven't anything except these clothes we have on! Dr. Randall was shouting that they talked of tarring the road, that would mean lots of autos, fortunately the Ridge was off on a side road, and the Ridge road itself was so steep tar would just flow right down it! Part way up the narrow Ridge road we stopped to let the motor cool, and Dr. Randall told us to look back at the view. We had climbed enough to make the country a lovely relief map, the shape of the blue water in the reservoirs clear within the massed green of the wooded shores, the contours of fields faintly swelling, lines of gray stone walls running over low hills, and in the distance, blue-green, then dust-blue, more hills. "Not much like Michigan, is it, Carey?" Gilbert said.

"We'd better get on," said Dr. Randall, "or Ellen will think I'm in a ditch. Somewhere along here my land begins. I ought to have a marker." He hit a boulder just then, and I bounced against a cross-piece that held up the top, hard enough so that I forgot to be frightened as he ground on around sharp curves and up slopes that seemed perpendicular.

"You ought to see this road in the spring," shouted Dr. Randall. "April with frost coming out of the ground. Took two horses to haul me out of that ditch at the bend there." Then without warning he turned in between white gates and stopped, brakes squealing, so abruptly that I just saved myself another bump. "Here we are."

A low stone wall with a small gate and stones laid for a walk across a green lawn to a low, sprawling white house. "The house is the original farm-house," Dr. Randall said as he walked toward it with us. "The wing at the right we added, but you see it duplicates the left wing, the ell they called it." At that time I

just thought that the house didn't look very elaborate and wondered why Dr. Randall spoke with such pride of its age. My
architectural taste had been trained in a small town in southern
Michigan, where a large new house was proof of solid success,
and lifting the mortgage or shingling the roof was my notion
of improvement for a small house.

Of course I know now that the Randall house is an excellent
example of the best early domestic architecture in this country,
vernacular style John Burchall called it. The ease and gracious-
ness of its proportions, the strength in its foundations, its corners, its lintels, the beautiful simplicity of its lines and its
arrangement all grew from the intention of the builders, their
devotion to the purpose for which they built. In a way such
houses are the physical form of the ideal of early American life,
a place for love, birth, growth, shelter, warmth, and at the
last, death for a man, a woman, and their children: they stand
often like this one of the Randalls on a hill-top, the windows
looking down on fields, pastures, tilled land and wooded acres,
from which the man and presently his sons extracted their iso-
lated, self-sufficient living. I wonder whether those women were
happier than the women of my generation, the women whose
lives on the Ridge I am trying to record here? One thing I
have noticed: the men and women who have set out during
these recent war-darkened years to practice a return to the
simple life of their grand-parents have made their living and
their pleasure not by raising sheep or potatoes, but by writing
books about their adventures, books which satisfied the nostalgic
day-dreams of the readers.

But I had none of these thoughts that first morning on the
Ridge.

"I'm glad you came out," Dr. Randall said, as we reached
the entrance. "Ellen finds it pretty dull. First time in her life

she's had to sit around and wait for something she can't hurry along."

"What's that Ellen can't hurry?" Ellen's quick, imperative voice sounded from the dim hallway, and Dr. Randall pushed open the screen door.

"Nature, my dear Nell," he said.

"You and your nature!" said Ellen. "Hello, Carey." Her hand was nervous and cold. "Has Father told you yet you're just a biologic specimen? Well, he will. Hello, Gilbert. I didn't really think you'd come! How many years since we first invited you? However do you think New York can get along for a week without Dr. Moore?"

Gilbert's non-committal smile lifted the corners of his wide mouth and he set down the suit-case to shake Ellen's hand. "How are you, Ellen? How's the Haxton Agency making out without you?"

"You can see how I am!" Ellen had stepped back into the living room and offered herself a little flauntingly for our inspection. I couldn't help staring at her, she looked so changed. No dark maternity dress with soft concealing folds for Ellen. She wore a red and white checked gingham, the belt tied in a bow under her full breasts, the skirt garishly snug over the distended belly, tipping up too far in front, disclosing her thin legs. Her fair hair looked colorless, like dry leaves, and she had dragged it back smoothly over her head and twisted it into a tight knot at the base, leaving her face exposed; her fine hazel eyes seemed to protrude between darkened lids, and her cheekbones and chin were too prominent under skin almost the color of her dry-leaf hair. She's like a caricature, I thought, and she's enjoying it! She cradled her arms over her body and laughed. "Jenny will take your bags upstairs, luncheon is ready, and if we don't sit down before the soufflé falls, the cook will murder us. Lawrence doesn't get out till late afternoon."

A maid had picked up the wicker suit-case.

"Is that all the luggage?" Ellen was urgent, pushing us to activity.

"That's all," said Gilbert, mildly. "Isn't it enough? I can carry it."

But the maid was leading the way up the stairs and I followed, thinking, I won't be silly and wish we hadn't come. How many suit-cases should we have, anyway? Ellen's nervous, I mean to try to like her, after all, they invited us, didn't they? The maid ushered us into our room, offered to open the suit-case, looked into the bathroom, thought everything was there, and left us. We peeked around. Twin beds, with pale green taffeta covers and green puffs in satin triangles, water lily pads and blossoms in the green panelled walls, sheer green net at the windows. Gilbert said, "What do we do with *two* beds?" and I giggled and hugged him before I ran to wash my hands. "We won't use but one," called Gilbert. We didn't, either, and Gilbert made fun of me because I rumpled up the other bed every morning before we went down for breakfast. "Why do you care what the hired girl knows?" he asked. "What do you bet her pa and ma sleep in just one bed?" But I couldn't help wanting her to think we knew how people did things.

Ellen didn't talk much during luncheon. Dr. Randall talked about the Ridge. The original farm had been two hundred acres, and then he'd bought up adjoining property for protection. He'd sold a piece of that to friends of Ellen's, Adelaide and John Burchall. Burchall was an architect, Adelaide had been Ellen's closest college friend, they had two children, boys. They'd camped out during the summer in a small building they meant to turn into a garage later, and now they were drilling a well, the first step toward their real place. We'd walk over after lunch and see how they were coming. Then we might call on the Willetts. I began to feel confused. How many families were there scattered around these Ridge acres? Now when I know them all so well it is strange to remember the bewilderment I felt that first week, and the difficulty (which really lasted until we had become part of the community) in sorting out husbands and wives in the correct combinations and with the correct backgrounds. Genevieve and Dexter Willetts, said Dr. Randall. Dexter's father had been the noted Dr. Payson Willetts, the surgeon, a friend of Dr. Randall's.

"Had a mind like one of his knives, too. He wanted Dexter to follow in his track and the boy would have none of it. He was delicate as a child. His mother took him off to Arizona or New Mexico. She always acted scared to death of the doctor. Poor Payson! He just wanted someone to stand up to him! Most of those thick-necked, sanguine men do. But Marcella Willetts just quaked and ran away and finally died, and Dexter, who adored her, blamed his father. I don't know how he got into teaching, I lost track of him for some years. Dr. Payson came out here with us occasionally. He liked Mrs. Randall, my wife."

"Mother was a match for him," Ellen said, reflectively, and for a moment the atmosphere changed, and I half expected the capable, energetic Mrs. Randall to come bustling into the pleasant dining room which she had planned and wonder who on earth these guests were at her table. Then Dr. Randall went on with his account of Dexter Willetts.

"He seems to be doing well. Instructorship at Columbia in economics. You haven't run into him there, Carey?" No, that wasn't my field. "He went to England for a year at Oxford and came back with this English wife. Australian, actually. He ran into her at the English Speaking Union."

"But veddy, veddy English!" said Ellen. "Old enough to be his mother, too."

"Not quite, Nell. Some ten years or so. She hasn't been very well since the birth of their second child. They live out here.

Dexter's father bought about twenty acres, the prize site next to this one, and what a horse deal that was, too, the old . . ." Dr. Randall laughed. "It's the other side of the Ridge, not the way we came up. He gave it to Dexter for a wedding gift. We'll stroll over to see their house."

"A little bit of England," said Ellen. "Actually, in some lights, it might be Sussex wold."

"Your English accent is not too good," said Dr. Randall.

"How do they really talk in Melbourne? Not like Genevieve, I'll bet."

The maid had set the dessert plates in front of each of us, crystal finger bowls with nasturtium leaves floating on the water, a cobweb of lace under the bowl on the delicate gold-banded plate. I tried to catch Gilbert's eye to show him how to set bowl, doily, and silver to one side, but he was looking speculatively at Ellen.

"Genevieve's accent couldn't be thicker if she was the Queen of England," Ellen was saying, as she served herself with strawberry shortcake. "After all, if this country's good enough to live in . . ."

"These berries are from my vines," said Dr. Randall. "Everbearing. It's been good weather for them."

"All right," said Ellen. "I'll drop Genevieve. But I'm glad I can't walk that far with you. She won't approve of you, either, Carey. 'Do you find it nec'sry to work, now that you are married? In England, except of course in the lower classes. . . .' "

"She'll be glad to hear you have retired. Take more berries, Carey."

"Tell her I'm going back in August, the minute Lawrence Junior is one month old."

"Says you," said Dr. Randall. I don't remember the rest of the conversation, because Gilbert was lifting a wedge of short-

cake, and Ellen exclaimed, "Unless you like to eat Alençon!"
The maid whisked the doily out of the way, and Gilbert just
said, "Thank you," without blinking. Later, when I told Gilbert I shouldn't have cared if it hadn't been for the malicious
expression on Ellen's face, he grinned at me and said, "Their
tribal customs differ from ours, that's all. Why should you
care?"

Queer how those trivial, forgotten details float up to the
surface. Of course this was the first time Gilbert and I had ever
been guests in the household of an outsider. Outside the family,
I mean. Visiting relatives is different. You're sure of yourself
then; your ways are as good as theirs, and usually bear the same
hall-mark. Visiting the Randall house was as much an experience
as my first trip abroad. Ellen Hunter, her father, the whole
pattern of living left by Mrs. Randall, had a quality of sophistication which I admired and meant to acquire. Gilbert was
indifferent, untouched. He was on the track of a real sophistication, in the root-sense of the word, a wisdom about men and
women. Perhaps women are more exposed to superficialities.
I don't know. But at that time Ellen Hunter seemed to me to
have just about everything: background, by which I meant not
just money and its evidence, but a family with character and
accomplishment; a start at her own career; poise, sureness,
brilliance, and a smooth husband who was doing very well on
Wall Street, to say nothing of a baby on the way.

Well, Gilbert and I were on the up-grade, too. By the end of
the summer I'd have a master's degree and could look for a
position; and nothing could stop Gilbert short of the very top
of his profession. Someday we'd have a home of our own, and
children. Finger bowls. Gilbert might object to finger bowls.

Lawrence Hunter, Ellen's husband, appeared earlier than
schedule, while we were having coffee. He'd had to collect a

power-of-attorney in the Bronx, he explained, as he bent to kiss Ellen, and he'd caught an earlier train.

"I wish you wouldn't let them make an errand boy out of you," said Ellen. "I suppose you want some lunch now."

"Had it at the station." Lawrence accepted a cup of coffee and stood, drinking it.

"If you'd told me you were coming out early, we could have waited luncheon for you." Ellen sounded irritated, but Lawrence smiled comfortably at her.

"I'll go back and come on the other train, if you like," he said, and Ellen laughed. Then he turned to ask me how I liked the place. "Nice view, isn't it?"

I had met Lawrence several times in town and never found anything to say to him. He was like the fraternity boys I'd seen on the campus back in Michigan. That weekend on the Ridge he was very pleasant, although there was always between us that non-conducting gap, a sheet of thin lead through which nothing personal ever passed. Gilbert got to know him better than I did. I just didn't interest him and he didn't interest me, except as Ellen's husband. Like Ellen, he had a head start in life. The Puller of Puller, Welseet and Puller was an uncle (the other was a grandfather) and Lawrence would just move up in the firm the way he'd moved from bassinet to Groton.

He was sanguine, smooth-tempered, slow-moving, and even then, before he was thirty, inclined toward plumpness. I remember when he came downstairs for our walk, having changed from his business suit into tweed coat and cashmere pull-over, how much soft flesh he seemed to wear over his bones! He wasn't handsome. His sandy hair had receded a little at the temples, so that his smooth, high forehead and well-set blue eyes had an engaging candor, like a young boy's, and his mouth lost its immaturity when he smiled, which was often. Ellen was lying in a long chair on the terrace, and Lawrence went back after we had started, thinking he heard her call. The sound of their voices came without words as we stood waiting, and I thought what a well-matched counterpoint it was, Ellen's quick, rather dry speech, and Lawrence's low, comfortable drawl.

When Lawrence joined us, we struck off along a wood path, Dr. Randall and Gilbert walking briskly ahead. Dr. Randall had a flexible, springy gait; except for his crest of white hair he looked, with his erect, slender back, as young as Gilbert. I wanted to hear their talk, something about a recent monograph by an Austrian psychiatrist, but Lawrence had no desire to walk at their pace, and he was playing attentive host, offering me unnecessary aid over roots and boulders, asking me polite questions, how long had I been East, did I like it, did I like the country, did I ride, was there hunting in Michigan, had I ever hunted in Carolina? I couldn't think of much to reply except yes and no, and after awhile he dropped his questionnaire. He was glad we could come out, he didn't want Ellen getting bored. "She's a wonderful girl," he said. "Got pep enough for a dozen girls. Believe me, I'll be glad when this is over. I knew she'd be bored out here, but her father insists."

There was something bewildered and likeable in his voice as he spoke of Ellen, and I thought, he's crazy about Ellen, perhaps that's what she sees in him, but my goodness, I'd be bored with him! I was glad when I saw Gilbert and Dr. Randall waiting for us where the woods ended and the path led through a gap in a stone wall into a pasture.

"This is another of my favorite sites," said Dr. Randall. "You get a glimpse of water and the hills. The road is under the brow of that second hill. There's an old foundation somewhere here."

The grass was reedy and sweet under our feet, birds flew up from the tangle of wild grape vine and brush, and a cloud shadow drifted in slow violet blue down over the slope of the hill. Lawrence moved ahead to walk with his father-in-law, and Gilbert and I stood for a moment.

"Nice, isn't it?" asked Gilbert.

Dr. Randall called back, "Here's that old foundation, you can see the cellar hole beyond that old apple tree."

We waited for him and Lawrence to move on.

"I like this better than woods." Gilbert stood with his feet far apart, his dark head at an angle, little squint-wrinkles between his heavy brows, at the corners of his eyes, and suddenly I was relaxed, free of the ineptness and constraint I had been feeling, sensible of sunlight and blue distance and the easeful contours of the land, hearing the faint different notes of the summer wind bending the grass heads, running through the leaves.

"That's because you grew up on a farm and not in a wood lot," I said.

"Don't you like it better?"

"I like anything better with you."

Gilbert gave a little, "Um-hm," which meant he was thinking hard about something else, and we went on, hand in hand, stopping at the gnarled, sprawling apple tree to look at the cellar hole. It wasn't a hole, it was only a small green hollow. "They picked the best location all right," said Gilbert. "They could see the Indians coming in plenty of time to hide." He looked back several times as we walked down the slope of the pasture, and said, "It would be fine to own a piece of land like that."

"Someday we will," I said, and Gilbert's firm, cool hand gave mine an affirming pressure before he let go, as we came near the others.

It was part of our plan, an unquestioned symbol of achievement, to own a small bit of the earth with a house on it. Your own roof over you, my mother had phrased it. I can still hear the sound of her weeping in the night because again some business venture of my father's had failed, there was no money for taxes or payments and once again her brief illusion of ownership, of security, had been destroyed. I have thought that my mother must rest well in her grave, knowing at last that she had her own roof over her.

And when Gilbert's father died, his mother had given the farm to the elder son who had stayed home to help his father, instead of setting out to make his own hard and different way, as Gilbert had done. Gilbert said he supposed his brother Tom had earned the farm, but I think they might have done something to show they were proud of Gilbert, instead of resenting his success. Gilbert never told me when he sent Tom money, because he knew how I felt about his family. He used to say that if he hadn't had to stop to earn money, so that he was slow in finishing his education, he wouldn't have met me. "You would have found some other girl, then," I would say, just to hear again his reflective, "I don't think so, Carey. I think I should have just gone on looking for you." Well, we had met, and this ownership of house and land at some future day was one sign of the security we planned for our life together. As if Dr. Randall had heard our thoughts, he called out, "Got your house all planned?"

"Not yet," said Gilbert.

"I tried to persuade the Burchalls to build up there. You remember who they are? The young architect and Adelaide, who was Ellen's friend, we're on our way to inspect their well. Adelaide preferred this location down the road. She doesn't care for far vistas."

"Adelaide's near-sighted," said Lawrence. "She's as near-sighted as a hen."

"She's a nice, practical young woman," said Dr. Randall. "Perhaps if you don't care for long views, you have more energy

for what's under foot. Look, they must have struck water
enough, the well drillers are pulling out."

Near the road was a small white building, the garage they've
been living in, I thought. Beyond that a clumsy red truck,
the long folded back arm of the drill rocking, chugged away
from an area of mud and shining gravel, workmen threw tools
into the body of the truck, and two small boys skidded on the
piles of mud, shrieking. Adelaide Burchall saw us and came
running to meet us, her brown checked dress snug around her
plump body, her curly brown hair flying, her cheeks so flushed
that the little freckles across the bridge of her nose, under her
round brown eyes were golden.

"Oh, Dr. Ranny!" she cried. "I'm so glad you've come!
We've got the most wonderful well! Come see it!"

"It smokes! The water smokes!" shouted one of the boys,
and the other yelled, "Water can't smoke! You're crazy."

Dr. Randall introduced us, but Adelaide was too excited to
do more than say hello and drag us all toward the round tile
which stuck up in the middle of the mud-pile. John Burchall,
her husband, must have been busy with the drillers; he didn't
appear until the truck had rumbled across the grass to the
road. Meantime we had each looked down the well, holding a
flash-light. There was something exciting about the crystal-
flashing movement of water in the narrow black hollow of the
tile.

"It's just like the Bible," Adelaide said, and her voice was
like a brook over small stones. "Believe on him, and out of his
belly shall come a river of living water."

The younger boy shook her arm. "That isn't his belly,
Mamma! That's a layer of gravel—"

"It's living water, Dick!"

"It ought to be!" John Burchall pelted across the mud,
yanked the other boy up from his knees. "Wipe that muck off

your pants!" John was a slight little fellow, with everything about him in motion; he hitched up his overalls, his thinnish neutral hair stood up on his narrow head, his eyes behind the horn-rimmed spectacles were agitated, his voice had a truculent over-emphasis, he could scarcely pause for Dr. Randall's introduction of Gilbert and me.

"John's just paid the bill," said Dr. Randall, amused. "That's why it better be living water."

"I told them this morning if they didn't strike water within another five feet, they could just pull up their hole and cart it off, I wouldn't pay one damned cent for it."

"They couldn't pull up a hole, Daddy," shrilled the younger boy, and Adelaide said, cheerily, "I knew they'd hit water today, I had a feeling."

"If I hadn't insisted on their testing it, they'd have gone straight through to China! They're used to dealing with amateurs. Why should they stop? The deeper they go, the higher the price per foot."

"It was simply marvellous!" Adelaide's round brown eyes were soft with pride. "John rigged this device to measure the flow every night while the men were gone, a sinker on a line, and he watched every bucket-full they dumped, and this morning he said, 'that is a new . . .' what was it you called it, John?"

"A new stratum."

" 'That means water,' he said, and sure enough, it did!"

John's eyebrows, above the rim of his glasses, said, "You see?" Then, being thus established, he could spare a moment of attention for his callers. He was sorry he didn't have the blueprints of the house to show us; he'd left them at the office, his secretary was working out the specifications.

"You can show them the location," said Adelaide, and John paced off the foundation walls, trampled grass between painted stakes marking them.

"Modified Colonial," he said. "We'll use the rocks from that wall around the field for the cellar. Here." He whipped out a pad and knelt to sketch on one knee the floor-plan.

"Show where my room is," demanded each boy.

"This is the ground floor," said John, and Adelaide looked over his shoulder, murmuring, "All those southern windows for the sun to come in all day long and a huge stone fireplace at the end."

"A house should be indigenous," said John. "I told Dexter he couldn't graft an Elizabethan cottage onto this landscape. Have you see the Willetts' house?" he demanded of me.

"We're strolling on that way presently," said Lawrence.

"Well, they like it," said Adelaide, brightly. "After all, people have to have what they like."

"What about standards?" roared John.

"Of course we have to educate people." Adelaide moved away from John and ran to one corner of the trampled plot. "See, the kitchen is here."

John tore the sheet from his pad and handed it to Gilbert. "That's the idea, roughly. Driveway sweeping around here, our camp turned back to garage and tool house. Come see the camp. It's rather ingenious, the way it solves all the problems of living in one four-walled space."

"Oh, yes," said Adelaide, "and I'll make you a simple tea."

"Sorry," said Lawrence, who was edging with slow determination toward the road. "We ought to get along. Ellen's alone there, after she has her nap—"

Adelaide sent her best to Ellen; she'd be over to see her in a day or two, she was so glad Ellen had finally seen the light and given up her work.

As we walked away, John was shouting at one of the boys to put that marking stake right back exactly where he'd found it.

"He's really a good architect," said Dr. Randall.

"Adelaide thinks so," said Lawrence. "Or else she puts on a good act."

"It's no act," said Dr. Randall. "Adelaide is an honest little person."

"I can't believe any woman who's been married to a man for six or seven years could think him as perfect as Adelaide lets on she thinks her John."

"She's something of an anachronism nowadays," said Dr. Randall. "A contented woman."

Lawrence had mounted up a handful of gravel and topped it with a stone. He stood off, swinging a stick he had picked up, and for a moment he looked at his father-in-law, frowning. "Too smug for me," he said. Then he knocked the stone down the road and caught up with Gilbert. I heard him begin another questionnaire, did Gilbert care for golf?

"She has an interesting background," said Dr. Randall, as we strolled down the dusty road. "Has Ellen told you about her?"

"Only that they were at Radcliffe together."

"Ellen backed her up then. One reason Adelaide values what she has so highly is that she had to make a fight for it."

I don't recall now just how much Dr. Randall told me on that walk and how much I came to know later. Adelaide's mother and father had been missionaries in China, where Adelaide and a brother were born. The father had been killed in the Boxer rebellion, the mother had lived in caves and escaped on sampans, or something equally wild and hazardous. The missionary society of the church had furnished the funds to educate the children, and Mrs. Crowly, Adelaide's mother, had gone around the country lecturing on China. Adelaide was intended as a missionary, in return for her education, and she had put on her own rebellion against that fate. Her mother, the missionary society, and the brother all lined up to push her straight off to Shanghai. They were especially furious because Adelaide held back her outright refusal until her tuition for the final year at college had been paid.

The family and the church had cast her off, and the Randalls had taken her in the summer after graduation. She and Ellen had a fine time looking for jobs, planning to conquer the world. Ellen had enjoyed the fight, her idea was that Adelaide now would prove in some spectacular way that she was too gifted, too brilliant for the career her mother and the Board had planned for her. Then at the end of the summer Adelaide just walked off and married John Burchall, at that time a drafting clerk in an architect's office. They lived on his invisible salary in some kind of tenement.

"Adelaide makes a virtue of necessity," said Dr. Randall. "She tackled laundry and bread with as much enthusiasm as she'd tackled calculus and philosophy. Ellen was furious at first, but Adelaide brought her around. They're really friends, those two. And John has come along well. He got a little money from his father, that's when they bought the land out here."

I must have made some comment about how romantic it seemed to be born in China, as I remember Dr. Randall's quiet, "Place doesn't make much difference to a baby, does it? All he needs is a mother. What looks romantic to us may have been only insecurity, instability, to a child. Frightening. Adelaide still has nightmares about it. You and Ellen are out for something your mothers didn't have. Well, so is Adelaide. Things move in cycles."

I protested, floundering among phrases which seemed to me passwords to a new existence for women. This wasn't just a cycle, this waking up of women. Economic independence, parasitism, suffrage, individuality, all those labels of the period, I tried to make them impressive. Dr. Randall patted my arm.

"You're like Ellen," he said. "She wears women like a chip on her shoulder, too. I tell her to go ahead and make the world over, it needs it, and then see what her own children will do. At least she's going to let me have a grand-child." Then he tipped back his head, his profile sharp against the blue June sky, cross-hatching of fine lines in the hollow of his cheek, the cords of his neck distinct and a gray shadow under his chin.

"Listen," he said. "That's a tanager. Do you have them in Michigan? Ah, you should see the fellow. See if I can spot him for you." .

I felt the confused protest of youth against age, the argument dropped, the weighty matter tossed overboard, drowned in bland indifference. He didn't find the tanager, but we had come to a gravel road winding up at a sharp angle through the tree.

"Here's the Willetts' hill," said Dr. Randall. "I hear Dexter. They're home. Dexter's the economics prof," he added, his eyes kind. Like taking a child's hand to lead him among strangers. "His wife's the Australian. It's funny, Genevieve's mother was homesick all her life for England, down there under, as they say, in the Bush. After her death, Genevieve got to England, and instead of marrying a nice county gentleman, the picture her mother had drawn for her, she comes over here with Dexter. Of course America and Australia both begin with an A, but otherwise they aren't so much alike as Genevieve sometimes insists."

The voices above us grew louder, and I heard a flurry of barks. We came, around a curve, out of the woods, and I had my first glimpse of the Elizabethan house Dexter had built for his Genevieve with her inherited nostalgia. Dark timbered, pale stuccoed, sitting in wide green lawns (always a little spotty, as if that New England hill refused to submit to greensward) it fronted toward the farming valley with fields and gardens like a rumpled patchwork quilt. The formal garden with clipped cedar borders, stone benches and bird baths, seemed

full of figures. A woman, kneeling, broad sun-hat hiding her
head, was working at the flower border, Lawrence sprawled on
a bench, Gilbert stood a few steps back, hands in pockets, a
nurse-maid went slowly along a path with a chubby dark child
throwing out his legs in the experimental wobbles of the early
stages of standing upright and moving, an older child, a girl,
ran across the grass with a small terrier at her heels, and a man
stopped beside the kneeling woman, a flat basket with small
plants between his hands. He saw us and came to meet us, a
tall, slender man with an easy, graceful way of moving, his
narrow, long face losing its lean gravity as he smiled.

"Hello, there! Nice of you to walk over, Mrs. Moore. My
hands are too dirty to shake." He had, even then, a nervous way
of pulling down his eyelids quickly, to hide the inquiry in his
deep-set, somber eyes. "Perhaps you'd know what this plant is.
We've lost the label. I brought them out from town for Genevieve's herb border." His thin fingers rubbed a leaf between the
tips and held it out for Dr. Randall to sniff. The faint aromatic
odor was like a small minor chord in the sunlight.

"I know that," said Dr. Randall, speculatively. "Let me
see . . . *Cumin*. Cuminum Cyminum."

"It's cumin," sang out Dexter, and his wife's voice answered,
under the brim of her hat.

"Cumin. Really! I remember now. My mother had it, before
the drought ruined her herb bed. Bring it here, Dexter. It's a
good herb." She pushed the dirt firmly about its roots with
gloved fingers. "It gentles humans and animals." She broke off
a leaf and held it out to Dexter. "Put it in your pocket. It
makes you faithful forever."

Dexter's eyelids twitched, but the next instant he was helping
his wife to her feet, and Lawrence was drawling, "I hope
you've planted lots of mint julep herbs, have you, Genevieve?
That's the one herb that interests me."

"The mint bed's in the kitchen garden." Genevieve turned toward us. She had a wide, pale, immobile face under her large hat, with slightly protuberant dark eyes which looked at me without curiosity, although her small, thin mouth smiled politely enough around her phrases of accepting Dr. Randall's introduction. I was a stranger, I didn't matter to her. I never did matter to Genevieve, although after what was no doubt to her a decent interval, twenty years or more, she accepted Gilbert with warmth.

She was taller than I had thought, almost a head taller than I am, and heavy, her soft figure bulging under the figured blue silk dress, the deep V front displaying smooth white bosom, so smooth there was no hint of structure underneath the flesh, just the deep cleft between the billowy breasts. She handed gloves and trowel to Dexter, and drew her fingers over her forehead, sighing.

"I shouldn't attempt gardening," she said. "But actually I can't resist it. I'm the only one in the family with a green thumb."

"I was afraid you were working too long," said Dexter, anxiously.

"I'll be quite all right as soon as I rest a little. Shall we go out on the terrace?" Dr. Randall and Gilbert walked off with her, Dexter waited a moment as the little girl called, "Daddy!" and ran toward him, and I watched her. She seized his thumb and looked up at me under her bang of light hair, her small, pointed face flushed and serious.

"This is my daughter Alicia, Mrs. Moore. Alicia, this is Mrs. Moore, a friend of Ellen's and Dr. Randall's."

The child offered me her hand with a sober, "How do you do, Mrs. Moore," and then tugged at her father's thumb. "Could you come, Daddy? I think Mister is getting him a mole."

"He thinks he is, you mean." Dexter smiled down at her as the dog's yaps changed to a somewhat buried note.

"I wouldn't like him to get a mole when I'm all by myself," said Alicia.

"If he gets it, you holler and I'll come." Dexter spoke with dry tenderness; with a little nod of agreement, Alicia went off toward the yaps, at a stiff-kneed, rapid trot: "She always walks like that when she's in a hurry, instead of running," said Dexter.

"What a nice little girl," I said, politely. "How old is she?" She had a composure, a lack of self consciousness which I was far from possessing, and I suppose a darkling comparison of my childhood and hers shadowed my thoughts. Not that I was aware of any shadow at the time; I just said to myself, she's old for her age, and my goodness, isn't her father crazy about her!

"Not quite five," Dexter said. "She's really quite a person." Then, with a small gesture, a shall-we-go wave of a hand, he moved toward the terrace. "Did Dr. Randall say you were at Columbia?"

We were chatting about Columbia as we joined the others on the terrace. Dexter knew one or two of the men with whom I had studied, and he was saying, "We may run into one another some day, for all the place is so large. Don't you think you need an economics course?"

Genevieve Willetts was sitting in a high-backed wicker chair. She had thrown off her sun hat, and looked very different, her astonishingly lovely hair, bright red-gold, springing back from her low forehead, wound in a heavy braid around her head. The pallor of her flesh took on life with that hair revealed.

"Are you taking economics?" she asked sharply. "Are you?"

I was startled by the way her dark eyes bulged with accusation, and Dexter said, with no emphasis whatever, "No, Mrs. Moore is working in science. I was just drumming up trade for my department."

"Oh, your department! It's simply a mollusk, devouring you."

"Not a mollusk, Jenny." Dexter picked up the handkerchief which the wave of his wife's hand had tossed into the air. "A Moloch." He started to tuck it into her hand with a gay gesture, and she grabbed at it, rudely, a quick smoulder of anger in her dark eyes.

"What's the difference? You're *so* academic! But no wonder. Did you know, Dr. Randall, Dexter's insisting on teaching this summer? Going in all those terrible weeks of heat. When I thought we'd have a long, quiet time to ourselves."

"It's only six weeks and I'll get back every afternoon."

"I wish I'd gone in for the academic." Lawrence was standing on the steps of the terrace, obviously waiting to be off. "There's the life for you. All holidays, everybody kowtowing to you. How about getting me a job, Professor?"

"No money in it, though. You better stick to your capitalists. I want one rich friend I can touch for a loan." Dexter grinned at him over the pipe he was filling, his nervous fingers spilling brown crumbs.

"But your book!" exclaimed Genevieve. "If you would only finish your book! Now that the house is finished, and this summer we are actually alone in it, without workmen all about, and your study is waiting for you."

"Summer school helps pay the workmen," said Dexter, with the patient tone of a man repeating himself. "No study of economics in the Colonial period . . . not even mine, Jenny dear . . . is going to be a best seller. I mean to take a whack at it again, later this summer."

"The Burchalls will have their turn at workmen," said Dr. Randall. "We just stopped there, they've got their well. It's a sort of second incarnation of the old Ridge, first our house rejuvenated for Ellen and Lawrence, then yours built, now the

Burchalls'. Gilbert, you and Carey should join the group. Young people building their houses, their families, their futures."

Gilbert, who was sitting in the Gloucester hammock beside Dr. Randall, looked up with the little stiffening of muscles which meant he had been interrupted in his own meditation. "Thank you, Dr. Randall," he said. "You're very kind."

I thought, you can't startle Gilbert into giving away what he's thinking; his mind goes right on about its own business. His eyes met mine for the briefest instant (a longer glance, for Gilbert, had too much intimacy, like touching me in public) and all the scattered bits of myself, anxieties, doubts, curiosity about these new people, flustered attempts at response, came rolling together like bits of quicksilver shaken into one shining globule. *Darling*, I thought. You and me, together! A kind of magnanimous pity for everyone who hadn't Gilbert, who wasn't Gilbert's wife, spread its soft wings, lifting me out of my awkward self-consciousness.

"I'm not being kind," said Dr. Randall. "We want the right people on the Ridge, it's my pet scheme, keeps me interested watching the places develop."

"Look out, Gilbert," jibed Lawrence. "My esteemed father-in-law is one of the keenest real estate men I know. He'll have you signing on a dotted line before you know it."

"You mean I'm a public benefactor, finding this land, opening up the old roads, paying the taxes." Dr. Randall clapped his hand on Gilbert's knee, his thin face animated. "Here you are, Gilbert, you've caught on in New York, you know you're going to stay right there. What's the next move? Get a little piece of land and—"

"The next move is Carey," said Gilbert, lifting Dr. Randall's hand and placing it firmly on the Doctor's own knee. "She's not started, yet."

"You know about Peter Piper, don't you?" Dr. Randall smiled at me. "Or was his name Piper? Peter, Peter . . . here's Alicia, she can tell us. What did Peter, pumpkin-eater, do, Alicia?"

Alicia was climbing the steps to the terrace, one step at a time. She looked out gravely under her bang. "He put 'er nin a punkin shell," she said.

"And?" Dr. Randall prompted her.

"An' the punkin shell turned into n' auto, an' she drove away with the pretty prince."

Lawrence laughed. "At-a-girl!" he said. "Modern version."

"That's Cinderella," said Dexter, protectively, as Alicia put her grubby little fingers over her mouth, her eyes alarmed. Her face changed instantly, and she exploded into laughter.

"Don't encourage her!" Genevieve sat forward in her chair, the sun making a nimbus of her hair, her face passive. "She's old enough to say her rhymes correctly. Please, Alicia, don't let that dog drag his filthy bone up here!"

Mister stood at the top of the steps, nose as dirt-encrusted as the bone he carried.

"That's what he dug up," said Alicia, looking at her father. "It wasn't a mole at all."

"Off with you!" Dexter swung the child around. "Take him out back of the house."

"When you laugh at her, she thinks she's been clever," went on Genevieve.

"She hopes she's been clever," said Dexter. "That's different."

"That time she was." Lawrence laughed again. "You put your wife in a pumpkin shell, but you don't keep her there."

"But I thought Ellen had given up that position and come home." Genevieve had a slight pucker between her brows, not quite a frown. "Or do they mean you, Mrs. Moore?"

Dr. Randall smiled at me, his lean face sardonic, and I flushed with my compulsion to assert my young self. "It wouldn't make any difference how many houses Gilbert had," I said, "I'd still want my own work."

"There, there!" Dr. Randall laughed. "I wasn't suggesting but one house."

"I can't see why anyone wants to work unless he has to, to eat." Lawrence strolled lazily across the terrace. "You try it a while, Carey. See how overrated it is. Interferes with everything a fellow wants to do."

"I'm afraid I'm actually just an old-fashioned woman," said Genevieve. She cast her dark eyes up at Dexter, who looked embarrassed. Then she fixed me with a hard stare. "I think it's the climate here, making women restless."

"Seems to me I've heard of English suffragettes." Dr. Randall pushed himself slowly up from the hammock.

"Oh, those! A few hysterical women!" Genevieve shrugged her plump shoulders. "Pouring glue in postal boxes. Imagine! Of course, if a woman isn't fortunate enough to marry. . ." She broke off. "You aren't going, Dr. Randall? Dexter, tell Lena we'll have tea now. It's almost time."

"We can't stay, Genevieve. Have to get back to my pumpkin shell." Lawrence waved as he moved off. "Come over and see Ellen. She'll be out here alone next week."

"As soon as I have one of my good days. It's something of a walk for me. Give her my love, Lawrence. I'm so relieved she has come to her senses. Give her my sympathy."

As we went toward the road, Alicia called shrill goodbyes to us, and we turned to wave to her. We passed the nurse-maid, the little boy a heavy, sleepy bundle in her arms, his dark head bobbing over her shoulder.

"He'd walk in his sleep if I'd let him," she said. "He's wild about walking, now he's found it out."

"He started walking so late he has to hurry to catch up," said Dr. Randall.

"That's only because he's heavy." The nurse-maid bristled, defensively. "You take a heavy child and they walk late. Light-built ones, like his sister, is different, that's what I keep telling Mr. Willetts." She gave the child a hitch and went on.

"Robert's more like his mother." Dr. Randall stopped as we reached the road. "Shall we take the short cut home, Lawrence? This way, then?" He took a long step over the ditch, and pushed back a tangle of blackberry vines and sumac. "We leave it overgrown at this end," he explained, "so hunters won't notice it in the fall. They may have hauled their winter wood this way a hundred years ago. It goes around the hill we came over, across the valley and comes up behind our house." Old leaves were soft under foot, the sun made a green mist through the growth of young hemlocks which filled spaces between birches and oaks, there were dark old stumps and trunks of fallen trees, the brown powder of decay around their broken ends. "He'll always have a slower rhythm. Robert, I mean." Dr. Randall was still considering the Willetts family. "Alicia is thin-skinned and lean, like her father. More precocious."

"Too bad Alicia didn't get that wonderful hair like Mrs. Willetts," I said.

"Striking, isn't it? And she hasn't a red-head temperament. She's a good wife for Dexter. She's made a real man of him."

"He seems very nice," I said.

"The ladies all fall for Dexter." Lawrence was close at our heels. "But watch out for Genevieve. Dexter's her little boy, hands off!"

"It takes longer to know Genevieve," said Dr. Randall, with a certain impatience. "She's an interesting woman, and they are our neighbors permanently, and I don't want Ellen's sharp tongue building up a prejudice."

"Well," said Lawrence, tolerantly, "Genevieve's not too tactful. But now that Ellen is to be a mother, Genevieve approves of her. They may get to be real chummy, who knows?"

I giggled at that, and Lawrence glanced at me, pleased that he had been amusing.

"Mrs. Willetts doesn't seem exactly a chummy person," I explained. "The way she stares at you!"

"That's just thyroid," said Gilbert, drily.

"Oh, come! You young men think you've got the answer to everything." Dr. Randall seized Gilbert's elbow and swung him ahead along the path. "A gland and a complex! What about a man's soul? What about his character?"

"Listen to them go it," said Lawrence. "You know, it's fine to see the old man take an interest in things. He's been pretty low since Mother Randall checked off. Good for him, having your husband to talk shop with. I don't mean he's been moody. He's made an effort, on account of Ellen. But I couldn't ever get him started like that. He's a brainy man. Your husband is, too, isn't he? One of these deep, quiet fellows. I'm just run of the mill." Lawrence wasn't apologetic; he just placidly stated a fact. "Did you know Mrs. Randall? You couldn't know her, just meeting her once or so. I miss her. She was fond of me." Lawrence held back a hemlock branch, a reminiscent affection in the smile that pushed up the ruddy flesh over cheekbones and crinkled the blue eyes. "Too bad she couldn't have waited for her grand-child."

"Too bad," I murmured, with the unimaginative casualness of youth. "Ellen must miss her, too."

"Yes. Ellen's a damned good sport, you know." Lawrence thrashed out with his stick at ferns, sending green tips flying. "She's a damned good sport. Just takes everything in her stride." He lengthened his own step, the thought of Ellen pulling him homeward, and I felt more at ease with him as I followed his broad shoulders down the path. Not very exciting, perhaps, but if you knew him, you would like him, just because under a surface sophistication, he's simple and—well—kind. He waited for me at the foot of the slope, where moss-grown boulders made a slippery fording of a brook, and gave me a hand across. "Now take a deep breath," he said. "It's a pull up this hill, and then we're home."

We came out at the rear of the Randall place, the woods ending abruptly at a stone wall, with vegetable gardens and an old white barn in a wide bowl, above which stood the house. Gilbert stood waiting for us.

"Dr. Randall's gone off with his farmer," he said, and to Lawrence's inquiry, "I haven't seen Ellen."

"I'll hunt her up. You two can amuse yourselves, eh? Comfortable chairs out in front of the house." He strode off.

"Hello," said Gilbert. "How you making out?"

"Fine." I tucked my hand under his arm. He crooked his elbow, squeezing my fingers. "I think we both are doing very well!" Then we laughed softly, standing close together, knowing a delighted wonder that there we were, on a hillside in Connecticut, the two of us, having come this far on our road.

"Let's find some place—" Gilbert looked around, measuring the distance to the house. "Back here by the wall. Tired?"

"Not now."

I sat down on the grass, my back against the stones, and Gilbert sat on a rock just above me. He never liked to sprawl on the ground. He used to laugh about it, and say he couldn't get up fast enough if anything happened. Then I waited, knowing by the crease betweeen his brows, the way his eyes had a dark, impersonal concentration, that he was either turning over the discussion he and Dr. Randall had started, or he had something to tell me.

"Do you like it out here?" he asked.

"It's lovely." I looked up at him, solid and firm against the brilliant summer sky, and saw excitement stir under his concentration.

"Do you like the people?"

"I think so. Lawrence is pleasant. Dexter Willetts seems very nice."

"Hey, I don't mean just the men!"

"They're all nice enough, I guess. I don't know them very well. You know it takes me a while. Why?"

"Carey, what do you think? Would this be a good place for us?" Gilbert hooked his hands around his knees, his strong knuckles standing out. "To start our own home?"

I twisted around, pushing one hand under one of his. I could feel the vigor of his intention in his muscles.

"We couldn't build just yet, of course. But Dr. Randall meant it, about that field—the one with the old cellar hole. He says we can hold it by paying a few hundred down. If you like it. . . ."

"Could we manage?"

"With you getting a good job in the fall . . ."

"Instead of being just an expense . . ."

"We ought to think it over," said Gilbert. "But it's a good place, since we can't buy much of a piece of land. We'd know who our neighbors are. Dr. Randall wouldn't sell just to anybody."

"Just to special people like us!" I cried. "Oh, Gilbert! Could we?"

I wanted to go back that instant, to look again at the field, but Gilbert said no, wait till morning, we wouldn't say a word. We had it as a secret so likely to explode that we didn't dare glance at each other the rest of that day, and the excitement I felt has submerged other impressions. I remember a brilliant star that moved across the wide many-paned window, first in one of the square panes, then in another. The Ways and Means Committee meeting, Gilbert called it. And the excitement of the future we planned, which step by step we seemed to overtake, fused with the excitement of our love so that everything, imagination, flesh, spirit, were fired with delight until at last we slept.

Breakfast was set for nine the next morning, Sunday. Long before that I woke with a start at the unfamiliar surroundings. Sunlight filled the room, warming the greens of walls and curtains, the satin puff had slipped into a billowy pile beside the bed, and where was Gilbert? A water pipe thumped, and I sat upright. Gilbert appeared at the bathroom door, jerking his face out of the towel with which he tousled himself.

"I thought you were going to sleep forever!" he whispered. "Come on!"

I padded across to him, flurried. "It's too early, Gilbert! We'll disturb somebody, we aren't supposed to get up yet."

"If they want to stay in bed all day they can." Gilbert looked severe, his freshly shaven chin set subbornly, his hair sleeked back. "Are you coming or not?"

I knew where he wanted to go. We had to see whether in daylight, under a morning sun, the plan we had woven in the darkness had any substance. I rubbed my cheek against his warm, hard shoulder, and flew for my clothes. We had good training in speed in those early, hard-working days. Twenty minutes from bed to breakfast; I always cooked the oatmeal the night before. I was ready, my hair twisted into a knot, jacket over my arm, by the time Gilbert had his shoes tied and his necktie knotted. We tiptoed down the stairs, we heard someone, a maid probably, in the dining-room, Gilbert had to experiment a moment with the night-lock, and we were off.

"The maid thinks we've gone off with the silver," I said, as we crossed the lawn. "Are you sure you know the way?"

"Sure. Don't you remember?" Then we both laughed, pleased with our escape, with the morning, with our small family joke; I never knew the way, and Gilbert had a sense of direction true as a compass. But the way was different that morning, as if walking it with Lawrence, I had not seen anything, and now, with Gilbert, I saw it doubly clear. There were cobwebs across the path, and Gilbert broke off a branch to hold like a baton to keep the filaments from their light, furry touch on our faces. The meadow, when we reached it, had cobwebs everywhere, their geometric delicacy spun on grass and bushes, dew still clinging to the threads in shadows where the sun had not yet struck. The long grass was cool and damp against my ankles. We stood at the edge of the old cellar hole, looking off at the valley, blue in the morning shadow.

"Well," said Gilbert. "I guess this is it."

He paced off a square around the old house site, leaving a dark path over the wet trodden grass, and came back to me. "About thirty feet square. That might do for a beginning. Wouldn't be hard to bring a road in." He went off to see if he could find any trace of an old road, and thought perhaps his feet found a track. "What do you say, Carey?"

I said yes, of course. I was reckless with happiness, and anything was possible. The future seemed an extension of that morning, warm with love, brilliant with sunlight. I have never been a hesitant person, weighing pros and cons. If I wanted something, I saw no cons. I thought I was a practical, intelligent woman, planning my life around a kernel of sound ambition and love. I know now that what seemed to be swift decisions were emotional responses, and that what seemed to be my steady onward direction was movement into which I was propelled by forces with which I did not know I had to reckon. I thought I was running straight toward a goal, and perhaps I was only running away! Like a runner, I tossed aside anything that might weigh down or hobble my speed.

But I am setting down this story of the Ridge to escape myself. Gilbert was always more deliberative than I; he wished to know the exact shape of his next move, its details, and the shape, too, of the alternative, of the objections. He went over figures. "No more tuition for me, if we spent nothing for clothes, if I got . . . well, say fifty a month to start with. . . ."

"Make it a hundred," I said. "I'm worth that much."

"Another thing, these other families are just getting established. They aren't too far ahead of us. We can keep up with them."

"You're a better man than they are!"

"And their places aren't too close, and yet they're around. If we went out and bought just anywhere, we might not have any neighbors. I don't mean we need other people too much, but we ought to be part of something."

Then it was almost nine, and we had to hurry back along the path we had come, Gilbert still figuring, and my mind full of bright fragments. I'd write my brother, "Gilbert and I are buying land in Connecticut, we expect to build. Near enough New York for weekends. Some day you must come east to visit us."

"I'll get Dr. Randall off alone after breakfast," said Gilbert.

"Oh, yes! Suppose someone else got that hill first!"

Dr. Randall was standing at the front door, hands in pockets of his brown leather jacket, thin shanks jaunty in gay cuffed golf hose, his face grayish, a little mottled, in the bright sun. He was off guard, shoulders sagging, a kind of suspended animation about him. When he saw us, he came suddenly alive, his back straight, his arched eyelids lifting, a shrewd kindliness in his smile.

"Been to look over your place?" he asked.

I laughed, and Gilbert said, cautiously, "We did walk past that land. Have we kept you waiting for us?"

"No, no. Lawrence has just come down. Ellen's having breakfast in bed. As a great concession to the next generation. Let's go in, I smell the bacon."

After breakfast Gilbert and Dr. Randall vanished, and Lawrence went off to the village for a Sunday paper. I was uneasy, this leisure in a strange house enveloping me in awkward folds, a garment not mine. A maid, coming down the stairs with a tray, said that Mrs. Hunter would like to see me, when I didn't have anything else to do.

Ellen was flat on her back in one of the ivory beds, her arms arched above her head, hands clasped, her sandy hair in two pig-tails with scarlet bows at the ends, the circles under her eyes darker than the hazel iris. Her arms were lovely, slender, tones of pearl along the narrow wrists; the hollows in the curve of elbows, and her throat, the curve of shoulder deepened by her posture, had the same pearl texture. I had never seen her before as anything except arrogant and aggressive, at first in town, and yesterday, as boldly pregnant. This morning she seemed younger and more feminine. More friendly, too, although the intimacy of the setting may have had that effect. The room was charming, pale yellow and ivory, with crystal and silver winking back sunlight on the dressing table, thick tufted ivory rugs on the floor, a quilted yellow satin dressing gown tossed over the foot of the chaise longue.

"Sit down, Carey, and amuse me. This is my Dad's notion, not mine. Lord, nine months is a long time!" She rolled over on an elbow to face me, as I sat down beside the bed. "I've just been multiplying by three. You have to leave a gap between them, too. But I don't want an only child, and two isn't quite enough, in case something happened to one of them. How many do you want?"

"I don't know," I said, hastily. "We haven't got that far yet."
"You must have thought about it. Oh, well, don't tell me!
But believe me, I envy the hen! She has the neat way with her
offspring. I tell you, Carey, if men had to bear children, they'd
have done something about it a few centuries ago. All this
blah about it's being a great spiritual experience! It's about as
spiritual as a broken leg. It's made me so dull I haven't even a
mind to think with! I haven't really done any work for weeks,
but I was determined to stick it out at the agency." Ellen
laughed. "There's one old maid secretary there who hasn't
dared look at me for a week, she's been so embarrassed."

I tried to match Ellen's attitude, brushing aside queer filaments of resistance, intangible traces of my past, unanalyzed,
unrecognized, like the cobwebs across the wood road. Snickers
and children nudging each other as a woman trudged past, her
coat inadequate to conceal the distortion she hoped to hide. My
mother, unwilling to leave the house except at night, sending me
on her errands, with a list written in her neat, small hand, nain-
sook and thread and cotton flannel and soda mints and drug
store nostrums.

"I think you were grand, working so long," I said. "After
all, we're supposed to be proud of it, aren't we?"

"So few women will stick it out. Look at Adelaide, just going
native as soon as she marries! She's smarter than John, too. It's
easier to stick if you don't have children, I know quite a few
married women like that. But I—" Ellen held up one hand, the
slender thumb standing away from the palm, and then, as she
doubled the fingers into a fist, sealing them down hard. "Father
says I'm greedy. I want everything! Why not be greedy? Lawrence doesn't mind. He says what I want suits him. He thinks
I'm crazy because I like to work. But he doesn't mind. Now
Gilbert really cares about your getting ahead, doesn't he?"

I said yes, he did. I wasn't going to talk about Gilbert, even if Ellen's restless, brittle thoughts had seized on him.

"He talks about it as if you were his son instead of his wife." Ellen laughed again, and rolled back flat on her pillows, her hands interlaced over the mound of her body. "I don't mean he's talked you over. Just his most casual references. Funny, too, when he's so hell-bent on getting ahead in his own career. Father says he has a great future."

Of course that pleased me, as Ellen intended. I knew Ellen Hunter wouldn't have looked at me twice, if it hadn't been for Gilbert. This rather confidential chat was a need of an audience, not a need of me. But I could tell myself stoutly, you wait, you'll see! And at the same time, I could be proud that Dr. Randall, one of the head physicians at the hospital where Gilbert had put in apprentice years, felt that way.

"It means a lot to have your father say that," I said, clumsy in my eagerness. "It's such a big new field . . . Gilbert says we just don't know anything yet . . . I mean about psychiatry. It's terribly exciting."

"It's all exciting," said Ellen, with sudden passion which tightened the skin over her temples and cheek-bones, deepening the fine lines which bracketed her mouth and repeated the curve of her eyebrows, a passion which set amber glow in her eyes, flecks of light in the greenish irises. "What we're going to do, going to have, going to be! Even children. One son will be a doctor, like my father. One can go into the firm with Lawrence. He'll be a senior partner by then. And my daughter will go to Brearley's, and then have a year in France for polish, before she comes out. Mother wanted to send me over, but Father wouldn't see it, and so I just went to college. Of course she'll go to college, too, my daughter, I mean, although Lawrence's family are rather old school, and think a good marriage is the female goal."

"Goodness," I said, "you have it all planned! Suppose your boys are all girls?"

"They won't be. The Hunters run to males. You always get what you go after in this world, don't you think? Or are you like Lawrence? He's a scream, when I get to talking this way. He looks around as if somebody was listening, and insists on adding 'D.V.' I tell him he's just plain superstitious." Ellen's laughter had a tinge of ridicule which made me uneasy. "You don't tempt providence by knowing what you mean to have, you simply show it where to go!"

(Don't be too sure, Carey, or you'll get your come-uppance. My mother's tired voice, like a thin spiral of smoke from ashes.) When I spoke, my own voice came out too loud, the way I used to boom out against Mother.

"If you know what you want," I said, "then you don't let anything interfere."

"That's it. Now, Lawrence is a stick-in-the-mud. He's a Hunter, and everything's been handed to him. Perfectly contented the way things are. But I keep him stirred up." Ellen's lip curled back, showing pointed eye-teeth. "If he plays things right, he'll have his uncle's place in the firm . . . and his uncle's fortune, too. We'll need a lot of money. When I go back to work, I expect a raise. I landed a new account for the agency just last month, cosmetics. You watch, I'll put a lipstick and a compact with rouge in the handbags of a million women!" Ellen flung her arms up over her head with a quick sigh. "When I finish this little job." She stared up at the ceiling, her face puckered, its animation gone.

"You're tired," I began, hesitantly, "you've talked to me too long."

"Oh, Lord! Talking never tires me. Does it, Lawrence?"

"Not that I ever noticed."

I had not heard the soft fall of Lawrence's moccasins on the stairs, but he was crossing the room, to drop the bulky paper on the foot of Ellen's bed.

"That'll amuse you for a while," he said. "Feeling all right?"

"I feel like Cheop's pyramid, same shape, same age, same general brightness. Don't sit on my bed, Larry! You know I hate that!"

Lawrence grinned at her. "I'm not sitting on it, baby. I can't stay long enough. I have to get some stakes and the surveyor's tape measure and the map your father made, and Carey, if she wants to come."

"Oh!" I cried. "Has Gilbert decided?" I jumped to my feet, and Ellen said, crossly,

"You might tell me what's going on! I have to lie here. . . ."

"And nobody tells her anything!" Lawrence tweaked one of her braids. "Your papa works so fast it's hard to keep posted."

"Are you two going to build out here?" Ellen sounded peremptory. "You and Gilbert?" Ellen stared at me, a long, deliberative look, and for all my flurry because Gilbert had so quickly committed us, I knew that Ellen turned over in her mind the advantages and disadvantages of having us as residents on the Ridge, and I had a quick, sharp resentment because I could not guess her thoughts, because she could look at me with that cold detachment.

"We won't build for some time," I said, disliking myself because Ellen could give me discomfort, almost fear. "Gilbert thought a piece of land might be a good investment."

"I think it's swell," said Lawrence, and Ellen added, "Oh, so do I! I am just surprised."

"So am I!" I said. Lawrence laughed, and the chilly awkwardness of the moment dissolved. "You didn't think we could afford it, and we can't!"

"It will be nice to have another working woman out here." Ellen was gracious, now. "Which piece is it?"

"South Pasture," said Lawrence. "You know, the old Beckner place. Come along, Carey, help drive the stakes." At the door he stopped. "I forgot, Ellen. I saw Genevieve and Dexter, on their way to church. Will we come to tea this afternoon?"

"You didn't say we would?"

"Nope. I said you'd call them up."

"I'll tell you!" Ellen sat up in bed, the red ribbons on her braids bouncing over her shoulders, her voice eager. "We'll have a supper party in South Pasture to celebrate!" She was making amends now handsomely for her moment of delay. "Your first party, Carey."

"Here, wait a minute," said Lawrence. "You sure you feel up to it?"

"Heavens, yes. It will be something to do! You can drive me around by the road. I'll have Cook pack up some baskets, we'll ask the Burchalls and the Willetts. Take a shovel, and Gilbert can turn over the first sod. Run along. I've got it all planned. I didn't know what on earth to do all day, and this is it."

"All right," said Lawrence. "Come along, Carey. We've got to get the land staked out or the party won't be legal."

My recollection of that evening in South Pasture is disorderly and incomplete. People in groups always leave a confused impression, especially when I know none of them well. Gilbert and I were the new-comers; all his life Gilbert was an onlooker rather than a participant, and it took me more years than I had at that time to get my self-consciousness pushed down where it wouldn't interfere with social enjoyment. And a group of people who know one another have almost a language of their own, even when they are reasonably hospitable to strangers, a language of joking references, of established relationships. Some of my recollections of the evening may merge with impressions collected through the years that followed. I remember that Adelaide Burchall had a special manner for Dr. Randall, a flat-

tering cajolery, a minor kind of flirtatiousness which pleased
him, and that she was efficient about the cooking over the charcoal fire in the stone fireplace Gilbert and Lawrence had set
up. Genevieve Willetts was feminine and helpless, shrieking
about a spider, complaining in her quick light accents that the
ground was damp, sitting in precarious dignity on the camp
chair Dexter opened for her, the green scarf over her hair very
effective in the twilight. She held Dexter on a short leash, but
he seemed to like it. I remember John Burchall charging about
with nervous officiousness. He had to rearrange the stones of the
fireplace because the draft wouldn't be good; he was scornful
of the charcoal, good wood embers broiled much better, but if
Ellen insisted . . . and she wasn't going to make coffee with
cold water!

"Johnny, darling, everyone knows you could do this better
than anyone else, but it's my picnic! Will you let me bumble
along?" Ellen bulked between John and the fire, John vibrated,
unwilling to yield, and Adelaide spoke up.

"John's really a professional at camping, he's been on so many
hunting trips."

"This is amateur night, then," said Ellen. I suppose John
withdrew, but he was back in a moment, did Ellen know the
sticks cut for broiling were wrong, alder would flavor the meat?
He'd get some maple. "As long as you don't cut poison ivy,"
said Ellen, and everyone laughed except Adelaide, who said,
very earnestly, "But that was in the late fall, when the leaves
had fallen, and no one could have told!"

"You have to hand it to me," insisted John, "I never do a
thing like that but once. Live and learn, that's me."

"Live and tell us what you learn, you mean," jeered Ellen,
and John rushed off, unperturbed. "There's nothing John won't
tell you how to do," said Ellen. "Yes, I admit it, Addie, part
of the time he's dead right."

Adelaide's expostulation ended in a laugh, and she gave Ellen a quick hug; she looked very pretty, her brown eyes round and bright, her cheeks flushed, a spatter of gold freckles on the bridge of her small nose, her pink dress a pleasant color in the meadow. She's fond of Ellen, I thought, but she works for John with every breath she draws.

There were other people in the group that evening, friends of the Hunters or of Dr. Randall, from the village which was scattered in the valley beyond the railroad station, or from other hills. They are just blurs, although I may have known some of them in later years. Rachel Thayer insists that she came to that picnic to celebrate our taking possession of our piece of land, that she happened to be spending Sunday with her uncle and aunt, and drove out with them. It was the first time she saw Dexter, she says. "You probably thought I was one of the children." She was only seventeen then, a small, dark girl, and perhaps the older people submerged her gay, flashing vitality. I can't remember her that evening, for all I try to find her face among the shadows. Perhaps she needed a year or two more before she had the picturesque charm which made her conspicuous, so that you looked at her twice, deciding that she wasn't in the least pretty, but she had something.

I remember the rose-coals of the fire as the evening twilight deepened subtly, moving up from the valleys to seal the hill against the sky, I remember Gilbert with his foot braced on the long-handled spade, turning the chunk of sod, Dr. Randall making a ceremonial of the moment. I remember Dr. Randall saying, "One more beginning on the Ridge. What a fine place this has become! What stalwart young men and women! I wish I were young again to see what you all accomplish." Then they drank to our house, with Gilbert demurring, that's a long time off, and John Burchall chattering at my side, he'd strike off a few sketches, see what our idea was.

I told him goodness, we didn't have any ideas, we hadn't even had the idea of being landowners until last night! Dr. Randall overheard me, and said, "It's a good feeling, isn't it, Carey? A man needs to be pinned to some spot on this earth. He needs to belong." And as John darted off to buttonhole Gilbert, Dr. Randall went on, "I have a sentimental mood tonight. I see all you young people as a sort of foster immortality for myself, established here on the land I discovered, working out your destinies, coming back here when, like me, you reach an end of usefulness, and watching your children move into the world you will presently leave." I was uncomfortable, not knowing what to say. My imagination didn't stretch to any picture of myself as old and watching my own or any other children. Dr. Randall gave a little shrug. "But I'm boring you. Just leave it that I'm glad you've joined the community."

"Oh, no!" I expostulated. "I'm just overcome. You're so nice to welcome us like this." Then I added, "You wait! You'll be proud of us, too!" Dr. Randall looked at me, his lean face grave and pale in the twilight. He must have guessed a little at the pressure which drove me, the goad of what for a better phrase I may as well call a profound envy. Not cupidity; I have never longed for wealth or possessions, I have wanted money enough so that I didn't have to worry about it, that's all. Of course the people I was affected by that evening weren't conspicuously wealthy, although they seemed all of them to have an economic security which neither Gilbert nor I had known and toward which we labored. Rather an envy of qualities and experience which they seemed all to possess and which I lacked. They seemed citizens of a world much larger than the small Michigan town in which I had grown up; they had travelled ... Adelaide had been born in China, Genevieve in Australia, and they seemed thus, from the start, invested with some value which I lacked. Dexter was on the faculty at the

University, John was a rising architect, Lawrence was on Wall Street, and Ellen, more than the others, had an assured sophistication. They filled me with a sense of inadequacy, which I tried to shove under the surface so that often I was too glib, too meaninglessly facetious in what I said. I didn't analyze my feeling, but I knew its sharp prod. Some day I'll make you recognize me. It has taken me most of a lifetime to understand what Gilbert knew almost from the beginning, that each individual is his own battlefield, that the bitter conflict for supremacy is within himself, not between himself and his neighbors, that the urge for recognition, for superiority has no satisfaction except when the soul recognizes itself, when it has found its inner ease.

What Dr. Randall said, after a moment, was, "Well, my own daughter won't listen to me, so why should you? But I'll say it anyway. Don't be too ambitious, Carey. Why do you care who's proud of you, if you're happy? In the long run. . ." He stopped, laying his hand for a moment on my arm. "There, don't button yourself up like a turtle! I won't preach to you."

Lawrence called just then. Ellen was tired, he was going to drive her back to the house, did anyone want a lift? Ellen protested, her voice high. She wasn't going so early, what if she was tired? That must have been a late stage in their argument, for as I went across toward the lane, Lawrence exploded in a grim undertone.

"If you don't get in that car, I'll put you in! I've got a say about what you do! It's my child, too!" In the dusk he moved down on Ellen like a threat, elbows out, head lowered.

"Don't be such a' fool!" she said, and then she must have seen me, for she laughed, Lawrence jerked open the car door, and helped her edge into the seat. "Sorry, Carey," said Ellen. "Lawrence is just a damned bully."

"You're such a damned fool, you won't admit you're human."

Lawrence banged shut the door, his whole big body tense with the vibration which sounded in his voice.

"I hope you haven't done too much," I said, scrambling for words to cover my embarrassment. Lawrence, who seemed so even-tempered, so phlegmatic! "It's been a lovely evening, we'll always remember it."

For answer Ellen turned on the headlights of the car, and the sudden glare gave a theatrical effect to the meadow, isolating the figures within its slanting cone, and bringing sudden night up like a dark wall. Dexter and Genevieve were caught in the brilliance, coming toward us. Dexter dodged, and Genevieve came on with a regal poise, as if she liked the way the light focussed on her hair and white throat.

"Is there room for Genevieve?" asked Dexter.

"I don't want to ride if you aren't coming!" Genevieve stepped into the shadow beside me. "Who is it? Oh, Mrs. Moore! I can't see a thing, not a thing!"

"Pile in, Jenny," said Lawrence. "Dexter, too, if he'll sit on a basket."

"I'll walk," said Dexter, and as Genevieve started a murmuring dissent, "I'll cut through the woods and be home before you are. Good party, Ellen. Good-night." He stepped back into the darkness before Genevieve's hand could reach him.

"I don't like his going through those woods at night," complained Genevieve. "What if he tripped and fell!"

"The punch wasn't that strong," said Ellen, and Lawrence asked, "You coming with us, Carey?"

I said no, I'd walk with Gilbert. Then everyone was going, with good-nights called out, and the cars from town turning into the road to follow Lawrence. Adelaide and John, a basket swung between them, set off on foot, John singing lustily, "Good-night, ladies. Good-night, ladies!"

Gilbert and I stood there, the trampled grass a soft mat under our feet, a small red eye winking at us from the spent fire, the hum of the car motors diminishing until it was only the whir of some insect in the night.

"Suppose that was really our fireplace," I said, sighing, "and the house was all built, and we could lock the door, now that the guests have gone."

"And all the planning, the contriving for it behind us? Don't be in such a rush!" He lighted his pipe, the dancing star of the match flame catching for an instant the reflective frown on his forehead.

"I was just thinking how all these other people could go home . . ." I said, apologetically. "I'm not impatient."

"I've been pushed around too fast all day," said Gilbert. "I could have had fun for a long time thinking about this land, and talking about buying it. Here we are, owning it! And we hadn't ever seen it till yesterday."

"Love at first sight," I said, sliding my hand into the crook of his arm. "Like us."

"Yeah," grumbled Gilbert. "But I waited a long while till I told you. Here, let's get out to the road before it's any darker." We found the road without difficulty, its pale surface shining dimly between the darker trees, and Gilbert laughed when I wanted to turn in the wrong direction.

"We can come out and look at our land," I said, as we stepped along in the darkness. "And plan the house. I'm glad we didn't wait!"

"Dr. Randall was insistent," said Gilbert. "You know, Carey, there's something wrong with him. A man his age doesn't retire, doesn't want to wind up everything. . . ."

"Oh, Lawrence warned you he was a super-salesman!"

"His color is queer."

"That's probably his natural color. Of course he's quite old."

"You're a hard-hearted little wretch, aren't you?"

"You're getting so you see symptoms all the time!" Gilbert's arm tightened around my waist, his shoulder, his thigh moving solid and warm against mine in the rhythm of our walking. "I won't worry about anyone!" I said. "I want everything to stay as it is now! Only more so. They're all nice folks, aren't they? And they were all so cordial to us. . . ."

"Why shouldn't they be?" asked Gilbert. "Gave 'em a chance to have a party. Gave Ellen a chance to engineer, that Burchall a chance to show off, all of 'em a chance to eat and drink. . . ."

"It was a nice celebration!" I insisted.

"I'll tell you what it was. I've got it. It's a vestigial remnant, a rite with its usefulness lost. Now when my grandfather bought his land, the neighbors got together and had a real barn raising. They stayed two days and got the barn shingled, and he and Grandma moved right in! Now, how many kegs of hard cider did Grandpa say that barn took?"

I leaned comfortably against Gilbert's shoulder. "We don't want a barn, anyway." Then I giggled, at my own silly joke. "Did you hear Lawrence? He was raising the roof, all right."

Gilbert had heard, he seldom missed anything. "Ellen's pretty arrogant," he said, reflectively. "Queen Bee type. She ought to watch out. Lawrence hasn't whirled downward from his nuptial flight . . . not yet. I was thinking about those couples . . . you couldn't find women more different. Ellen's the Queen Bee. The Willetts . . . she's the limpet, sponge, clinging ivy, no, I tell you, Dexter Willetts is her island she's going to live in, now she's given up England. And the Burchalls, by God, that Adelaide is going to make something out of Johnny or know why!"

"And us?" I asked, burrowing my fingers under his hand where it pressed against my side. "Tell about us."

"Tell you what?" Gilbert quickened his pace. "Here we go, marching along together, that's us."

"I wouldn't trade places with anyone of them, would you? Not with anybody!"

"No," said Gilbert. "But you can't really imagine yourself as being somebody else. All you can do is to borrow some of their trappings and see how you'd like them. You can't step out of yourself, no matter how hard you work your imagination. Suppose I try to be John Burchall, going around telling the world, with Adelaide rolling her brown, adoring eyes at me! I just feel embarrassed, because I would, if I acted that way, and I want to take Adelaide aside and tell her not to be so conspicuous even if she's a hundred percent for me. That's not the way John feels! I know that, but I can't imagine just how he is, inside."

"You can guess near enough. You're very smart about people! That's why you're going to be a famous psychiatrist."

"That's why I think sometimes I've got a nerve to try it," said Gilbert. "Setting myself up to doctor men's minds, their nerves, their emotions. What a colossal nerve! Why, Carey, I don't even know what goes on inside your head. Sometimes, when we've been . . . you know . . . closest, I suddenly hear your mind ticking away, but I can't hear what it's ticking about! We're as separate as if we'd never known each other. See!" He swung me suddenly against his body, his hands under my shoulders, and held me, his face close to mine. "Love me?" His mouth was on mine, and quick passion uncurled in the deep nerve centers of my flesh. After a moment his hands dropped, and he stepped away from me. "See!" he repeated. "We rush together, we go a little mad, we don't think, we just feel. . . ."

"You can spoil anything by talking too much about it," I said, in a flurry of indignation. "You needn't kiss me for an experiment!"

"I didn't. I kissed you because I wanted to. But I didn't know I'd make you cross. See?"

"I'm not cross, only I wish you didn't analyze everything all the time."

"That's what I mean! I don't know why you feel that way." Gilbert started along ahead of me. "I won't talk any more."

Suddenly I was contrite, and ran after him stubbing my toe on a rock, catching at his arm to keep from falling. "I don't know what ails me!" I said. "Too much excitement!"

I know now what Gilbert was trying to find, and I know, too, what caused the irritation which twanged so inexplicably at my mood. But that night we put it aside, we left it behind us, another of the small moments over and around which the current of our warm, young love swept us. Then I forgot about it. I was incapable of projecting myself into a future in which we, Gilbert and I were different, essentially, from what we were then. We would go on, hand in hand, and the only change to come would be in what we accomplished. My vision of that accomplishment did not stretch far beyond the next month, the next year . . . it was an urge, a direction, rather than any defined plan. Emotion, sensation, took the place of thought so far as my personal life with Gilbert was concerned. There was nothing cautious or deliberative in Gilbert's love for me. But loving me, having made me his wife, he made me a part of the future which he built so carefully, with such secret apprehension of possible disaster, such growing knowledge of change and difficulty.

Most people have only the present, so far as any sharp and actual consciousness of living is concerned; they may have some mulling over of the past, regret or disappointment or recollected triumph, and they may have plans for their future . . . houses, or schools for the children, or annuities for their old age. But their personal life is like the hunger of the body, an immediate need, requiring food today, accepting the daily fare. Gilbert, in some way had come much earlier than most of us into a perception of the steady movement of life, time to him was not just a clock measuring the hours today, it was the cycle of birth to death, and tomorrow flowed out of yesterday and today, carrying the consequences of past time into the future. He thought of us in that whole cycle. He had broken through his reticence, his loneliness, his shyness for me, and he wanted to know me not only as my lover, not only as partner in our struggling economies, but fully, as a human being.

Well, perhaps that kind of knowledge is the mystical union with his God toward which a mystic yearns, and human beings never reach it. Perhaps at the end Gilbert understood me better than I knew myself . . . and if he did, perhaps he forgave me, knowing the part fear played, knowing the curious, dark sources of the impulses which drove me. But I have started to tell the story of the years between that first experience on the Ridge, the story of the men and women who lived there with us, and I must wait until I have set down that story before I come to Gilbert. I couldn't have foreseen, from that first glimpse of these others, Lawrence and Ellen, Dexter and Genevieve, John and Adelaide, the future they had even then in the making, tragedy, hopeless passion, endurance, the beauty of high courage. I remember that Gilbert said once, "The lives of so many people seem as inevitable as if they were just propelled violently along a trajectory from the womb to the grave. And yet even a bullet or an arrow may be deflected . . . and who knows what current of air, what movement of the spirit may alter that trajectory?"

I started this story of the Ridge to escape myself, and I see now that if I am to avoid this constant return to Gilbert and to myself, I must leave us out and tell the story of the others without explaining how I came to know so much that happened. Unless I put myself firmly out of the picture, I shall stay in its center, and my own shadow will stretch its darkness across the light for which I search. And as yet I cannot bear the swinging of the pendulum between the past and the present, with the long arc steadily shrinking until the pendulum is still, and there is only the empty present.

Enough now to explain that Gilbert and I did build our house a few years after that Sunday when we bought the land, that for a time we spent the summers there, commuting into the city, that we rushed out for holidays and Sundays, that gradually, as my work engrossed me, and as Gilbert's practice increased, there was a diminishing of that first enthusiasm, the trip seemed too long, the time we could stay too short for the effort of transplanting ourselves, the value of that isolation seemed less than the people or affairs we sacrificed. We rented the house for a few seasons to Rachel Thayer, not guessing then why she wanted it, and even after we closed it, Gilbert refused to sell, saying he might go back when he was too old to work. But we were there enough to see the progress of the drama of the Ridge, to piece together what happened between the acts we watched.

There is a line of poetry I have heard Gilbert quote. "Are we no greater than the noise we make along a blind, atomic pilgrimage?" That links with his comment about the trajectory from the womb to the grave, and his insistence that some current of air, some movement of the spirit may alter that trajectory. I think again of the way each person reduces himself to a minimum impression, no more than a flavor of personality. If life puts the skids under you with birth, and that's all there is to it . . . I won't believe it. Gilbert spent his working years trying to pry people off their skids! He couldn't have believed it. But here I am, back again to Gilbert and myself. I'll make an end of that by beginning the story of Ellen and Lawrence Hunter.

Book Two

ELLEN AND LAWRENCE

I.

*E*LLEN's first child was born in August of that summer, a boy, confirming her idea that she could plan her life as she liked. She came back to her father's house on the Ridge when Larry was two weeks old, bringing a nurse, and Lawrence had his summer holiday of a fortnight. He was in high spirits, perhaps a little clumsily so, as if he felt responsible for Ellen's state and turned on additional buoyancy to lift her back to vitality. "Chip of the old block, that Larry," he said. "Got my brick-dust hair, even got my bald head! It's going to be good fun, teaching him to ride."

Ellen, who had expected that once she had actually produced the baby, she would revert to her usual state of somewhat tense well-being, was inclined to blame Lawrence because she didn't bounce back like a rubber doll.

"There's nothing the matter with you," her father told her, "except that your body has done a big job, and everything's depleted. If you'd just nurse the baby, you'd have some pleasure and one less trouble."

"I won't, as I've said." Ellen drew a harsh breath under the tightly bandaged breasts. "I've done enough for him! What do you think? Have Libby bring him into my office every three hours? Why, I feel now as if he'd sucked up every drop of life I ever had! And he's such a little thing to do all this to me."

"He's a fine big boy," Dr. Randall said. "All creation involves disintegration and decay. Waste products. Toxic. You remember how tired you get just working out one of your advertising campaigns? That's only mental creation. Now your body's been host to germination and growth for months. Takes time to rid itself. . . ."

"You make me sound like something putrid."

"Don't be sentimental," said Dr. Randall. "It's just a matter of chemistry."

"That's what I mind! I'm sick of being a matter of chemistry, I want to get back to being myself, Ellen Randall Hunter! It's all very well for you to stand there looking smug about your scientific explanation! You're a man. You never have to go through it. Listen, Father! It's not the pain. You know I'm no coward. It's the humiliation of being just a thing that's being used! Not even a good, honest tool. Nothing but a . . . what was it you said? A host. A damned incubator, and then wrecked in the bargain. I don't like being used! You never told me how it would be. That's why there's so much that's sentimental draped around the whole messy job! Don't you call me sentimental."

"You're a bad tempered little girl," said Dr. Randall, gently. He walked across to a window, and stood there, the sunlight marking the planes of his thin face with austerity. "You know, my girl, your sex really has the advantage of mine. Of course you're being used, and you know it. We all are. That's what life's up to, using us. It's a rare male who knows how, but unless he gets some faint glimpse of that how, he's never content. It becomes necessary to struggle for that glimpse when you get as near the end as I am. You won't listen to me today, nor for a long time, but someday you'll hear what I say. I'm not out of patience with you, but I don't like your talk."

Ellen grinned at him. "Sure, I'm bad tempered. Why not?

You'd like to see me all soft and squnchy, wouldn't you? So would Lawrence, the big lug, strutting around because he's a father, and a lot it cost him, didn't it? And the worst of it is, I've got to do it all again. I won't have an only child." She leaned softly into her pillows, the curious recurrent drowsiness darkening her thoughts, dulling her senses, before she quite formulated a question she had started . . . why did you stop with me, if you'd had more. . . . Her father wouldn't have answered, he couldn't say your mother felt as you do, she wouldn't repeat the experience. I'm not like Mother, she was spoiled, she ran things to suit herself. . . . With that thought, as loud as the closing of a door, Ellen slept.

Dr. Randall lowered the shade to the edge of the opened window, he stopped a moment beside Ellen's bed, laying a finger on the thin wrist. Good steady heart, a little slow; skin cool, moist. Her eyelids puckered faintly, and he withdrew his finger. Ellen sighed and shifted her head for deeper sleep. The August afternoon was breathless and still, made for lethargy and healing. Dr. Randall went down through the quiet house, out through the front door, clicking the latch slowly lest he disturb the silence. Summer haze blurred the distances and bleached the cloudless sky, it dimmed the brilliance of the thick foliage of trees and shrubs.

Down the eastern slope toward the gardens he saw the baby's carriage shrouded in white netting and beside it on a canvas chair the stocky blue figure of Libby. She was knitting, her fingers moving the needles with slow determination, her face, as he came near enough to see, flushed and moist. Libby had worked with him for a long time, a practical nurse coming on cases after the need for pert young trained nurses was over. She'd been slim and pretty and just over from Ireland when he'd first known her, with clear blue eyes and a long Irish upper lip. She'd spent her life taking care of other people's babies and

her own father and mother. Her father was a lazy Irishman
who never went on a job without getting hurt, and who spent
more time fighting for compensation than he did working.
Libby's head drooped, and then flew up with a jerk. She saw
Dr. Randall, and stood up promptly to peer with him through
the netting at the small, domed head with its wisp of reddish
hair on the fragile pulsing skull, the tiny mottled fists curled
against the chest.

"Regular as clockwork," said Libby, moving away from the
carriage. "Never had a better baby. Sleeps, eats, thrashes, moves
his bowels, sleeps. He's no trouble." She smiled, the gaps in her
teeth showing, and Dr. Randall thought, I've got to get after
her again about fixing her teeth, spending all her money on her
folks when she might be a good looking woman still. "He's
more a Hunter than a Randall, that's it. Takes it easy." She
went on with her knitting, her elbow pinning the ball of yarn
to her side, her needles moving brightly. "Some of them fight
from the minute they draw a breath. They won't sleep, they
throw up whatever you give them, they hold back on number
two, they know too much to take it easy. Ellen was a tartar. I
guess you don't need to be told that."

"She's asleep now," said Dr. Randall.

"Kicking against the pricks, that's Ellen."

"Have you seen Mr. Hunter?"

"No, not since lunch." Libby pursed her lips, counting
stitches. "He went off in the car."

"If he plays golf today, he'll get a sun-stroke."

"Not that one. Tough as a salamander, he is. Better golf
than some of the ways new-born fathers amuse themselves."

"Sounds as if you'd been keeping bad company, Libby."

"I've spent forty odd years with the human race."

Dr. Randall looked at her tolerantly, and tweaked one of her
knitting needles as he strolled off. "You're a big bluff," he said.

"Keep an eye on Ellen, will you?" He went down past the vegetable gardens, where the farmer worked, clearing away the rows of crumpled yellow pea vines, piling the litter on a wheelbarrow.

"This heat's pushing everything," he said, leaning on his fork, blowing sweat off his upper lip. "I put the hose to it every night, but that sun cooks the tomatoes right on the vines."

"Handsome corn," said Dr. Randall. The plants were motionless in the windless sunlight, the broad leaves shining and sharp in their crisp arcs from the stalks, the seeded sheafs at the tips full beaded sprays, the silken tips of the ears among the leaves just darkening with ripeness.

"Yeuh," said William. "Corn likes it hot."

They talked about the garden for next year, the piece of new land William wanted to plant. Be bad if they had a late spring, didn't drain off till late. They agreed you had to take a chance, and with a final, "Don't work steady in that heat," from Dr. Randall, and William's, "The compost pile's in the shade now, I take my time dumping the barrow," the Doctor went on, across the stone wall and into the woods. He wished Lawrence took more interest in the farm. He trailed around after Dr. Randall when asked, he listened blandly to the small projects or triumphs, but none of it meant a thing to him. His youth, perhaps, or his urban background.

Something satisfying about growing things, the recurrent rhythm, the steady looping progress, a sure thing to plan for, to wait for, a knowledgeable use of the future. Lawrence didn't have anything he was interested in. That wasn't exactly true, he had a vast, good-humored vitality which meant that he was never aware of boredom, he liked just moving around in his life. He was a direct and simple man, l'homme sensuel, not a sensualist in its derogatory meaning. Dr. Randall stopped his slow walk, to let his thoughts have their own movement. He didn't mean that Lawrence was just natural man, no more than an animal. The fellow had his own code, his own standards. He wasn't complicated. But he's kind. That's important. It may work out all right, if Ellen doesn't push him too hard.

Funny, thought Dr. Randall, I don't really know how Ellen feels about Lawrence. One of those things a father didn't ask his daughter, not out and out. Ellen was a good deal like her mother. But I've no business to assume Ellen's exactly the same! How many times had he given himself that warning? Admit it, he was afraid that his daughter would grow into maturity and age as her mother had done, with her emotions always centripetal, always tending toward a center and that center herself, a narrow brittle whirl excluding everyone except the self.

Of course there's a difference, he thought. Ellen, in her generation, hitches her ego to theories about women and jobs and expression. And poor Florence, his wife, had been hitched to nothing, so that the trivia of her life, social functions, details of domestic affairs, clothes, artificial social prestige, had always to be distended in her effort to find something for her energy.

Florence had done her best for his career, proper contacts, charming dinners, all that, she'd been relieved when he had suggested that he keep a separate room, he was so likely to be called out any time, disturbing her. He had been a means to an end, she had wanted a husband, a house, one child and no more, dignified position as married woman with successful husband.

Well, he'd had a good life, if it was lop-sided. He'd thought back over the whole of it, after Florence's death. Other women, a few, at first. Temporary, unsatisfactory, not what he wished. Unless he broke with Florence. He might have done that, if she hadn't had that long illness. By the time she was well again, he had made his decision. She was satisfied; if one of two human beings in the curious relationship called marriage liked the shape it had taken on, wasn't that as much as you could expect? He probably had found as much satisfaction in his work as one man could expect in life, anyway, with the hospital, the private practice, the younger men he'd helped. He'd worn out earlier than he liked, no use in dwelling on that. What he was trying to figure out was Ellen and her marriage.

He slapped at a mosquito, and moved on slowly. The sunlight filtering through the thick foliage overhead spattered the path with its small disks, the shade had an illusion of coolness. He'd like to have Ellen get more than Florence had. He'd thought for a while, after he'd first brought young Gilbert Moore to the house, that maybe he'd be the right man. He still wasn't sure. Of course Moore had a girl out west, nice enough, same background and all. But those youthful engagements are not always final, and certainly Ellen had an awareness of the fellow she hadn't ever shown toward Lawrence.

Well, what happened? Something Florence did or said? Who were Gilbert's people? Oh, he was intelligent, but absolutely naïve and gauche. And poor. He might get over that in time, but he'd never have the same values, really. Dr. Randall didn't know whether Florence had said all that to Ellen, or only to him, whether Ellen had been so much like her mother she had thought it for herself, or whether Gilbert just wasn't available. That might be the answer; he and his young wife seemed off to a good start. Must be a sign of age, this looking backward all the time. The thing was settled, the question was how will it come out? Lawrence's very lack of subtlety was a kind of protection, it kept him comfortably oblivious to whole areas of feeling where a more sensitive and involved personality might suffer. Good thing Ellen wanted more children. If she had enough else to occupy herself, she wouldn't be so likely to find Lawrence dull. A good back-log for her life.

Dr. Randall pulled off his canvas hat; for a moment or two the air against his damp forehead felt almost cool. Ought to get a thunder shower after a spell like this, he thought. Usually this walk through the woods was pleasant, but today the motionless monotone of green above and around him seemed to compress the heat until he fancied he could feel it separate for his slow progress, and flow together as he passed. There was a relief in reaching the open fields, and he skirted them, keeping in the shadow of the hedges, looking around to see whether the Moores had done any more work on their land. Gilbert had mowed the grass, and had dug out the old cellar hole; he had staked the driveway to the road, and dumped his rubble along that. "It may grow up to weeds again before we can start building," he had said, "but it's fun working on it." No signs of recent work, the two of them were pretty busy in town.

It's a grand time of life for them, thought Dr. Randall, clumping along the dry, soft, uneven road, helping tread it down. Everything's in the future, not out of reach, your fingers already know the touch of just what you wish to grasp, there isn't time enough in the day, the week, the year, for all you wish to do toward your fine goals, achievement is the meaning of life. You don't wonder what it's all about then; you know.

He had come to the end of Gilbert's driveway, and he stood there a moment, smiling. The lathes marked a wide exit, and at each side Gilbert had built a gate post of black rocks from the pasture wall, fitted together and squared off. Dr. Randall laid his hand on the warm stone, and looked down the road. He could hear the Burchall boys yelling, but the violent activity of early summer around their place, the sawing and hammering and trucking, had ended. He went along the road, the dust rising in puffs about his feet, his step quicker now that he had come so near the end of his walk. After he came to the curve and drop of the road he could see the new Burchall house, surprising still there where for so many years he had seen only a bit of woods, its white clapboards so brilliant they seemed the source of the light which made him blink.

The ground yellow and raw in all the graded slope about the house suggested a hostility held by the earth against the intruder. John Burchall had been sure he could start his lawn the minute the uprights of the house were in place, he'd scrapped with the workmen about stepping over places he'd rolled and seeded down, he'd run his sprinkler until he'd sucked dry his whole water system and got sand under the valves of his pump, but he hadn't sprouted any of the grass seed. All Adelaide said was, "In any ordinary summer, John would have had a good lawn by now!" That was Adelaide for you. Dr. Randall chuckled as he turned in the gravelled driveway. She'd blame the Lord before she'd blame John. It was a pleasant house, a little like an albino now with no blinds, and presently the earth would accept its presence, grass and shrubbery would pull it into place.

"Hi, Dr. Ranny!" Adelaide's brown head popped out of one of the dormer windows. "Come on up and see how you like my paint job. Come in the back door, the front hall's still sticky."

He glanced at the extraordinary disorder of the kitchen as he entered. The Burchalls had moved into the rear of their house as soon as the floor had been laid, because it was so much cooler and less crowded than the garage where they had been camping. Books and papers in one of the wall cupboards, a drafting table with John's sketching paraphernalia at one end and white enamel plates and cups, milk bottles, packages of breakfast food at the other. Two saw-horses with a length of two-by-four for a bench. Cots set up in the dining room. A curious odor prickled in Dr. Randall's nostrils, smoky paper and shavings, and the air inside the house seemed degrees warmer than out of doors.

He walked quickly along the path of reddish carpet paper across the expanse of gleaming floor in the long living room, glancing at the stone fireplace, sniffing, and hurried up the stairway.

"Adelaide!" he called. "Something's burning!"

She came to meet him in the hallway above, brushing damp wisps of hair away from her forehead, her limp print apron clinging to her soft round breasts and thighs and knees.

"Not now," she said, "not now it isn't." She laughed, and tried to fan herself with her paint brush, and then, with a little squeal, bent to mop up a trail of blue specks with the edge of her apron. "Come see my woodwork!"

"But it's hot as blazes and I certainly smell something," insisted Dr. Randall.

"That's just the furnace," said Adelaide. "John wanted to try out the heating system before he settled with the plumbers." She giggled. "It worked all right."

"But today of all days!"

"He said it was so hot anyway it wouldn't make any difference. Look, isn't that nice? I had just that one door to finish. When the paper's on the walls, the color won't be quite so bright."

The white plaster of the sloping ceiling shimmered against the robin's egg blue of wainscoting and closet door. "Very pretty little oven," said Dr. Randall. "Come on out doors, you stubborn little idiot, you want to make yourself sick? Where is John, anyway, letting you do this?"

"I was just coming down," said Adelaide, her sneakers squeaking on the floor as she walked beside Dr. Randall. The freckles were distinct on the bridge of her small nose, and her brown eyes rolled up at him, droll and admitting. "John beat it," she said. "He said he had to go to the village anyway, and when Lawrence stopped, why John just hopped into the car."

"Smart boy."

"We haven't a thing for supper. It was lucky Lawrence came along." At the foot of the stairs she stooped to lay an experimental finger on the threshold of the hall. "Sticky," she said. "Oh, Dr. Ranny, isn't it a lovely room!" She tiptoed along the strip of paper as if she balanced on a tightrope of delight. "You can see it better without the furniture, can't you? Too bad we have to clutter it up with chairs and things. I can feel the proportions of it now. John says it will look larger after it's furnished. And after the walls have color. We're going to let the plaster season for months. I like it white, anyway, it's so light."

"In short, you like everything about your house," said Dr. Randall.

Adelaide nodded. "Every single thing, and you needn't make fun of me. I even like the mortgage, Dr. Ranny! It's a good investment, isn't it? Gives us something to work for."

Dr. Randall wondered whether the pucker between her brows, the strained look about her nostrils was really anxiety, or only the effect of heat. "John's done a good job," he said. "Nothing shoddy. He's right, of course, the best is cheapest in the long run. Let's find a cool spot, if any, out doors."

Adelaide thrust her paint brush among others in a can under the kitchen sink, and held her wrists under water from the shining faucet. "I *am* dirty!" she exclaimed, and scrubbed her hands and face, blowing at the water like a child.

Dr. Randall watched her as she found a dry corner of a towel which hung beside the sink and pushed her hair away from her ears and temples. He wasn't sure about Adelaide, whether she was without vanity and female wiles, or whether she deliberately affected a lack of self concern, like her attitude about John. This was the life she had chosen, this was her man, her house, and by the good Lord everything was right! Perhaps Ellen was responsible for his occasional doubt, with her insistence that Adelaide was actually smart, that she had mapped out just what she meant her life to be, the opposite of everything in her mother's rootless, shifting, hazardous career.

"I haven't even asked about Ellen!" Adelaide looked very young, her face cooled and shiny from the scrubbing. "Come outside." She slipped her hand under Dr. Randall's elbow, and they kept step together across the small rear porch and around the corner of the house. "I haven't seen her for two-three days. I just haven't had time to find me a clean dress and go over. Is she . . . but I know she's fine."

"She's all right. A trifle impatient."

"Oh, well!" Adelaide dismissed that. "You tell her I'll be over tomorrow, unless the furniture van comes. John's ordered all our stuff brought out. But it may take days!"

Below the terraced, raw ground around the house, beyond the gravelled driveway, in the shade of several old trees left years ago by some farmer perhaps to make a resting spot for his horses and himself in the corner of his field, were faded canvas chairs and a limp hammock dangling between two of the trees, and a rope swing, the ground scuffed bare beneath the seat.

"I wonder where my two are," said Adelaide. "I sent them down here." She tucked herself into the hammock, which bulged snugly around her plumpness, and Dr. Randall skirted a toy wagon and a shovel, to seat himself with care in one of the chairs. "John's going to bring back a piece of ice," she went on, "and I told them we'd have lemonade."

Dr. Randall shifted to get his rickety chair balanced, and, if possible, to keep a bar from paralyzing the small of his back. "Folding chair's a good name for these contraptions," he grumbled.

"Next year we'll have to have new lawn furniture. The boys sort of wear things out." Adelaide set her hammock swaying gently. "Oh, boy, does this feel good! I'm never going to move again."

"You don't keep still, even lying in a hammock," Dr. Randall said.

"You mean I lack repose?" Adelaide made a little face at him, and dug her heels into the net, swinging faster. "Never mind, as long as you're fond of me. You are, aren't you?" She made her brown eyes wide and round.

"Sure I am." He was, too. Nice little lively piece, like a partridge hen with the gold flecks in her brown hair and eyes, and she didn't treat him like an old fossil, either. Take the other young women . . . Carey Moore, for instance, was too respectful, kept reminding him of his age. And Dexter's wife, Genevieve, didn't treat him any way at all, he just wasn't within the range of her attention. Except when once in a while she remembered that he was a doctor . . . had been a doctor. Lord, he thought, how much I hate it. Before he went on to analyze what that sudden gulp of distaste meant, Adelaide said, as if she had already said it once or twice:

"Dr. Ranny, is she? Is Ellen really going back to her job in town?"

"Oh, yes. Yes."

"I thought maybe she'd stay out here, once she had her baby. It would be nice . . . for me, anyway. I should think she'd want to. But John says I shouldn't expect everybody to want just what I want. I don't think I do, do you?"

"Perhaps no more than we all do."

"Except where something seems just so real or right there isn't any question about it."

"One man's meat." He smiled.

"No, sir. Some things are absolute, good food or poison."

"But good food spoils, and the deadliest poisons, in proper doses, are useful medications."

"You can beat me arguing," said Adelaide. "So can Ellen. But I don't care! You can't change my mind."

"I'm not trying to. But you'll be a smug old woman if you don't look out." Dr. Randall sounded irritated; he could see Adelaide down the years, growing plumper, firmer, more settled, he could see his daughter Ellen growing harder, sharper, fiercer in her grasp, and annoyance like prickly heat, unlocalized, but comprehensive, spread over him, regret at what they might make of themselves, pity for the lost promise of their youth. What ails me, he thought. Must be the heat.

Adelaide had thrust her head up from the hammock, a little listening frown between her brows. "I thought I heard a yell," she said, and swung her feet out to the ground. "Did you?"

No, he had heard nothing.

"I wish the boys would yell," said Adelaide. She made up her mind not to go in search of them, Dr. Randall saw traces of the brief conflict before she set the hammock swinging again. "I won't be a tagger," she said. "Only it is awfully hot, if they're in the sun somewhere."

"It's hot if they're in the shade, too," said Dr. Randall. "I heard them a while back, when I was crossing the Moores' place. Gilbert's got quite a lot of his digging done, hasn't he?"

"I haven't been even that far," said Adelaide. Her eyes brightened indignantly. "John saw them last week. He offered to draw them up plans, and Gilbert said he was going to build his own house! Isn't that absurd? What does he know about planning a house? John wouldn't have charged him full rates, either, his being a neighbor. . . ."

"Well, Gilbert and Carey may want to work out their own notions."

"Um," said Adelaide. "You mean I'm trying to run them, too, don't you? But it isn't smug, Dr. Ranny, when I know John's a real architect, now is it?"

"Ah! You did hear what I said, after all?"

Adelaide let her sneaker scuff over the grass. "I don't think I'm smug."

"Smugness would include the inability to admit that it was smug, wouldn't it? But I didn't say you are a smug, not now. I know John would design a better house than Gilbert can. What's he going to do now? Does he need the job?"

Adelaide tipped back her head, the warm, firm column of her throat glistening as she laughed. "Sure, he needs lots of jobs. He's going back with his firm, he just took off these two months to finish our house. I thought if he could get some country houses to do, he wouldn't have to take that trip into the city every day. But the firm's eager to have him back, they're expecting a big year, John says."

"So you're going to live here the year round."

"It's home!" Adelaide was emphatic. "My children are going to know where they belong. I won't be lonely, I'll be too busy all day. I did think it would be nice if Ellen moved out here, too, and we could do things together afternoons."

"Well, you'll have the Willetts," said Dr. Randall. "You'll have to chum up with Genevieve. You'd do her lots of good."

"Um. Of course, we're neighbors." Adelaide's tone was bland. "But don't you think, Dr. Ranny, she's one of those women who just doesn't care about friends? She's so completely married . . . I mean . . . absorbed."

"Partly her health."

Adelaide made a small disparaging whff sound. "John says she suspects women, you know, of designs on Dexter. Dexter's all right, but my gracious, he's not that attractive!" Her brown eyes brightened with curiosity, as she tempted Dr. Randall into some betraying gossip. But he sat forward in the canvas chair, balancing himself gingerly before he rose, urged into movement by a return of the irritation he had felt earlier. There was in

Adelaide's neat, energetic, clear-intentioned self a kind of intolerance for differing personality, for differing desires. He told himself it was her youth, her eagerness about her own affairs, but he disliked it, the more so when it interfered, a slight and only momentary block, with the current of his own emotional attitudes. He knew what Dexter was up against in that marriage; his deep affection for Dexter resented this sudden indication that portents he had thought disclosed only to his trained and sensitive concern, were obvious enough for shallow wise-talk between John and Adelaide.

"There's something almost feminine about Dexter," Adelaide went on. "Perhaps because he's intellectual. I think academic men are that way, don't you? I know you like him, you've known him such a long time. All I mean is I don't expect we'll ever be very intimate, not even when we're old residents, too. And every time their little girl, Alicia, comes over to play with my boys, something happens. She's . . . well, touchy, and they're all boy, and she tries to boss them."

"Alicia hasn't played much with other children." Dr. Randall looked away from Adelaide, scowling at the crude poster effect of the new house, the white clapboards, the green tiled roof, the yellow raw slope of ground all garish in the sunlight, thinking that it was all like Adelaide, self-contained, lacking grace. Something atavistic in women like Adelaide, a return to the primitive female, this hostility to everything other than her own!

"Oh, you can see that! She's a scream, the words she tries to use."

"She's an unusual little girl," said Dr. Randall. "Gifted, I think."

"Thank goodness, Henry and Dick are ordinary boys." She swung herself out of the hammock with a quick jump, and stood beside Dr. Randall. "Isn't it perfect?" she said. "Perfect. I'm glad you came over, I'd rather talk to you than anybody I know, except John." She slid her hand into his, small, firm-fleshed, brown, and for a moment his eyes lingered on it, the sturdy fingers amusingly dabbed with blue paint, saw the swollen dark vein at his own wrist, the brittle, ridged nails as his long fingers closed over hers in a friendly pressure. He was a crotchety old man, taking irritable exception to her chatter. He knew her for what she was, a warm, healthy, enthusiastic young woman, pretending to be more ingenuous and direct than she was. Why should he mind her limitations? "Listen!" she said. "Isn't that the car?"

They listened, and were not sure at first whether what they heard was more than an insect stirring in the sleepy, still air. There was a whirring sound; it ceased, and then started again, increasing this time to a swarm of insects. "That's it! Coming up the long hill."

Dr. Randall could hear the motor thumping, and then the Maxwell puffed into sight, stopping at the foot of the drive-way, and males spilled out on each side, Lawrence easing his bulk around the wheel, John leaping down on the opposite side, small boys . . . were there only two of them? . . . and finally Dexter Willetts, looking warm and urban in a gray flannel suit, his briefcase in one hand.

"Get your cart," John said, "right smart about it, or the ice'll be gone!"

"Why," cried Adelaide, "have you boys been to the village?" They scooted past her, and she advanced swiftly upon the group near the car, Dr. Randall trailing. "Dexter! You've been in the city? It must have been terrific on the train!"

"I was glad to have a lift. Last day, though. Summer school's over."

"That's good." Adelaide poked a finger into John's side as he leaned into the rear of the car. He jumped around, the paper bag he had lifted tearing, oranges rolling bright blobs of color under the wheels, down the little slope. "I wish you'd tell me when you take the boys with you," said Adelaide. "I had no idea where. . . ."

"How could I tell you when I didn't know? They were half way to town, little devils, hoofing it along in that heat. 'Nobody told us we couldn't go, Daddy!' I couldn't come back to ask you, now could I? Don't poke me like that again, the next package is eggs."

"Why not drive up near the back door?"

"Now, listen, Adelaide! Do you want Lawrence getting a couple of punctures the way I did this morning? The drive's peppered with shingle nails. If I could get my hands on the fellow that dropped them, I'd make him crawl on his hands and knees till he picked up the last one! He was sore because I caught him with his truck half full of my good lumber, brass pipes, hardware, God knows what. I told him he could line his pockets off other jobs, not when he worked for me!"

"He even had a gallon of paint oil," said Adelaide, her arms crooked for packages which John piled briskly into her grasp. "And he had the nerve to say, 'I didn't suppose you'd want that junk!' Imagine, throwing nails in our driveway!" She tucked her round chin over the edge of a bag bulging with breakfast food and toilet paper. "It's not heavy," she said, as Dr. Randall offered assistance.

"Did you see this act of sabotage?" Dexter stepped hastily aside as Henry clattered down the drive, kneeling on the small cart, one leg over the side furnishing side-wheel propulsion, Dick screaming behind him, "Wait for me!"

"I saw the nails." John's shoulder blades were sharp under his blue and faded shirt as he wrestled with the block of ice on the floor of the car, the arch of his thin back was taut. Lawrence said, "Wait a second!" Dr. Randall braced the cart against the running board, Lawrence shoved, and the block slid out, the burlap cover dripping and musty.

"There!" John leaped around to pick up the handle of the cart. "You steady it, Dick."

"You going to do this all summer?" Dr. Randall looked into his car, that saw-dusty puddle would dry off, give it time. "You'd better let your neighbors drive up, one by one, till they collect all your nails."

"I've got a better scheme." John slapped at his pocket. "Where'd I put it? On the back seat, in the corner!"

Lawrence handed it out, a small horse-shoe magnet, and John dropped it into his breast pocket. "Fasten it on a cord, stake out the road in sections, drag it."

"Can I do it, Dad?"

"Lemme do it, Dad!"

"Isn't that a good idea!" Adelaide was moving slowly along the road in the direction of the house. "Let's all go up to the house and use some of the ice in good cold lemonade."

"I'll just stroll on home," said Dexter. "Thanks for the lift."

"We'll drop you off," said Lawrence. "I'm on my way before John sets me raking his road! You better come along, Pop, he's got a retaining wall to build before supper, too."

Adelaide set up a quick flurry of denial, but John shouted over the creak of the small cart as he pushed it into motion, "Damn good thing for your figure if you did a little honest work!"

"I'm just not the type." Lawrence expanded comfortably under the wheel, and Dr. Randall, sliding into the rear seat, was amused at the irascible haste with which John shoved at his ice-cart, his sons scooting along to keep their heels ahead of the wheels. Dexter slumped beside Lawrence.

"Tell Ellen I'll be over," called Adelaide. "Give her my love."

Lawrence trod on the gas pedal, and the car bucked forward. "If ever I offer to taxi that lunatic around again, shoot me first, will you?"

"Too energetic for you?" Dexter let his head roll toward Lawrence, his muscles lax.

"Crazy as a coot! You know how long he dragged me around hunting that damned magnet? I'll bet it was over two hours. Found it in a loft in Wicker's junk shop, temperature a hundred and twenty, dirt a foot thick, under pounds of rusty iron. You never can tell when John's going to break out with some fool notion!"

Dr. Randall leaned forward, bracing a hand against the back of the front seat. "He's got enthusiasms," he said, amused. "Keeps him interested."

Lawrence muttered profanely, and then they all bounced as a wheel hit a boulder.

"We'll have to have some work done on this road," said Dr. Randall.

"Get John to fix it," said Lawrence.

"What I wonder," Dexter spoke reflectively, "is about that workman. Did he dump nails on the Burchall drive? I suppose John did catch him pilfering . . . but no one ever dumps nails in our road. How about it, Dr. Ranny?"

"We probably aren't smart enough to catch them." Dr. Randall saw the sardonic flicker of response in the side-glance Dexter gave him, and felt without words the little warmth of satisfaction he often felt with Dexter, the sense of communication established. Lawrence wouldn't know what he was talking about, Dexter knew he had suggested that John created situations, being actively suspicious, antagonizing, cocksure. It was a rare thing, feeling this sudden click of real communication. One of the fine satisfactions in a narrowing life. Sometimes with that

Gilbert Moore . . . although Gilbert was more cautious about revealing his response.

"Don't bother to turn in," Dexter was saying. "Drop me here." Lawrence stopped at the entrance to the Willetts place, the narrow road winding in through the deep midsummer shade, its curve as it climbed looking as if the trees had closed in dense and leafy silence across it. "Thanks for the lift." He stepped out, straightening his relaxed, long body, setting back his somewhat stooped shoulders. "I'll be seeing you, now I'm through the college grind." He stepped off along his road with an assumed briskness.

"He looks all in," said Lawrence, driving on. "Messing around with books all the time. No kind of life for a man."

Dr. Randall settled back in the corner of the seat, one hand on the frame of the car. Wouldn't suit you, my lad, he thought, but he said nothing, looking at the solid bulk of Lawrence's shoulders, the firm, sunburned pillar of throat above the opened collar, the dome of head showing sunburned through the thin sandy hair. Good organism, he thought, eupeptic, smooth functioning; might develop high blood pressure as he grows older if he doesn't keep down his weight.

"He's got some crack-pot notions he's picked up out of books, too," Lawrence said, as the car slid quietly down-grade from the Willetts' hill toward the hollow where the Randall road would begin to climb. "Why, if I didn't know Dexter, I'd think he was one of these damned radicals, some of the things he shoots off. League of Nations, excess profits . . . God knows what. I told him if he'd get into business for a week, he'd see how fast his book ideas would scatter."

"Dexter's an idealist," said Dr. Randall.

"But he's really a good sort," protested Lawrence.

Dr. Randall laughed, but Lawrence, shifting gears for the sudden gravelly ascent, didn't hear him. By the time the car stopped at the gate in front of the house, Lawrence had dismissed everything but an amusing eagerness to locate his new son, to see Ellen.

"I've got some letters for Ellen," he said; "they'll pep her up a bit. Where's Lib and the kid? They were down there by the garden." He strode toward the house with his easy, long step.

Dr. Randall glanced off toward the western horizon, where the glazed sun, enlarged by the murky air, rode near the crest of hills. Must be almost six, an hour till dinner. The dahlias along the border were lifting their ragged, half-blown heads more crisply now, in the shade. If he were in town, at the office, his office nurse would be saying, "Five more in the waiting room, Doctor, you can't see them all today," and the city heat smell, dusty, oily pavements and sweat, the sweat of motor exhausts and tired human beings and decaying produce would stir around her flounce as she cleaned bottles or swabs or whatever he had just used from the table. "Don't let any one else into the waiting room," he would say. "But I'll see the five. . . . Who's next?"

He'd thought he'd like nothing better than long days with nothing to do, no pressure, no pushing against the inexorable rush of hours, none of that forever trying to cram into the narrow space of a day more than any day could hold, like the nightmare of hurling things into a trunk that would never close, or struggling to make a train which was always leaving. Perhaps he had dropped out too abruptly, if he had had a chance to let himself ease gradually into idleness . . . perhaps he was too old to alter all his habits. Ridiculous to figure ways of killing time when he knew he was on short rations, and yet that was what he kept catching himself doing! Pleased that the afternoon was gone . . . I ought to do better with what's left, he thought. Take his own advice, which he had delivered so briskly to elderly, querulous patients. Get yourself a new interest! Get yourself a hobby. Stop brooding over yourself! Find some device to anesthetize yourself. That was what he had meant, wasn't it, although he dressed it up? You are troubled because the forces which have kept you moving since you were conceived are playing out, you can't comprehend what it was all about now that you near the final curtain. You can't find out, stop looking! Go South, learn bridge, collect something, anything, distract yourself, anesthetize yourself!

Perhaps he'd been wrong, and the final job the human being had to do was exactly to come to terms with himself. Perhaps his own case was different; the knowledge that men are all mortal never seemed to trouble the conscious thoughts of men, not even doddering old octogenarians. But if a man had heard his death sentence, and knew damned well no messenger would ride up with a pardon from the governor, well, that was different. Work was the only anesthetic Dr. Randall would like, and that he could no longer have. Or was work an anesthetic? It didn't so much dull the pain a man felt—not pain now, so much as emptiness, bewilderment—as it prevented him from turning in upon himself. Curious that the more demands made on you, the better. Hands reaching for you, frantic, feverish, fearful, eyes watching for you, apprehension, panic, suffering clearing in that quick, humble giving over of the burden to the physician, such clutching hands didn't pull you down, buffet you about, instead they held you in a proud and upright strength. No wonder some doctors get to thinking they're God Almighty. That's what ails you, he told himself; you've got to find out how to stand up by yourself, without being bolstered up.

William came around the corner of the house, carrying the small tripod for the lawn-sprinkler, the hose snaking out behind him.

"I don't know as it's worth running this." he said, scowling at patches of seared grass. "Cooked the sap right out of it." He set the sprinkler firmly in place in the center of the plot. "Gets much worse, we'll have to plow up the whole lawn. Just when I had it real good, too."

"The roots aren't burnt yet," said Dr. Randall. "I've seen it look worse than this and come back another spring."

"Will you turn it off bimeby?" William dusted off his palms on his overalls. "Time I got along home." He turned his slow, proprietary glance toward the flower border, and beyond that, toward the western horizon. " 'Nother scorcher tomorrow," he said. "Good thing August is a slack month. Have you ordered those berry bushes yet?"

"By Jove, no!"

William's weathered face creased in severe reproof.

"I have to get them in by the end of September. I hear that nursery over Amawalk way has good raspberry and blackberry vines."

"I'll drive over there tomorrow," said Dr. Randall. "You come along, help pick them out."

"If I can get the time." William walked off toward the corner of the house, with the easy, loose-kneed gait of a man accustomed to uneven ground. "Don't forget to turn off the spray. I'll set her running."

Dr. Randall grinned. William liked nothing better than catching him in some remissness. See, you couldn't run this place without me! Good feeling for a man to have. The spray made a hissing noise, and Dr. Randall stepped out of range as the arms began their revolving, and the fine arcs of water leaped and fell, the sharp, fresh smell of moisture cutting through the heavy air. He sat down on the granite doorstep, facing the wooded valleys and the line of hills beyond, dark now with coming shadowed twilight as the afterglow held its dull crimson above them. The unpolished granite of the step still surprisingly warm seemed friable under his finger tips.

"I will lift up mine eyes unto the hills, from whence cometh my help." Now how did that go from there? "The sun shall not smite thee by day. . . ." He'd have to look it up when he went into the house. He supposed those old fellows who wrote the Psalms were hunting for the answers, too. He'd never thought of them that way before, with this sharp recognition of what drove them to their poetry. Don't think you'll ever find out, they had said, in effect. Trust in the Lord.

From one of the upper windows came the sudden indignant wailing of young Larry, ending as suddenly. Got his dinner now, thought Dr. Randall, leaning back against the stone. He smiled, thinking how the baby's soft, greedy mouth would seize the nipple, how the blue eyes would stare up at Libby as she bent over the crib, holding the bottle at the proper angle. The thought of his grand-child stretched his mind over unknown time, it was like the wide distance of the familiar and beloved landscape at which he looked, time and space combined to expand the tight coil within which he had tormented himself, he was relaxed and at peace.

2.

In September Ellen and Lawrence moved into town, leaving young Larry with Libby and Dr. Randall on the Ridge until Ellen found new quarters for the enlarged family. Dr. Randall had given up his apartment in the spring, and in spite of some pressure from Ellen, had shown only indifference to any winter plan. He might stay in the country all winter, he said, vaguely.

"He's queer about it," Ellen said to Lawrence. "He swears he feels all right, but if he does, why did he give up his practice?"

"Might be your mother's death," suggested Lawrence.

"Don't be so sentimental! Oh, of course he was fond of her,

I don't mean that. But he wasn't dependent on her. I suppose we'll have to find a place large enough to take him in with us."

"Well, that's all right. He's a nice old boy. We get along fine."

Ellen sat at the dressing table, brushing her hair with quick strokes, her arm moving across the reflection in the mirror of Lawrence sprawled comfortably on one of the twin beds. The hotel room seemed somehow jaded, after the dignified personal quality of the country house, almost as if the succession of summer transients left weary imprint there.

"You get along with anyone," said Ellen. She laid down her brush, and her fingers moved deftly, braiding the fine strands, her face averted, secret. She knew how it would be. Men always ganged up against a woman, her father would be on Lawrence's side, oh, very subtly. Lawrence wouldn't actually understand what went on, but he would feel aided and abetted. Her father was fond of her, but he had his generation's ideas about women, and she knew just how he would watch, with that noncommittal, observant look of his. She wanted to be let alone, to do as she liked. A parent never could let you completely alone, you always seemed a child to him, he kept that awful sense of responsibility about you.

"If you don't want him," began Lawrence.

"I didn't say that!" Ellen tossed her braid over her shoulder. "It's complicated, that's all. You know, if we give a small dinner, if we're invited out. . . . But we'll have to manage, somehow." She changed the subject before the slow process of Lawrence's thinking developed a question about her attitude. "I'm going to have my hair cut. It's coming out terrifically since I had the baby."

"So's mine." Lawrence leaned toward the shaded table lamp. "See?"

"Yes! It's a hard thing, being a father!" Ellen knotted the

sash of her thin silk dressing gown, and rose, stretching herself a little, pleased with the slim, light, erectness of her body. "Look at you, bulging out of your pajamas! And me, scrawny as anything!"

Lawrence caught her hand and drew her toward the bed, pulling her arm to his face, his lips soft in the hollow of her elbow, his eyelids flushed. "I've missed my girl," he said.

"Be a good boy," said Ellen, coolly, but she sat on the edge of the bed, leaning against his knees. "For a while longer." He dropped her arm, the flush running over his high temples to the edge of sandy hair, his mouth thinning into a wry grimace. "I just don't feel up to it." Ellen made herself small and drooping, and a moment later lowered her lids over a swift brilliance of triumph as she felt Lawrence relax, and slide his arm easily around her waist.

"It's all right," he said, almost in apology. "Only it's a hell of a long time . . . I get lonesome!"

"That's not the worst thing you could be," said Ellen. "Not half as bad as what I've put up with!" She waited long enough for Lawrence to remember all that, and then went on, "But let's not talk about that! It's most over. Let's talk about what we're going to do." She was animated now, her voice quick and pleased. She did not permit herself to think in words, I can do what I like with Lawrence, but like a toxic in her blood stream, feverish and subvertive, lay the dark knowledge of her power. "I've been thinking about it, all these weeks I've had to lie around doing nothing. And I think what we should do now, you and me, is to buy a house."

"We've got one," said Lawrence. "Same as, anyway. Your father's."

"Not in the country. Right here in town."

"Good Lord, Ellen, that takes money!"

"We've got some, what Mother left me. We're going to

make lots more. . . . You can work harder and sell more bonds!
If you have a big mortgage to pay off, you'd have to work
harder!" Ellen went on swiftly, persuasively. She had bewildering details. One of the men in her office knew about a charming small house over east in the seventies, she'd written him, it
was still available. Tomorrow they could look at it. All her life
she'd wanted a house in New York. Her mother had wanted
one, but Father was mule-stubborn, he had an obsession about
owning land in the country, he'd thrown away thousands on
those useless acres in Connecticut, who wanted to live in the
country? Look at Adelaide and John, Adelaide was shutting
herself out there, away from people, from anything stimulating,
it was criminal! What good would that do John's career? With
a lovely little house, Lawrence could invite people home for
dinner, the children (Ellen paused here, turning her hand
slowly inside Lawrence's, pulling at his thumb, smiling around
at him ... "At least two more, darling!") would have a home,
a background, the right kind of place for their childhood.

"Sure, it sounds fine," said Lawrence. "All but the money
end. We aren't millionaires."

"Maybe we will be! Your uncle ought to do more for you.
He's never turned over any of his best clients. If he sees you're
in deadly earnest ... he thinks you're easy going, and you
aren't, really, are you? You want your wife and your children
to have the very best!"

"I thought we were doing pretty well. I'd rather wait till we
get more of a head start."

"I don't believe in waiting for anything! The thing to do is
to take what you want and then keep it!"

"But suppose I got sick ... or you did ... or something."

"Suppose we didn't!" Ellen laughed, she twisted sideways to
reach his head, pulling it toward her, kissing him, a quick, hard
kiss. "You're sweet!" She slid to her feet, and snapped off the

table lamp. "Tomorrow we'll go look at the house! That won't do any harm."

"Your pop told you to go slow for a week or so."

Ellen tossed off her dressing gown and stretched out experimentally. "Good bed," she said. "Nice and flat." She pushed the pillows higher under her head. "I feel better by the minute, now we're back in town."

"Kinda noisy, after the country."

"Known as the voice of the city," said Ellen. "I like it." A composite sound, all angles and crossing lines, steel wheels on steel tracks, noise caught in narrow streets, movement, vibration, in a rhythm you could detect if you listened, a mechanized dance, a march. "It's exciting to pick up things again. They've got a new account for me at the agency, Walker wouldn't tell me what. Walker'll be glad to see me. But I know two other men there who hoped I'd die in child-birth."

"Hey!" Lawrence gave an explosive grunt. "They aren't that bad."

"It's true! I'm better than they are, and they hate it. But a woman has to be twice as good as a man to get anywhere." And I am. The thought, tightening her nerves, keyed her to combat. I am good! She waited, but Lawrence made no answer. In the darkness she heard the creak of his bed, the heavy thump of his body as he flopped around, seeking comfort. "Twice as good, and then you have to fight every inch of the way! But you can't get a man to admit it."

"I'll admit anything." Lawrence yawned, a long huhhh. "Getting yourself all wound up! I thought you were tired."

Ellen caught the constrained exasperation in his voice. She considered several rejoinders, cool reproof for the tone, a denial that she was wound up, a gay of course she was wound up, it was fun to feel that way again after being unwound so long. But before she had settled on her words, Lawrence spoke again, an amused hesitancy this time in his slow question.

"Say, do you suppose the kid'll know us when he sees us the next time?"

"A baby that age doesn't know anybody!" Off at the margin of consciousness Ellen felt a forked flicker of irritation; she would have denied hotly that it existed, a darting snake's tongue of jealousy that Lawrence had moved out of range, that she just wasn't what he was thinking about at all! "You don't think Larry knows you, do you?" She made her voice soft and tolerant, and with unexpected vividness she saw the baby in Libby's arms as she and Lawrence drove off to the station that afternoon, and Libby's upper lip, long and disapproving that Ellen could leave her child.

"Of course he knows me!" Lawrence boomed out. "He'd got so he'd grin when he saw me, how's my old man."

"Gas."

"You didn't see him." Lawrence gave another yawn. " 'Sfunny," he said. "I didn't know I'd miss anything that size so much. Well, your father's right on hand, if anything goes wrong."

"We simply couldn't bring him to this hotel!"

"Don't you miss him?"

"Of course I do. But Libby's much better than I am, she knows about babies, and just as soon as we find a place..." Ellen trembled slightly, pushing back defensive words; Lawrence would like to see her all sentimental softness, madonna with child. There were other ways of loving your son! "That's why I want us to see that house right away. It has a little yard in the rear, with a tree. Good days Larry could be out there in the sun ... and later, he could even have a sand pile there."

"And I'd be so damned rushed trying to pay off the interest on the mortgage I'd never have time to play with him."

"We have to work if we want a family!"

"Yah!"

"You will look at it," coaxed Ellen.

"I bet he's going to be a big fellow," said Lawrence, drowsily. "He's got an awful grip already."

Early in December Ellen and Lawrence moved from the hotel to the front bedroom on the second floor of the house in the east Seventies. The decorating was not yet finished, but the house was livable, and Ellen said she could see to things better if she didn't have to waste time travelling across town. The rear bedroom was for Dr. Randall, because its two windows opened toward the south, and had sun except when the buildings on the next street cut it off. The nursery was the south room on the third floor, the maids' rooms were above that. Ellen had an intense possessive fervor for every inch of the place, from the green door on the level of the street which the previous owner had substituted for the original stone steps leading to an entrance on the first floor, to the broken flags in the neglected little yard at the rear. She spent her luncheon hour matching samples for draperies, hunting for lamps in special small shops, planning color schemes with a clever and inexpensive decorator, a woman who was just beginning her business career. With the good pieces she selected from the family goods in storage she had a fine start, they really didn't have to buy a single expensive piece of furniture.

Christmas they spent on the Ridge, as Dr. Randall insisted, and by the first of the year Ellen had them all in town, with a cook and a second girl to run the house. Lawrence had said at first, "You'll run yourself ragged, trying to do so much." But she hadn't, she throve on the activity, her satisfaction in the setting she designed for herself and her family deepened the

eager confidence she felt about her work. The advertising campaign which the firm had handed to her was to push a new
cosmetic company. Put rouge, powder, lipstick into the handbags
of a million women, make them make-up conscious. Her imagination was facile, concocting phrases for the copy-writers, suggesting sketches for the artists.

Often at the end of the day she walked east from the Fifth
Avenue bus, swinging along lightly, enjoying motion after the
day at her desk, enjoying the anticipation which quickened her
pace as she came into the block beyond First Avenue, saw the
narrow green door with its brass knocker, perhaps heard a tug
whistle from the river. Sometimes she rang, just to test the
promptness with which the maid appeared; more often she let
herself in, listened for household sounds from the kitchen in the
rear of the basement, glanced at her reflection in the mirror
above the chest, and climbed the stairs, narrow up to the turn,
then three wide steps to the foyer. There she could look into the
living room, with its soft gray walls (she'd been careful about
that warmth in the gray), oyster-white woodwork of mantel and
bookcases, dull green with hints of gold in tapestries and crisp
folds of draperies. Or she could look into the dining room, with
its soft gleaming Sheraton table and chairs, the silver tea set
which had been her mother's on the side table. Sometimes Lawrence would look around from the wing chair, tossing aside his
evening paper, but more often he came in later. Then she'd
climb more stairs up to the nursery, where Libby would be giving young Larry his supper. Ellen would watch him, but she
didn't pick him up. "Upsets his stommick," Libby said. Sometimes Libby had news about a new tooth, or an extraordinary
moment of new activity or recognition; sometimes she had an
item from the restrained feud between herself and the second
maid, "shoving my kettle back from the fire, so I don't know
how long since they stopped boiling. I gave her what's what."

"I'll speak to her," said Ellen. "But, please, Libby! Please be tactful."

"Somebody ought to keep an eye on the help." The toss of Libby's head meant, What I could tell you if I let myself go!

"I can't be in two places," said Ellen, firmly. "But I know the baby's all right." That appeased Libby for the moment, and her implied disapproval of Ellen's way of running her house and her life made another amusing little story for Ellen to tell.

The house had reached the state of near-completion where Ellen began to wish an audience for it. Late in January Adelaide wrote that she was coming in town for a day, new suits for the boys and a trip to the dentist, she and John were crazy to see the new house. "We'll have them for dinner," said Ellen, and Lawrence suggested the Moores and the Willetts, too.

"Curiosity might drag Genevieve into town. She wouldn't let Dexter come alone." Ellen considered. "It's a good group to train the servants on. I wouldn't care if things weren't perfect . . . not with Adelaide . . . and the Moores wouldn't know, anyway! I don't mean they're boors, but you'd know Carey had some kind of queer background."

"She and Gilbert come from the same place," said Dr. Randall.

"Gilbert came first." Ellen smiled at her father. "All right, I'm being snobbish! But at least there's nothing naïve about Gilbert Moore. Well, it won't make an exciting dinner party, but it's a good one to begin with."

The night of the dinner Ellen was late; a conference at the office had dawdled past five, and then she had stopped at a florist's. She fidgetted, pushing her toes against the floor of the taxi-cab when a traffic light held them. She rang, and then, impatient at a moment's delay, found her key and unlocked the door. Katy was running down the stairs, her cap askew above a round, shiny face, her hands busy with the knot of the checked kitchen apron which protected her uniform. She had it off and under an elbow, saying, breathless, "I'm sorry, Mis' Hunter, I had my hands full of the silver."

"Hang up my things, please," said Ellen, half way up the stairs. "And be sure to pin those shoulder straps! Did you put fresh water in the vases? Has Mr. Hunter come in? Everything all right?"

"Yes, ma'am." She followed Ellen and watched as Ellen ripped the cover from the florist's box. Yellow roses, just uncurling from tight buds, for the crystal bowl in the center of the table. "We had to call the butcher three times before ever he sent the chickens," she said.

"Um." Ellen stepped back to look at the effect. "I thought they'd be good with that cloth. Hurry up, Katy, with the rest of the silver. Not so near the service plates. Like this." Nine was an awkward number, but she couldn't think of any extra woman to combine with this group. Couldn't ask Father to have dinner out when these were the Ridge crowd. Later, when she had more special guests . . . a more formal dinner party. . . .

She hurried into the living room with stalks of laurel for the tall white vases, one at each end of the mantel. The dark, pointed leaves made a good accent in the room. Her quick glance inventoried the room, crisp folds of satin draperies drawn across the windows, small logs behind the brass andirons . . . queer how city firewood was always nondescript, someday they'd have a load brought down from the country. Cocktail shaker, glasses . . . she hoped Lawrence had remembered the gin, he said he knew where he could get some good stuff. "Take the box down when you go," she called, dropping it in the foyer as she hurried up to her room. From the hall she called, "Libby! Is the baby having his supper? I'm late, I've got to tear!" She didn't wait to hear Libby's answer.

She stripped off her suit, and stood a moment at the door of the closet, her hand moving along the dresses on hangers, rocking them gently. She'd like to dress up, say that hyacinth blue velvet. A long dress did something for a woman, the soft brush of fabric against an ankle . . . Her house really demanded a touch of elegance. "I'll be a sight," Adelaide had said. "Unless I lug in a suitcase and take time to change. You don't care, do you?" Ellen knew just how Adelaide would look at her, that shrewd, unspoken comment in her round brown eyes. Showing off again, Ellen?

"Hello, there." Lawrence was at the door. "I thought you decided not to come to the party. D'you know Larry has a new tooth? A pip!"

Ellen seized a dress, any dress! "I couldn't help it," she said. "Did you remember. . . ."

"Sure. Had to try a couple of places. I'll have to get me a regular bootlegger who'll deliver. I felt as if a cop was following me all the way home."

"Don't mix too many cocktails," said Ellen. "Not for this bunch."

"I'm surprised you want drinks at all."

"It's a nice city touch." Ellen ran across to close the door. "Do go along, darling! I haven't time to talk!"

Before she had finished dressing, she heard the distant tinkle of the bell. She stepped into her pumps, and opened the door a crack. If that was Adelaide, Ellen would call her upstairs; I want to see her when she looks at my house! But that wasn't Adelaide's quick, emphatic voice, it was Carey Moore, no mistaking that middle-western twang.

"I'm afraid we're early," she was saying. "It isn't half-past yet, is it? We didn't know how long it would take to get way over to this number." Then Gilbert's quiet tone, smoothing over the embarrassment in Carey's words. "We walked around the block once, and I said someone has to be the first arrival."

The door across the hall opened, and Dr. Randall emerged from his room. "Oh!" He glanced at Ellen, uncertainty in his manner. "I thought I heard someone . . . but you haven't gone down yet."

"Goodness, you don't have to wait for me! I'm coming in a minute. It's your favorite Moores." As Ellen dusted powder over her face, and whirled before the mirror to be sure she had fastened all the hooks of the black velvet, she frowned, wishing that Father wouldn't be so punctilious. He made her uncomfortable, the way he was so careful never to get under foot, never to intrude. Acting as if he had to tuck himself out of sight on a high shelf in a closet! He had demurred at the whole plan, he wanted to stay in the country, he didn't want to live in this house, he'd had no training as a guest, he said. Ellen had to drag him in, she didn't have time to worry about him alone in the country, especially after the queer turn he'd had at Christmas.

There, her hair was smooth, the pearls looked nice against her throat, black velvet made her skin have a lustre like the pearls, what was the word, nacreous? . . . no, that wouldn't be a good word for her copy, no one knew it, anyway it didn't have a pleasant sound. She wasn't pretty, but she was smart to look at.

She whisked powder off the glass top of the dressing table, turned off the ceiling light, looked about with the sharp eyes of impending inspection, and nodded, gratification like honey on her tongue. A good room, informal and intimate, with touches of luxury in the heavy silver toilet set (she never used it, the brush was too soft!) and the chaise longue done in satin to match the dull gold of bed spreads and curtains. Not that she ever had time to use the chaise longue, either! Nothing about the house had a hasty, thrown-together by a commercial decorator look.

Ellen heard the door-bell again, and with a quick glance into

her father's room (she'd done that well, too, more a sitting
room than bed-room, with his flat desk and comfortable big
chair) went quickly down the stairs. Adelaide's head was coming
up the stair-well from the entrance, and Ellen waited for her.
Adelaide kissed her, chattering.

"Isn't this wonderful! Gracious, are we impressed! That
darling door, right on the street!"

"Did you cut that entrance?" John came up close behind his
wife. "It's not the right period for this house, of course."

Below them, Katy was admitting the Willetts. "Leave your
things there," called Ellen, "and come right up!" To John she
said, "We haven't changed a thing. But I like the door!"

"Oh, it's convenient. But as an architect. . ." His eyelids
twitched, and for an instant his eyes met Ellen's with a sharp
tingle of conflict. He'd have to show off more than ever tonight, because of the house. She must be careful, thought Ellen.
The hostility between them was an old habit, but they kept it
out of sight. She moved past him to greet Genevieve, who
mounted slowly, the light burnishing her red-gold coronet of
braids.

"I'm so glad you'd take the trip in town," Ellen said, "it's
our very first party, and we wanted the Ridge!"

"It's my first trip away from home for months, actually."
Genevieve lifted her soft bosom in a deep breath, having
reached the top step. "Dexter runs back and forth so much, it
seems nothing to him, but I just hibernate all winter."

"This is something to come in for." Dexter looked a trifle
worn, as if he'd brought his wife all the way by hand. "How
well you look, Ellen! And what a fine place! You're the only
friend we know who has a town house!"

"It's charming, Ellen!" Adelaide went on into the living
room, her chatter like gay little banners. "Just like a stage setting! If you had my two boys, you'd never have all this ele-

gance! And cocktails! Why, Lawrence! Hello, Dr. Ranny. Do you know how much I miss you? Every afternoon I hope you'll stop in, and then I remember you're way off here!" She still clung to his left arm as he shook hands with Genevieve and Dexter, and Ellen made a little rush across toward Gilbert and Carey, who were standing side by side as if they posed for a photograph with the piano for background, Carey's eyes hurrying from one detail of the room to another, like a child who mustn't stare and can't help it. What a little frump she is, thought Ellen, however did she catch Gilbert!

"It's been ages since I've seen you!" Ellen stepped up her cordiality. "When was it? How's the new job, Carey? Does it keep you just tearing through the days? Of course the house has been a terrific extra job for me. Do you like it?"

"It's impressive." Katy was opening the French doors into the dining room, and Gilbert stared with mild interest. "Do you have all five stories to yourselves?"

"Our apartment would go right into this one room, wouldn't it, Gilbert?" Carey's words ended in a nervous little laugh. "I can't imagine people in New York having an up and down stairs!"

"Ours is big enough for the time we have to stay in it." Gilbert looked at Ellen, his dark brows almost meeting above his quiet gaze.

He's not really impressed. Ellen's thoughts set up a twittering like sparrows. He always looks at me like that, weighing me, unperturbed, watching me, not liking or disliking me, from the beginning he's done that, and I can't stand it! What did she want of him, anyhow? A country boy, no polish, just brains. Behind her Lawrence's easy laugh, the clink of ice in the shaker, John Burchall's sharp words, "What'd you do, make a killing on Wall Street? Come on, let us in on a good thing!" were louder suddenly than the twittering of her thoughts, Gilbert was talking, too, and for a sharp instant she knew what she wanted. Recognition. That smooth, steel, male strength in Gilbert opposing, beating down the wily, devious female strength in her.

"Have you heard about Carey's good news?" Gilbert raised his voice a trifle, insisting on her attention. (Had he heard that chitter? Oh, nonsense!) "She's pulled down a fellowship, so she doesn't have to hunt for a job."

"At Columbia?" Ellen saw the way the faint strain in Carey's face disappeared, the hint of anxious shyness in her manner dropped away. "How marvellous! What do you do?"

"It really is marvellous," said Carey. "I don't have to teach ... just assist in the laboratory, and I can work for a doctor's degree. We haven't settled on my special research problem yet ... but we will. Gilbert's helping me make up my mind. It saves me years of working up, because I get training and experience and come out with a label, all ready for something big!"

"You're going to be a doctor?" (I could have been a doctor, thought Ellen. Father suggested it. All those years of grind!)

"Not that kind. Ph.D. Science. Bacteriology. Blood chemistry. Maybe I'll make some stupendous discovery!" Carey's laugh was nervous again. "Don't get me started on it, I'm so excited I'd just go on forever! It must seem pretty dull to you."

"If anything's dull ..." Lawrence pushed between them, the tray a wedge, the golden liquid rocking in the monogramed glasses ... "try one of these. Guaranteed to remove all dullness."

John capered just behind Lawrence, balancing a large plate of canapés on one extended palm, and Ellen, with an explosive "Oh!", seized it just as it canted dangerously.

"Hey!" protested John. "I used to be a butler."

"Not for me, you didn't." Ellen held to the plate, and John followed her as she made her way around the room with it.

Adelaide and Dr. Randall were side by side on one of the low divans before the fireplace, Dexter and Genevieve on the other, Genevieve with her mouth turned down, the men laughing at Adelaide's account of some household catastrophe.

"Did you do this room all by yourself?" asked John, "or did you have a professional?"

"What would you think?" Ellen sipped her cocktail, looking over it at the room. This was the way she had seen it, a charming background, although Carey Moore sat too stiffly on the edge of that gold chair, and Gilbert, standing with Lawrence there near the piano, managed to keep an air of aloofness, of refusing to be merged in a group.

"It's really very good," said John. "Not too formal, these high ceilings give space even when you get a bunch of people. Ole Lawrence must be working his head off to meet the bills. I say, Lawrence!" John shouted across. "Did you make a killing on the Street? I asked you that once and you dodged!"

"Johnny, be good!" Adelaide smiled up at him. "Just because we've just been swamped . . . January's an awful month, when you've built a house and furnished it, I think . . . you shouldn't let everybody know that we can't help thinking about what it all costs. Isn't it funny . . ." she leaned back in the divan, her head close to Dr. Randall's shoulder . . . "that it's not polite to bring up money, when it's often quite important."

"Spoil the front people put up, if they talked honestly about money," said Dr. Randall.

Genevieve leaned forward. "It's very American, isn't it, this emphasis on money?"

"Hey!" Lawrence moved between the divans, offering dividends. "What do you use in England?"

"Actually, your upper class here is the wealthy class, isn't it? Now, in England. . ."

Dexter extended his glass, his thin hand not quite steady.

"If you go back to beginnings," he said, "you'd find the best families were always the best looters. Only it was land first, not cash."

Lawrence looked at him warily, and Ellen was glad that Katy appeared at that moment to announce dinner. Lawrence had Dexter marked as too red, she didn't enjoy ever the way Dexter's speculative, ranging mind seemed to show up the short tether on which Lawrence operated.

"Dinner!" she said. "Shall we go? See how you like my dining room."

"It's lovely, Ellen!" Adelaide gave her elbow a squeeze as they all eddied slowly across the foyer and into the dining room. "I don't see how you've done it! Imagine having a baby and a house like this the same year! No one but Ellen could manage that."

"Libby has the baby." Lawrence, drawing back a chair for Genevieve, was pleased with his little joke.

"Of course," said Ellen, too quickly, "I couldn't swing things without competent help." She caught her father's alert glance, and broke off the rest of her retort, that Lawrence, like most men, thought because she had servants and a nursemaid, she did nothing. "You sit here, Gilbert," she said, "and Carey beyond John, and Father, there between Adelaide and Genevieve."

"That's the trouble in the country," Genevieve complained mildly. "You can't keep a maid. They have no resources of their own, they begin to be moodish, and then they leave."

"Look at the advantage I have," said Adelaide. "Being my own maid. If I get moodish, I can't leave! Of course I have Mrs. Danieloski one day a week. There's a woman for you!" Adelaide's eyelids crinkled with ingenuous mirth. "She has twelve children, *and* a career. She goes out by the day."

Ellen gave a slight shrug. Part of her attention was on Katy, as the girl removed the service plates, one by one, and set down

the shallow soup plates. All right, Adelaide, she thought; boast
about your way, I hear your taunt, I'm not picking it up, not
tonight. If I weren't so fond of you, I'd think you were smug!

"Those peasant women are strong as . . . as anything," said
Genevieve.

"Well, peasants?" Dexter broke his roll with a sharp little
crack. "Bill Danieloski owns his own farm. At least, he's buying it."

"Damn Poles 'll own all of Connecticut if we don't watch
out," said Lawrence, as Ellen saw the quick, bridling reproach
with which Genevieve looked at Dexter. Genevieve had a way
of accumulating injuries when she and Dexter were out, Ellen
had seen that working often. Lawrence, having tossed off a
remark he had made before (and had he thought of it himself
or heard it?) was tasting the soup. He nodded across the table
at Ellen. It was good. Thin black bean soup with sherry.

"Oh, yummy!" exclaimed Adelaide. "You always have the
best food, Ellen!"

"She knows how to hold a man," said Lawrence.

"Now just add that the way to a man's heart is through his
stomach," said Ellen, "and feed the brute, and you'll have a
good collection of bromides."

"Lots of truth in those old saws," said Lawrence, unperturbed.

Ellen turned toward Gilbert, at her right. Queer, how seeing
Lawrence in a group, projecting him against the others, seemed
to give her this obscure irritability, as if, having seen to all other
details, she had failed to get a proper polish on her husband!

"What have you been up to since last summer?" she asked.
"I suppose you're terribly busy?"

Yes, he was, rather.

"Tell me about it!"

Nothing to tell, just plodding along, getting established.

Clinic at Bellevue some days, private practice. What was Ellen doing, back on her job?

"I suppose it seems awfully trivial to you, compared to Carey's work," said Ellen. "But it's great fun! Only don't start me talking shop."

"Why not? Nothing's more interesting."

"All right. You asked for it!" Ellen was gay, telling about the huge campaign the firm planned, the full page advertisements in all the women's magazines. Dazzle him a little with how much they cost, how many readers would see them, how shrewdly she had designed them. "I mean to make oh, a million women feel undressed without rouge! Not so long ago the rouge-pot and the lip-stick were a sign of sin! Now they're to be a sign of smartness. A way to be alluring." She gave him details, photographs of some of New York's upper crust, with testimonials. "You'd be surprised how easy it is to get them! Sketches . . . slogans . . . 'My dear, you never looked so beautiful!' "

"Snob appeal, sex appeal," said Gilbert. "You've got it."

"Now you're making fun of me again!" Why should she care what he thought? From the beginning she had pushed against that faintly ironic, impersonal attitude. She felt like a peddler who has spread out all his wares, only to find that Gilbert, who should have been fingering them over with envy and desire, had strolled off about his own secret concerns. He was a self-centered egoist, and why she bothered with him at all!

"I'll tell you what amuses me," said Gilbert, waiting a moment as Katy reached for his soup plate. "Here you are, carrying a torch for women, arise, ye slaves, and all that, and at the same time you're selling them the idea of painting themselves up to be more captivating, like the harem ladies."

"It's a disguise," said Ellen. "Your modern woman wants a lover as much as her mother did! She just wants other things, too." She leaned forward a trifle, the pearls dropping away from her soft throat, one arm extended on the table, the wrist delicate and blue-veined under the satin skin. Gilbert's eyes touched her hand, and lifted, and momentarily Ellen had a stir of pleasure, a light breeze ruffling the feathers of her vanity, as if Gilbert had turned back to glance at the wares she displayed.

"Don't generalize from yourself," he said. "You aren't typical." Then his glance moved across to Carey, his wife. Ellen tucked away his brief comment, a small coin for all her effort, but evidence that he had, under those dark brows, in that challenging impersonality, some conception of her. She'd ask him what he meant, she'd make him say. Sometime. Carey was sitting very straight in her chair, looking like a little girl dressed for Sunday School, her smooth, dun colored hair in a figure eight on the back of her head, her dark blue silk with its lace collar, her profile showing a polite smile as she listened to Lawrence and Dexter.

"Good times are ahead of us," declared Lawrence, "now the Republicans are in the saddle at last. We'll get rid of the Red menace, we'll. . . ." If Gilbert had only married the right woman, jumped Ellen's thoughts, someone who could help him socially! He's the best man here, Father thinks so, too, but how can Carey help him? Then John said, "How's the baby? I keep forgetting you've got one," and Ellen turned to answer him. She could spar with him and at the same time watch Katy, who entered now, a trifle winded, bearing the platter with Ida's best fried chicken; she could hear Ida's heavier tread on the rear stairs as she mounted with the vegetable dishes. For future dinners, more formal, more glittering, there should be another serving maid. Too bad Libby refused to help out. Couldn't risk any insistence on Libby, she was too necessary to Ellen's scheme of things.

The talk was general now, no more téte-a-tétes, friendly talk of neighbors with Adelaide telling stories of her boys, Dexter telling of a deer that came out at twilight every evening as he walked up from the station, Dr. Randall telling of the first winter he'd owned the Ridge, and the bitter crust over feet of snow, like the ice age. Ellen's imagination left them, leaping into the future, when her charming room would contain distinguished guests, bankers, artists, women in lovely gowns, Lawrence looking his suave best in white tie and satin lapels, sophisticated, brilliant talk. . . . "She gives the most charming little dinners, my dear."

Book Three
"STRONG BIRD ON PINIONS FREE"

REMEMBER that first dinner at the Hunters' house in New York partly because it was the only time Ellen ever invited all of the Ridge people in a group and partly because I had never before seen the interior of a New York house. I didn't want to go because I didn't have anything suitable to wear and I had to get up so early the next morning for an experiment I had started in the laboratory. Gilbert never wanted to go to a dinner anyway. But we decided to go, he because he thought I needed a change from work and I because I thought he ought to learn to be social.

I didn't have a very good time. I was self-conscious without being self-assured. Although I had met everyone there the previous summer, they seemed that evening not individuals but a solid mass, formidable because their ways differed from mine, because against them I was bound to reveal myself as ignorant and inept. Such trivial agonies! Standing stiffly beside Gilbert, not knowing whether I should sit down or join the people on the divan by the fireplace, smearing my fingers with cheese on the cracker I couldn't swallow, dropping the serving spoon when the maid thrust the platter of chicken between me and John Burchall.

Even the news about my fellowship didn't matter to anyone, except perhaps Dr. Randall, who said, "Well, you have your

start, Carey. Now don't spend all your life in a laboratory."
Dexter Willetts remembered it, too, for it was that night he
spoke to me about Rachel Thayer.

"I know a girl who's majoring in chemistry," he said, and
across the table his wife fixed her large, shadowed eyes upon
me, straining to overhear. "Didn't you meet her at that picnic
on your land? Rachel Thayer."

"I met so many people that night, they're just a blur," I said,
too flippantly.

"She was there. I'll tell her to look you up. She's got a good
head, she doesn't know quite what to work toward, you could
talk with her, perhaps."

I told him where my office was. (My office was a table in the
corner of a room shared by a dozen other assistants, but I liked
the sound of the words.)

"She's only nineteen," Dexter went on, "but she's a senior
next year. I think you'd like her."

That was the way my long association with Rachel began. She
is the only important character in the later events on the Ridge
who was not seated at Ellen's table that evening, and she was
just enough younger so that she would have seemed unlikely
to be involved with any of us. She says it wasn't casual accident
that turned her into one of my assistants, and took her back to
Connecticut, that she knew what she wanted and would have
found a way to achieving that desire.

"Let's walk home, shall we?" asked Gilbert, as we stepped
out to the street, into the sharp, dark night. Arm in arm we
walked briskly down the long blocks, dark and shadowed except
for the pools of light around each lamp post, light that shimmered with hints of invisible arrows, the promise of snow which
the sharp air held. "Did you have a good time?" he asked.

"Someday I'll make them sit up and notice me, won't I?" I
demanded.

"Sure." He tucked my hand down under his in a deep pocket.

"Do you like Ellen?" I asked. "What were you talking about so deeply?"

"Were we? When? Oh, at dinner? Ellen was just showing off . . . her job, her house. She's a voracious woman. Carnivorous, that's what she is."

Although I didn't know just what Gilbert meant, I was pleased that he was disparaging. "Her house is lovely, isn't it? Just like pictures in one of these magazines. . . ."

"If you like things as complicated as that. Servants and folderols and couches you'd never put your feet up on!"

We walked along in silence, my hand warm under his, and I thought about the difference between us. Gilbert had a self-contained steadfastness, not at all a self-approval, so much as an acceptance of what he was, down to the smallest detail of how we lived, what we were; his only desire for change, if you could call that change, was that he meant to win a wider margin of security for us, and he meant to climb steadily in his profession. I think that Gilbert kept with him always as a yardstick the recollection of his narrow, poverty-weighted youth, the recollection of his slow, laborious emergence, and measured by that yardstick, what he now had seemed good, not a miracle, because he had achieved it himself, but a deeply satisfying state. What Gilbert wanted was always a response to something within himself, not a response to outer stimuli. He never compared himself and what he had with men he encountered and their possessions. He would look at Ellen's house and observe the progress of her dinner party with detached interest, just as he might have watched the natives of some African jungle. Different people, different ways of doing things, different sets of values, all remote from him.

I wasn't like that, and sometimes I would burst out against Gilbert with an irritation I didn't understand. I was like a window shopper, who can not look at elegant costumes or furs or jewelry without in imagination trying them on, thinking how wonderful I would look in that, how people would notice when I passed! Not that I really longed for clothes or wealth. But I had a vague restlessness, a feeling that somewhere beyond the close margin of our busy, and for Gilbert, absorbing days, was another world, brilliant and exciting, its inhabitants polished, distinguished, everything! Ellen seemed to belong in part to that world, and in imagination I tried that on! In imagination I was polished and distinguished, never awkward or tongue-tied or too feverishly flippant. I suppose that if I hadn't had some brains, and if Gilbert hadn't been steadily encouraging about my work, and if I hadn't, out of what at the beginning was just a necessity to earn a living, and then a satisfying use of energy, had grasp enough on reality to see that work, Gilbert's and mine, was the one ladder we might climb to reach the vague heaven of approval and recognition and esteem for which I longed—if I hadn't happened to be thus equipped, I might have developed into a dissatisfied and complaining woman, one of those who thinks life has treated her unfairly. I can see now that this longing of mine had its bitter root in earlier days in college, where I was too shy to be popular, too shabby and plodding to be elected to any office, or bid by any sorority; earlier still, in my home town, where I lost too early the comfortable acceptance of home and family and self which any young animal has toward his corner, and took on my mother's fear of all the neighbors must know about us. But I couldn't talk to Gilbert about any of it, and that was another kind of fear. If I had talked it out—

"A house just big enough for you and me," said Gilbert, suddenly. "That's what we want. No clutter." He'd been talking with John, or rather, John had been telling him what to do. Prices were going up, a boom time was ahead, we ought to build right now, a bank or a building and loan society would help with finances. We talked about it all the way home, and went on after we had gone to bed in our little bedroom opening on a court, and that night or another winter night we must have decided to take the risk. "It looks foolproof," Gilbert said. "We work harder, that's all, and we have the fun of the house while we pay for it."

Although the first impact of the Ridge and its inhabitants stands out so sharply in my memory, the next years run together in a blur, and I am not sure of the sequence in phrases or small bits of action which my mind turns up. I look around at the house, and know that its present state is the accretion of years, as our taste changed and our income increased. Somewhere encysted here is the original house, and I can not separate it from the present. The same thing is true of myself. It doesn't matter when I bought the rugs or curtains or chairs, but it does matter that I dig out what happened to Gilbert and me.

Trying to recall the past in orderly, full flow of day by day, or even year by year, is like looking at the sky on a spring evening when mist in the lower air obscures all the stars except those of first magnitude. Slowly you recognize a few of those, placing them in their constellations, and slowly your mind pulls through the mist the lesser stars that should complete the figure. Orion's belt, swinging toward the north, the bright star that marks his shoulder, and somewhere, near Polaris . . . there, isn't that it, that blur, the small cluster of the Pleiades? Just so my mind fixing on certain moments, not knowing why they stand out, can fill in the pattern, drawing through the misty past the emotions, the people, the circumstances which make the constellation.

The years of my apprenticeship in laboratory work all run together, although I can feel under the arches of my feet the round of the stool on which I perched for long hours, can feel against my socket the metal eyepiece of the microscope, can smell the hot rusty iron of the gas plate. I remember my excited pride when one of the doctors sent in a memo, "Give this specimen to Carey Moore. I like her work."

Gilbert gave me a microscope for a birthday present, and fitted up a laboratory bench in a corner of the garage, which as yet held no car, so that I could work on my special problem during the University summer holiday. "The only way I can have my wife stay home," he said.

I remember the smell of hot sun on the woolen stuff of my cap and gown the day I walked in the convocation procession to receive my doctor's degree, and the queer, deflated feeling later, when I waited at the corner of Broadway for Gilbert, the crowds jostling past me and dispersing. He had gone off just before the lines of graduates had formed behind their marshalls, to telephone to Dr. Randall, who had not turned up as he had agreed, to watch the ceremony.

I was cross with anxiety by the time Gilbert came dashing out of the subway kiosk. When he called Dr. Randall, the maid was so incoherent and frightened that he had gone at once to the house. He hadn't seen my big moment! "I'm sorry, Carey, but I thought I'd get back in time." Ellen had been whisked off to the hospital, a month before her baby was expected, something had gone wrong; Dr. Randall had run out to hail a taxi for her, he'd either stumbled or he'd had another heart attack. After Lawrence and Ellen had driven away, the maid had found Dr. Randall all hunched up in front of the house, unable even to ring.

"You might have let someone else pick him up!" I was amazed at my own words. "Frightening me like this! You've ruined my day. You might have put me first for once."

"I said I was sorry." Gilbert's heavy eyebrows met, he tucked his chin against his collar.

"But you aren't sorry! You just think I'm unreasonable! I ought to be delighted that you can fly to the rescue of Ellen Hunter and her father. A morning that will never come again in all my life, one I've worked for years to reach, and you didn't care enough to stay!" The simple, self-pitying anguish of a child crowded out any other feeling; I had been alone, deserted, unsung, at a moment which I had foreseen as triumph with full recognition. If Gilbert had said, but I was as disappointed as you were, if he had laughed at me for my tirade, I, too, might have laughed at the child who cried out. But what Gilbert said, curtly, was, "You got your degree, didn't you? At least I didn't hold up the ceremonies."

He was distressed about Dr. Randall, and concerned about Ellen. Libby had given him full details, and he knew how serious her condition must be. He was tired and he had come rushing back to find me as soon as he dared leave the Doctor. He wasn't going to help me out.

"We can't stand on this corner the rest of our lives," he said. "We better find a place for lunch. Food might help."

We sat opposite each other across a bare table in a crowded, noisy restaurant, and I ate stubbornly, determined to prove that I could be as indifferent as he was, while stormy fragments of sentences, accusations and denials, kept splintering through my head. When Gilbert had finished his coffee, he went off to a telephone booth, and came back, not even looking at me, as he reported. Libby said there was no word from Ellen yet, Lawrence had called her at twelve; Dr. Randall was still lying down, but he said the pain had gone.

"It will certainly be a surprise to Ellen if anything goes wrong with her plans."

"You have to give her credit for taking that risk." Gilbert was counting out change for the check. "How'd they make that

eighty-five cents?" He picked up the spotted menu card, and
I jerked it out of his fingers.

"How can you?" I tried to keep my voice low. "Say a thing
like that and then fuss over a nickle! You mean I won't take
that risk!"

"I meant only what I said." His hand shut over mine, steady-
ing the card, and he verified the bill. "Yes, they're right." Deliberately he laid a coin beside his plate, and walked to the
cashier's desk. Then he waited at the doorway, and the waitress
who clattered our dishes onto her tray looked at me with such
bored impatience that I had no alternative but to follow Gilbert.

"It's my afternoon at the clinic," he said. "I may be late getting home tonight. Why don't you take it easy this afternoon?"

We stepped aside from the doorway to let a group of boys
come clowning out of the restaurant, and before I could answer,
Gilbert was off across the street toward the subway, moving
with his usual unhurried, balanced sure-footed walk, the walk
of a man who knew where he was going and just how and when
he would arrive. Tears burned under my lids.

When Gilbert came in that evening, I was paring potatoes at
the sink of the grubby little kitchen. I glanced around at him,
as he stood in the doorway, and at the expression of his face,
screwed up a little into uncertain inquiry, tentative, I dropped
my knife and rushed at him, sliding my arms under his, feeling
his long sigh lift against my breasts. "That's my girl!" he said,
and we kissed, and said no more.

Why should I remember that day so distinctly, when it seems
to have only an inconsequential and brief difficulty, only a momentary knot in the thread? I wonder now whether Gilbert
understood better than I did what made the knot? I wonder,
too, that human beings manage to get along with one another
as well as they do, when in all those years from childhood up
to middle life, years before the die hardens, the pattern is set,

the years when choice and change are still possible, they know so little what are the obscure and potent forces from which they speak and act and feel.

Yesterday I sat for a long time on the bank of a small lake, resting before I started the climb back to the Ridge. The quiet water was opaque and blue, holding on its surface only the reflection of the sky, at its rim the reflection of overhanging trees. There moved across space above it, floating on the steady air with scarcely a dip of the shallow arcs of his wings, a hawk. He seemed to float without effort, in a wide, descending spiral, and I thought, to his hard and brilliant eyes the water is transparent, he can see all that is submerged, streamers of weeds and rocks and heedless fish. And I thought, this is my hawk-flight, riding the steady air of all the past years, with time, not space, making transparent what I could not see when I was too close a part of it. I waited for the hawk to swoop and break the water, to rise with a shining fish caught in his talons, an omen for my own search. He may have spied me there, for he checked his spiralling, banked, and then soared until my eyes lost him.

So, looking through years which have thus become transparent, I see that I was troubled by a kind of jealousy of Ellen, not the ordinary jealousy, but a resentment that she was arrogant and unafraid, that she could take child-birth in her stride without losing step in her work. She had said to me, "I should think you'd have some children now, while you're young. Why, with work like yours, you'd scarcely have to miss a day, no one minds what you look like in a laboratory, your smock makes a swell maternity dress!"

I'd tried to explain, resentfully, that I had to make a place for myself, I couldn't just be part of an established firm that went right on as hers did, I couldn't risk division of interest, of attention, not till I was really established. And because I had a hidden anxiety that Gilbert might, never in anything he actually said, but in a look or a word withheld, have let Dr. Randall think, and through him, Ellen, that he too would like a child, I wanted proof for myself and for the world that Gilbert cared as much as I did about every step of my progress. Ellen would like nothing better than to feel sorry for Gilbert because he was defrauded. He couldn't ask a friendly question about her young Larry without her eyebrows lifting in carets of significance. "He's awfully good with children, isn't he?" That was Ellen's way of taking me down. Gilbert was doing very well, the name Dr. Gilbert Moore got into print occasionally on state commissions, the slow, stable growth of his reputation had started, and if Ellen couldn't build her husband up into a bright figure, she could at least dim Gilbert with commiseration.

All this I can see now, looking down through the past like the hawk. At the time I hid the truth under layers of excuses. I was over-wrought, tired. Gilbert wanted me to have what I wanted, that was our bargain with each other. I can see now, too, that what happened to Ellen later that summer increased my apprehension, so that the tension which had already come into my relation with Gilbert took another screw-turn or so. I wasn't going to be betrayed by my flesh, caught, tormented, made into a wretched invalid as my mother had been, as Ellen so narrowly escaped.

We had planned to move out to our house on the Ridge the following week, to spend the summer. I was to return to the University in the fall, to give several courses in laboratory technology, and I wanted the summer to work out my schedules carefully, and perhaps to go on with some of my own research. Gilbert was to spend three days a week at White Plains, substituting for a resident psychiatrist. I was packing away our winter coats and woolen blankets in camphor balls and tarred paper the night Gilbert came in, late, and stood looking at me as I wrestled with unruly paper and cord. "You might help, instead of just staring!" I said.

The tickling odor of the moth flakes made me sneeze, and the ends of the paper flew exasperatingly out of my clumsy folds. Gilbert pushed my hands away and tied the package.

"I just can't get ready to go tomorrow," I said. "I don't know where so much stuff comes from!"

"We can't go tomorrow," said Gilbert, his voice flat and dry.

Dr. Randall was dead. Gilbert had found him when he'd stopped at the house that afternoon to ask how things were going. "Good thing I did, too," he said, grimly. He'd come home to tell me. If I'd make him coffee, then he'd go back. No, there was nothing for me to do. Ellen was too ill to be told. But he refused to talk, except to say, "Poor Lawrence! He's come apart at the seams, he's just plain no use without someone to run him."

Libby told me later how much Gilbert had done. She needed an audience for her grief and her indignation. "You'd think sudden death was a crime!" Police and coroner, reporters, threats of an autopsy. "It's a disgrace the way a man can't go to his Maker without such shame! And Mr. Hunter as helpless as young Larry, what with his worry over Ellen and all! If it hadn't been for your husband!"

Ellen's second child had been born prematurely, the day her father died; Ellen had a series of hemorrhages and days of septic fever. Because of her condition, Dr. Randall's funeral was private.

Some days later we finally got out to the country. Ellen was out of danger, the baby, a four-pound girl, was apparently going to make the grade and live, and Lawrence said he'd be all right, he'd get back into regular hours at the office, nothing to do but wait for Ellen's recovery.

"I don't know how I'm going to break the news to her," he said. "When do you think I ought to tell her?"

"You'll have to decide that yourself," said Gilbert, and for a moment the glazed sleep-walker expression came into Lawrence's face again.

"It's really easier for her, because everything's all over," I said, and Gilbert gave me a quick, impatient frown.

"I hope so," said Lawrence. "She would have known just how she wanted things done, you know."

"Now don't begin that again!" Gilbert was curt.

"No." Lawrence rubbed the heel of his hand hard against his temple. "You know, it's a funny thing. You think you don't want a third party around, no matter who, but he was different. He was a kind of balance wheel. He kept a kind of check rein on Ellen." He broke off, his forehead scarlet up to the receding line of sandy hair, his eyes startled.

"He was one of the best," said Gilbert, quietly.

On the dusty, bumpy suburban train later that morning, Gilbert leaned back, his eyes closed. I pretended to read, but I watched him. He wasn't asleep, and his face looked smudged with fatigue.

"They've just worn you out!" I said. "I don't know why you had to take the brunt!"

"Nonsense. It was a relief to have things to do."

"I know you feel bad. But after all, he was an old man, quite old, and he'd had to stop his work."

"So what do I do? Not mind that I've lost my friend?" Gilbert opened his eyes and stared at me, somberly. "The way Ellen won't mind, because everything's over and she can put it all out of her thoughts? Do you think you can sidetrack all pain?"

I can remember the angry confusion I felt, and the way a strong impulse to hide and protect the very self which Gilbert had attacked kept me quiet for a moment until I could shift direction.

"Wasn't it queer, what Lawrence said, as if he is actually afraid he can't manage Ellen without the Doctor? Did you notice?"

Gilbert shut his eyes again. "He didn't intend to say that, he's not given to examining himself."

"He evidently knows who runs the house. But maybe it's a good thing he has Ellen to run him. He certainly was helpless this last week! And he doesn't seem to be nervous, he's always seemed so smooth and . . . oh, you know . . . never a doubt, what he did or thought was all right, he knew how."

"Within limits, that's true of Lawrence." Gilbert was silent for a time, and I picked up my book again. If he didn't want to talk, he needn't. I was just assuring myself that he hadn't really implied that he didn't like my attitude, when he spoke again. "Lawrence is a well trained performer," he said, "as long as he has the proper cues. Change the cues, and he's lost, because he acts from habit, not from thought or imagination. He's not so much weak, as rigid, inflexible. He can't improvise in a strange situation. That's the great disadvantage of being as well brought up as Lawrence has been. He functions smoothly within a smooth and artificial groove. Jar him out of the groove, and he's bewildered. That's what cracks up lots of folks, isn't it, not being able to improvise when the familiar cues stop?" Gilbert twisted his mouth into a grimace, interest and irony and weariness combined. "I'll docket that notion for further thought," he said. "Now I'm going to catch up on my sleep."

I looked down at the pages of my book, but the question Gilbert had flung at me ran annoyingly in my head, taking on the rhythm of the wheels as some irregularity of the flange hit the metal tracks. Do you think you can side-track all pain? Do you *think* you can *side*-track all *pain*? Why, I was just being sensible, wasn't I, trying to help Gilbert out of his unhappiness? He needn't have sounded so—so hostile. Deliberately I bent my mind to the meaning of the words on the page. Gilbert was tired, that was all. After a few days in the country . . . I'd be carefus what I said. . . . It was foolish to feel this forlorn isolation, with Gilbert right here beside me. We were both edgy, that was all. I made my lips shape the words I read, until they were louder than the unanswered question.

After that several summers combine in a general recollection. They were alike in that we spent them on the Ridge with Gilbert commuting to one post or another, with freedom during the summer for me as long as I held the university job. They are too much alike for me to separate them into a neat chronological order, to remember the time sequence of the impressions which move into vividness out of the blur as I stare backward.

That first summer Ellen did not come out at all; Libby brought the little boy to the Randall house, which now, of course, belonged to Ellen, and Ellen spent some months at the sea-shore, getting fatted up for further slaughter she said, by which she meant an operation intended to repair internal damages.

It must have been that year that Rachel Thayer came to stay with me for several weeks to help organize in final pamphlet form the material we had been collecting on leucocythemia. I know that Rachel was with me at the time that Adelaide Burchall's household had a siege of chicken-pox or measles, and Adelaide telephoned to ask if I would take Dick, the younger boy, in case he hadn't been exposed. I remember how pleased Rachel was and how she brushed aside my qualms.

"You must have had measles when you were a child," she said. "You won't catch anything! Dick is really a darling. What if he does interrupt our work a little? Tell Adelaide to put his toothbrush in his pocket and send him along."

Something in the way Adelaide had said, "Yours is the only household without children and I'm sure Dick won't be any trouble, he's a thoughtful little boy," had set me spluttering. Adelaide's incredible, implying blandly that since I have no children, nothing I may have to do is of any importance! Of course I have no choice, if I refused, she'd never forgive me! I think people should carry their own responsibilities. Then I stopped spluttering; Rachel would think me unneighborly, ungracious.

Dick came over tugging a battered suit-case which fell open on the steps, spilling out clean shirts and underclothes and books and a box of red and black checkers which rolled off the step into the grass. "Oh, murder!" cried Dick, scrambling his wardrobe together, his ears pink. Rachel ran down to help him gather the checkers, and he squatted on his heels, fitting the disks into the box. "Oh, murder, if I've lost some of those men!"

"We'll find them. Here's a red one and a black. There, isn't that all?" Rachel sat down on the step, and Dick slapped the cover over the box.

"I guess I won't put that back in this ole suit-case," he said. "Would you mind taking it for me? I didn't know as anybody played checkers, but I thought I'd bring 'em along." He planted one foot on the suit-case to squeeze it shut, and Rachel reached over to snap the catch down. "Do you live here?" he asked.

A trivial incident to recall so distinctly. I can see them there in the sunlight, the wind ruffling up fine ends of Rachel's dark hair, fluttering the corner of her blue smock, and Dick looking at her, a tentative acceptance of her friendliness easing away the embarrassed reluctance with which he had come up the walk. But in a small way it stands for the quality in Rachel which was her charm. More than anyone else I have ever known, she had a warm friendliness, a sensitive perception of others. She was intelligent enough, she had her own inner integrity, but she found her expression, her pleasure, her satisfaction in experience shared with other human beings. She had no competitive urge, no need to assert herself. Sometimes when I think of Rachel, I wonder whether in the breaking off for the short span of the individual life the fragment of self from the whole, she kept a truer prescience of herself within the whole, lacking the illusion of complete isolation which torments most of us. I don't mean to be mystical. But the way in which Rachel was, for the moment, fully concerned with the small boy and his confusion, the way she let him understand that he wasn't a clumsy intruder, has always been Rachel's way.

Some people are gregarious because they are bored or frightened when they are alone. They act as if they weren't sure of their own existence except as they find it reflected in the mirror of another human being, they can't stand up except in a supporting crowd. When I first knew Rachel, I put her in that class. "She's one of these perpetual undergraduates," I said to Gilbert. "Likes everybody, wants everybody to like her, has no discrimination."

"She has a stronger social sense than either of us," Gilbert answered. "She's more at home in the world."

"She hasn't any ambition whatever. She's as skilful and clever as any girl I ever trained in laboratory work, and beyond doing her work to earn her living, she never gives it another thought!"

"Now you're measuring her against yourself!"

"If a woman has brains, I like to see her use them, that's all."

"Too bad they don't take women in the diplomatic service. She'd be good there. She's . . . what is your chemical term? . . . a catalyzer. Brings separate elements together into a smooth blend. You watch her in a group and see how well they get on while Rachel's around. Maybe she doesn't use her brains, I don't know. She has one talent that she does use, the talent of making people think well of themselves. That's a gift."

"If she were more discriminating, her admiration would be worth more!"

"She's discriminating, in her own way," said Gilbert. "She's no fool about people, she likes 'em, each of 'em, for different reasons. I'll tell you, Carey, what it is about Rachel. She takes folks as they are, she doesn't have any urge to make them over. Leave her alone, she's a nice girl."

Dick stayed with us most of the summer, for just as his brother began to sit up on the screened porch, John Burchall came down with the disease, and then Henry had swollen glands. The first few days Dick examined himself frequently, hoping that each mosquito bite might be a sign that he was breaking out, and could go home to share Henry's important state. Rachel and I worked for several hours in the early mornings at the laboratory bench in the garage, and every time I glanced up, I'd see Dick loitering past, jerking his head away and moving along faster, the very cowlick at the crown of his dark head suggesting his forlorn confusion. "Can't you find something to do?" I would ask. "What do you do when you're home?"

"Henry and I do different things." Then he would disappear for a while.

"Poor kid," Rachel would say. "He's homesick."

"We can't stop everything else just to entertain him!"

"No." Rachel would turn back to her work. "I suppose it's good for him to be on his own a little, Henry's sort of run the pair of them."

"Henry's just like his father," I said. "He has to run things. I don't know where John and Adelaide got Dick! He's not like either of them. He looks like a gnome with that big forehead and solemn eyes!"

"He's got a beautiful head," insisted Rachel. "Give him a couple of days and he won't be so solemn."

Rachel played checkers with him. The two of them carried over from the Burchalls the long wooden box with the croquet mallets and wickets, and spent a long afternoon setting out the wickets, and playing. Gilbert was at home one rainy day, and suggested making a kite. I remember the patience and the deftness with which the little boy worked, the two of them at the dining room table, the diamond-shaped frame between them, the small, grubby boy hands and the square strong man hands folding the edge of paper down over the cord, and Gilbert telling about kite races the boys had run.

"I can make another kite for Henry, and when he's well we can race 'em. I could take this over and fly it up outside his window, only that might make him feel worse because he wasn't flying it."

"As I recall Henry, it would."

Unexpectedly, Dick thought that remark was funny, and laughed so hard he had to set down the sauce-pan of flour and water paste. "As I recall ole Henry!" he said, and Gilbert grinned at him.

Adelaide telephoned every morning as we sat at breakfast, and Dick strained up on tiptoe to reach the mouth-piece, his monosyllabic answers to Adelaide's maternal inquisitiveness coming in staccato jerks. Yes, sure, nope, sure, the small of his thin back incurved with the effort of being tall enough for the instrument. As he observed, "I guess you never expected any children to talk on your telephone, did you?" The first few mornings Dick waited for the bell to ring, and jumped when it did. By the end of the week he rushed off the minute he finished breakfast, saying as he went, to Rachel, "If my mother calls up, tell her I'm fine and dandy, and I haven't broken out, and I hope she's the same."

"It doesn't taken a child long to get over his grief," I said.

"I wonder," began Rachel; the telephone interrupted, she answered it and I carried a tray of breakfast dishes into the kitchen. Rachel followed me after a few minutes. "It was Adelaide, very cheerful." She picked up a towel and began to dry the cups, rubbing with a slow, absent-minded stroke. I never could understand how Rachel's hands could be so sure and competent with the tools and mechanisms of the laboratory and so clumsy in domestic tasks. "She said something about buying Dickie some underpants, she couldn't send over any till the house was fumigated. Her voice isn't good on the telephone. She uses too many italics." Dick pressed his nose against the screened door.

"Was that my mother?" At Rachel's yes, he pressed harder, bulging the screen. "Does that make my nose look funny?" I started to caution him about the screen, but he ducked away as suddenly as he had appeared.

"Dick's protecting himself," said Rachel, "from disappointment. I know how he feels! You have to be awfully old before a voice on a wire is any good when you are lonely for your mother . . . or your friend . . . or your lover. . . . It's the wrong symbol, that clacking at your ear, when you want touch or smell or sight, or all of them at once! You rush to the telephone, all eagerness, here at your ear is something like the voice you know, out of blankness, you can't grasp any image to fit that voice, and when it stops, you're much lonelier, much farther away. Why, Carey, even a little dog is smarter about love than that! He'd rather have an old slipper that belongs to his love than a voice distilled through space by metal and electricity! The old slipper keeps an essence. . . ." Rachel thumped the cup down on the shelf, and then examined it anxiously. "Goodness, I most cracked that! All I mean is that babies and pups and

small boys and me agree that if we want somebody we want 'em
. . . in person."

An odd little outburst, which I remember now as one of the
few times when Rachel talked about her own feeling. Then I
found her amusingly young, and said something obvious about
how pleasant it was, if you were separated from say, your husband, to talk with him even if you couldn't see him.

We saw nothing of Dexter and Genevieve Willetts the first
part of the summer. Genevieve was sure that her children would
have the measles. Alicia had played with Henry and Dick the
very day Henry developed a fever, if she came down with
measles and gave the disease to the little boy, Genevieve
would never forgive Adelaide for being so careless! She must
have known Henry wasn't well, but that was Adelaide all over,
just sticking her head in the sand like an ostrich! Dick ought to
be quarantined, and if we wanted to run the risk of exposing
ourselves, we could, in so many words, just stay away from the
Willetts! All this from the front seat of the car, with Dexter
driving on and Genevieve's unfinished sentence dangling.

"Henry didn't know he was going to get the measles," said
Dick, after reflection. "Anybody might be going to get anything, and not know it, couldn't he?"

Gilbert laughed. "You said it. There, in a nut-shell, is the
way the hypochondriac figures it out."

Dick asked, "What's a hypoklondike?" and Rachel asked, "Is
she really one? It's easier to worry if you aren't very well, I
suppose."

"Or is it easy to be sick if you worry?"

"At least we know where we won't go calling," I said. "The
Ridge is pretty quiet this summer." I was sorry after I'd said
that. I tried to steer away from anything which would set Gilbert thinking about Dr. Randall, and it wasn't easy, so many
things struck the note which started the deep vibration of his

loss. Gilbert didn't say anything, but his face, even his posture, had that slight change I had come to know, an evidence of stricture, a bracing against pain. What I told myself was that although Gilbert had lost a friend, there was no sense in his feeling unhappy about something he couldn't help. Perhaps I thought then that Gilbert could fold up his affection for Dr. Randall, his confidence, his habit of communication, and put it away, out of sight, out of mind, just as you fold up and put away the garments and the papers death has made useless.

"Who wants to go calling?" asked Rachel. "It's fun this way."

"Yah, who wants to go calling on that ole woman?" echoed Dick. "All she ever does is holler at Alicia, 'Tell those Burchall boys to go right home! I simply can't stand that screaming another moment!'" His mimicry caught something of Genevieve's accent, and Rachel giggled.

"You don't make much noise by yourself," said Gilbert.

"Wanta hear me?" Dick, with the young animal's quick response to attention, opened his mouth for a war-whoop, but Rachel tumbled him off the step to the grass.

"Never mind," she said. "We'll believe it." Then she pulled the boy up to his feet and they went off, trailing Gilbert, whose task, at this distance, I don't remember, something the Willetts had interrupted. I do remember thinking that the summer was working out very well, that Rachel's gaiety had a way of setting tone, that Dick was no longer homesick, and that Gilbert really didn't mind, although he'd been unenthusiastic when I had said I'd like to ask Rachel out for the summer.

With the opening of the summer session at the University, Dexter went into the city four or five days each week. Occasionally as I stood at the kitchen table preparing breakfast, I'd have a glimpse of his tall, lean figure streaking along the road to catch the early train. I'd think that I might have been hurrying for the same train, and then I'd assure myself that although the university work was a sure thing, my own original work, if I made a good job of it, would really mean more for my future. I hadn't noticed at what hour Dexter came back from the city until one afternoon when a sudden violent thunder storm rolled over the hills. I ran through the house to close the windows against the down-pour. The whole house shivered under the thunder, there was excitement in the noise, in the chill, sweet smell of rain, in the way the panes of the windows seemed to melt into the flooding water and the sheets of rain made a dark steely wall around the house. I thought I heard voices and ran down the stairs in search of them.

Rachel and Dexter Willetts were standing on the front porch, backed against the house wall, the rain slanting almost to their feet.

"Oh-h-h!" Rachel gave a sighing laugh. "I can't breathe! We ran so hard!" She was flushed and her hair was a dark, shining cap, flattened with rain.

"Hello! Are you soaked?" I ran out to drag a chair away from the corner of the porch.

"Here, let me!" Dexter took hold of the chair and we tipped it on end. "We just made it before the deluge. Whee-oo! Listen to that one!"

"Come on inside. You can't stay out here."

"I ought to go on," Dexter said, uncertainly. "If you'd lend me an umbrella. . . ." He gave Rachel a quick, oblique glance.

"No one would expect you till this is over," she said. "They'd know you'd take shelter somewhere." Rachel's words were matter of fact, and it wasn't until later that I wondered about the knowledge which lay beneath them, knowledge that Genevieve timed her husband on his walk home from the afternoon train, that any delay filled her mind with horrid pictures of disaster.

"This won't last long," I said, and held the screen door open.

Rachel slid past me. Dexter followed, the stiff angles of his elbows, his cocked head hinting uncertainty. "You aren't worried about measles are you?" I asked. "There's not the slightest danger, now. Dick's just staying on till his folks are well. Where on earth is the boy, anyway? Wasn't he with you. Rachel?"

"He ran on ahead." Rachel untied the sleeves of the sweater she had knotted over her shoulders, and dropped it on a chair. Her fingers pushed up the limp sleeves of her yellow cotton dress. In the half dusk within the house she seemed to gather whatever light there was, the yellow of her frock, the warm bloom of her slender, rounded arms, of her slim throat. Her face had the softness of a child's, without definiteness of planes, her eyes were clear and very blue, and her full, curved mouth was humorous and gentle. "He had to rescue something . . . his bicycle . . . I don't remember."

"Why not call up Genevieve?" I asked, as Dexter stood at the threshold of the living room, still hesitant. "So she'll know where you are." As I spoke, the bell of the telephone sounded in a high, light vibration, not like its usual ring, the wires crackled, and there was a sharp, ear-numbing clap of thunder so close that for a moment we seemed at the heart of violent noise. Dick clattered in from the rear of the house, shirt plastered to his shoulder blades, eyelids blinking off rain. "Oh, boy, was that a hum-dinger! I bet that most hit us!"

"I can smell it!" Rachel settled herself in a corner of the divan. "Isn't that sound of the bell different? Like the molecules stirring against each other!"

"No use my trying to telephone now," said Dexter. "Genevieve wouldn't touch a 'phone with this going on. I suppose it isn't exactly safe," he added hastily. "Since lightning hit that tree last summer, you know, the hemlock in front of the house, Genevieve's been a little nervous."

"Alicia's scart, too," said Dick, scornfully. "She was sitting on the fence with Rachel and me, waiting for you, and then at the first rumple of thunder, she beat it home."

The green-white glare of lightning emphasized the startled contraction of Dexter's face. "Alicia? Way down the hill?"

"That was an hour ago," said Rachel. "She's safe home, she and Mister went off like a streak!"

"Good Lord! What was she doing, so far from home?"

"Well, first she was looking for Mister, he'd run away, and I was riding around on my bike, and so I gave her a ride on my handle-bars, and then I told her how we waited for you afternoons and she waited too."

"It was bright sunlight then," said Rachel. "Don't look so horrified! I couldn't hold her, she wriggled down and just tore!" She sat forward, the color deepening in her face, her mouth a downward bow of consternation, her quick glance under her lashes at me almost frightened.

"I didn't suppose she wandered off our own place, that's all." Dexter swung on his heel and took a long stride to the door. "It's not coming down quite so hard," he said, quietly, and opened the door.

I called to him to wait a minute, and found in the hall closet Gilbert's old crooked-handled umbrella, and then stood watching him as he leaned into the wind, the rain cascading from the buffeted umbrella and drenching his coat and his long legs before he had waded even as far as the road. I didn't want to turn back into the living room, because I was embarrassed. I was fond of Rachel, I felt the responsibility which an older person feels for an affectionate, admiring child. It's nothing, I told myself. Dexter was one of her teachers, it's dull for a young girl out here, certainly there's nothing clandestine in sitting on a fence with Dick . . . to say nothing of Dexter's daughter, too! Another flash of lightning lacquered the drenched foliage of the trees along the road with garish green, and I waited for the roll of thunder.

"The storm's moving past us," I said briskly. Rachel was at the window, one hand lifted to hold back the curtain. I sent Dick upstairs to change into a dry shirt.

"I'm sorry Mr. Willetts was worried." Rachel let the curtain drop into its folds. "He'll be drowned before he gets home! Why, what could happen to Alicia? Should I have taken her home, Carey? I never thought of it. But he—he sounded cross with me."

I remember the relief I felt. Rachel was troubled only because of Dexter's abrupt departure, not because I had stumbled into awareness of a secret rendezvous.

"He was uneasy about his household," I said. "Alicia's the apple of his eye."

Dexter stopped the next morning to return the umbrella. "Not much like last night, is it?" He stood in the doorway, sunlight brilliant behind him. No, he couldn't come in, had to stop at the cleaner's with his suit.

"I knew you'd be drenched!" Rachel came down the stairs, buttoning the cuffs of her blue smock, and Dexter nodded at her.

"I needn't have run off like that. Alicia gave me what's what. She says she's a big girl now. She wants to come down after lunch to beat Dick at croquet. Is it all right? I can pick her up when I come past."

"Dick's been teasing to go up to your house," I said. "I didn't want to worry Genevieve."

Dexter laughed. "Alicia says she'd rather have measles than be so lonesome for the boys. We've been careful long enough, I'm sure. Don't let her be a nuisance. Thanks. Good-bye." He swung down the walk, sleeves and trouser legs of the suit he carried flapping over his arm.

"I'm surprised Genevieve consented," I said. "I bet it took an argument."

Alicia must have turned up every afternoon during the next weeks. Once in a while I would hear the children as I sat at the desk polishing the pages of my pamphlet, writing out the results of the morning in the laboratory. If I looked out, I sometimes saw them moving intently about their small affairs. Alicia was almost as tall as Dick. She wasn't pretty, but she had a kind of charm, partly because her movements were so deft and sure, partly because she had a way of looking at you with grave, friendly, interested eyes, much as Dexter looked and with the same impression he gave, that for all their friendliness, the eyes revealed little of the secret, intricate and shy person who looked through them. For the most part she followed Dick in busy amiability, with little black Mister chasing the two of them. Occasionally the tone of their voices would change suddenly, climbing into shrill, explosive yells mixed with Mister's excited yelps, and Rachel would run out, calling, "Children! Where are you? Dick!"

"It's really funny," Rachel told me. "The only thing they quarrel about is Henry! Alicia will say, 'If Henry was here, he'd beat you at croquet, you know he would!' and Dick will scream at her. She hid the red mallet and ball today, because they mustn't be used except by Henry. And Dick told her when Henry got well he wouldn't let her play with them, he'd be too old to play with girls. She asks me every day if Henry isn't coming today, but she waits till Dick isn't around before she asks me. When they stay off Henry, they're good as gold together."

That trivial, forgotten fragment fits into place now as part of the pattern. At the time I said, "Do keep them off Henry, then! They ought to be glad he's not around bossing them!"

In the late afternoon Alicia would drop her games to watch

for her father. She never asked what time it was; she seemed to have the kind of time sense which an animal possesses, or a seed deep in the earth, a tropism, a response to hints too subtle for an adult conscious mind to feel. Mister followed her to the edge of the road, and the two of them stared down the hill. Sometimes Rachel walked toward the village, a child on either side, sometimes she called Alicia back to sit beside her in the shade. When the wind was right, the whistle of the train, with its insistence on one prolonged minor note, made a fluttering ribbon of sound over the trees. Presently Dexter would appear, portfolio swinging, his long stride quicker as he came around the bend in the road. Alicia never ran to meet him, she never flung herself at him nor burst into chatter; she was satisfied that he had come.

Usually Alicia had something to show her father, a small stone she hoped might be an Indian arrow head, a snail shell, a golden feather dropped by a flicker, each a sign to establish contact after separation. Dexter always had time to examine her token. He'd stand there talking for a few moments, easy, relaxed, and then go on with Alicia. Often Rachel was laughing as he went, at some last words. I felt ashamed of myself because the suspicion started by Dick's phrase, "We waited for you every afternoon," wriggled out in a new form; if Rachel and Dexter wished to meet, they couldn't have arranged it more plausibly. Rachel was always on hand, but that seemed natural, and her friendly admiration for Dexter was transparent as crystal.

"He's just about the nicest man I know," she said, ingenuously. "In college he's so smart he scares you, but out here he's just funny and nice. I like to watch him with Alicia. I don't wonder she adores him." Crystal-clear, not a shadow of concealment. She tucked a hand under my elbow. "He's not any nicer than Gilbert. I don't mean that! Only Gilbert's different, he's so busy with his own thoughts he doesn't pay much attention to anybody else, does he? He looks you up and down once, and then he has your number! No use my trying to be interesting!"

"Gilbert likes you," I said.

"Um. As long as he puts up with my being under foot!" Rachel's face altered, happiness giving it an effect of soft focus, a complete expression of mood. "It's just perfect, being here with you this summer! From the minute I wake up! Working with you, having the children around, listening to you and Gilbert talk, this lovely place . . . oh, I am lucky! I wish it could last forever!"

"You're a nice child," I told her, "and you can certainly go on working with me, even if summer doesn't last forever." I had the comfortable glow of well-being which approval sets a-light.

The summer did come to an end, of course. Adelaide telephoned to say that they were through with the plague, the house was being fumigated, and Dick could come home. She'd never have asked me to take him, if she'd known how long the siege was going to last! When I said that we had liked having him, and I thought he'd had a good time, Adelaide was suddenly caustic. She hoped we hadn't spoiled him until he didn't want to come home! He hadn't sounded the least bit homesick. As Gilbert said, Adelaide was tired, she'd had a long spell of nursing her invalids. Rachel and I helped Dick pack. The suitcase he had brought was inadequate for his accumulations, the pasteboard box bulged: books, games which Gilbert had brought out from town, a partly finished model of a yacht, a humming bird's nest, even the kite, in spite of its jagged hole where its final flight had ended on the telephone pole.

"You're a squirrel, Dick, and not a boy at all!" Rachel told him, and Dick blew up his cheeks, his eyes tight squints, with unexpected, dismaying tears squeezing out at the corners. "I tell you," she said, quickly. "Leave some of this stuff, you'll be coming over often, you can get Henry to help carry it home."

I remember how golden the freckles shone on Adelaide's face, with its pallor of confinement, and how she pinned her arms around Dick's shoulders, shaking and hugging him, tears running over the freckles, her excited laughter, her "Dicky! Oh, Dicky!" mixed lament and greeting.

"Gee whiz!" Dick squirmed. "You're splashing all over me!"

"Aren't you glad to be home?"

John Burchall came up behind Adelaide, looking much as usual except that his sparse light hair was too long, and his eyes were red-rimmed. Had he, too, been crying, I wondered.

"I'd ask you all to come in," said Adelaide, "but the house is a mess! The practical nurse we had in to help wouldn't lift a finger except to cook gruel and such, and I couldn't get anyone else in till tomorrow."

"You'd be gassed, anyway," said John, blowing his nose and sneezing.

"Yah, it stinks!" Henry came through the door, a shrunken cotton bathrobe falling away from his skinny naked front. He stared inquisitively at the accoutrement which Rachel and I had helped Dick transport. "Where's the croquet set?" he demanded. "Didn't you bring back the croquet set?"

"Sh!" said Adelaide. "You better get back in the house, Henry, you haven't got much on."

"What makes it stink?" asked Dick.

"The fumigating gas," began John. "All nonsense, the amount of formaldehyde they insist on using, the way they seal up all openings."

"Where's the croquet set?" yelled Henry. "Dinche hear me ask you a question?"

"Goodness," I said. "We never thought of that, we had so many things. . . ."

"I thought of it," said Dick. "I thought maybe we could play over at the Mooreses, just for a while, see? You could come over there with me, and. . ." He had started out in a loud tone, hurriedly, and had run down, as Henry advanced on him. Adelaide caught him by the slack of the bathrobe, and slapped the edges together over his stomach.

"Why, Dicky," she said, "that's silly, and you can't go on bothering the Moores any longer! You must get the croquet set at once!"

Dick turned his head slightly, his eyes hunting for Rachel, his face scarlet and lugubrious.

"If the boys want to play there," began Rachel, eagerly, "it's no bother, is it, Carey? Alicia Willetts comes down every afternoon, and I told Dick we'd play partners when Henry was well enough to come over."

"That's very sweet of you," said Adelaide, in a voice which meant the opposite. "But Dick will have to learn to stay home." Her upper lip had a queer tremor, and her round brown eyes looked almost black. "You better carry in your bundles, Dicky."

Without a word Dick lifted the suitcase and marched into the house. Rachel set down on the step the box she had carried, and I tried to cover the embarrassment which prickled in my skin with a chatty invitation, they must all come over as soon as they were straightened out, we'd missed them, we'd be going back to the city soon.

John said that as soon as he had energy enough, he'd have to get back on his job, the Lord only knew what had gone on, there were two houses in Riverdale half constructed. "Tell them about that night, Addie, when I was out of my head."

"Goodness, did we have a time!" Adelaide's voice crisped with pride. "John was going to get right up, fever and all, and go down to Riverdale. The doctor had to give him something to quiet him."

"I don't remember a thing about it," said John. "But it shows how I feel about my work, doesn't it? If that's what I rave above when I'm delirious."

"Everyone knows what kind of architect you are," Adelaide gave a brisk little nod. "You rave about it even when you don't have a fever."

"Mamma, tell 'em what I said when I had a fever! Tell 'em!" Henry joggled Adelaide's elbow, and she laughed.

"Not now. You take Dick's box in, and help him unpack. You must go in, too, John, you've been walking around a long time!" She was like a bantam hen, cheeping her brood into the house, out of danger. "I'm terribly grateful, Carey. I hope your work didn't suffer." She didn't look at Rachel. "I hope I can repay you someway . . . someday."

"Do let Dick come over if he wants to," I said, "we're very fond of him."

"Of course." Adelaide's mouth was firm now, no tremor of the short upper lip. "But he mustn't impose on you. He and Henry are really great homebodies, anyway. That's what we got this place in the country for. John always says boys are like puppies, no good unless they'll stay home. It seems inhospitable not to ask you to come in, but you do understand?"

I said yes, I understood perfectly, and we'd hope to see them soon.

Rachel and I walked for a way without comment. The dust of the summer road rose in lazy puffs from our steps, the weeds and bushes along the ditches at each side of the road were tarnished with dust and scraggly with the coming on of fall. "I suppose we should have beaten him up a little," said Rachel suddenly, "so he was thankful to escape from us!"

"They can come and get that croquet set themselves," I said. "I'm not going to lug it home." Adelaide needn't have been so rude, I told myself. She always acted as an abrasive on me. She was so sure about everything! No doubt of her own values, her own way ever rippled the surface of her assurance. She wasn't arrogant or dominant, as Ellen was; she was compact, rounded, impenetrable, with no more awareness of outsiders than a closed clam, and about as much tact.

"I don't think Adelaide liked me," said Rachel. "She looked as if she'd like to fumigate Dick, too, to get him rid of us! Can't a little boy like anybody but his own folks, for heaven's sake? Did you see the way he looked when he went into the house? I could have cried. He held his head so stiff, and that little hollow just there at the nape of his neck . . . so defenceless. . . ."

"He's Adelaide's boy," I said, crossly. "After all, you knew that!"

"You're always very practical, aren't you, Carey?" There was no criticism in Rachel's voice, just a warm speculation. "I'm not. My common sense doesn't live in the same house with my feelings!"

"Well, you needn't worry about Dick's feeling lonely. It won't take him five minutes to forget he ever was away from home. Look how easily he settled in with us."

"All right." Rachel was downcast. "I'm going to miss Dick, and you needn't tell me I'll get right over it! I hate missing anyone. It's . . . it's being in a dark hole full of cobwebs. When I go back to town next week, I'm going to ache all over, missing everything right round the clock. I'll think, now we'd be having breakfast, all of us round the table, you with that pleasant, abstracted morning-look, what-am-I-planning for today, and I'd probably be letting the toast burn—"

"Nonsense!" I laughed at her. "You'll be too busy finding a place to live, getting into our fall schedule in the laboratory, meeting new people."

"I wish I was calm and sensible, like you." Rachel sighed. "I sound foolish, I know."

"You sound nice and young," I told her.

"Is that it?" We had reached our own place, and somewhat to my relief, Rachel said she'd spend the rest of the afternoon in the garage work-room, packing away the slides she had been using.

The ending of that summer does not separate itself from so many endings of summers since then. It must have been that year that I telephoned to Dexter Willetts after Rachel had gone, to say that she had left a box for Alicia, with a doll Mister had carried off and a sweater. "She was going to give them to you, but she missed you somehow, her last day."

"Has Rachel gone?" asked Dexter, abruptly. "I didn't know . . . Genevieve went in town with me, and we were late getting out."

"Oh! I'm glad Genevieve is feeling better," I said. She hadn't been well enough to walk as far as our house all summer!"

"We went in to consult a doctor. I should have insisted on it earlier. He was so positive . . . cardiagrams and everything . . . that Genevieve is like a different woman! It's a tremendous relief to find your heart's sound as a nut!"

I told Gilbert about it. "Did she think she had heart trouble?"

"She's had it all summer," said Gilbert. "Ever since Dr. Ranny's sudden death. Dexter caught the same train I did one day last week, she'd had an attack, he was late for classes and he looked as if he'd had the attack himself. I gave him the name of this specialist."

"And never told me a word about it."

"That was professional," Gilbert grinned. "Now it's gossip."

"Was Genevieve faking?"

"No. She's bound to suffer, she just experiments with how she suffers."

"Then she is faking!"

"No. The pain is real enough, it hurts just as much, whatever the cause."

"If Dexter weren't so sympathetic, maybe Genevieve would snap out of it."

"Perhaps Genevieve's ill health satisfies some need in Dexter," said Gilbert. "Makes him feel useful or strong, gives him a chance to make amends."

"He just has to put up with it, because he's married to her, and he's that kind of man, gentle. Sometimes you go too far, probing around for reasons. You spend so much time with mental cases, you get to thinking everybody's one!"

"It's only a matter of degree. What's the matter, don't you like getting at motives?"

"You see! Now you're trying to analyze me!"

"What are you picking on me for?" Gilbert laughed and came to sit beside me on the steps. "I've scarcely seen you all summer, people under foot all the time."

"Just Rachel," I protested, "and Dick for a while."

"It's all right, if you want them."

It may have been that night, or some other night, that we talked over Rachel and Dexter. I may have said, "You see, if you go ascribing motives to folks, you're suspicious, when really there's nothing but what you see! I thought Rachel was scheming to meet Dexter, that she was working up a love affair, all because I had forgotten how a girl feels. I mean that quality of innocence, complete, shining innocence. Like a child's, only some children haven't it. No sex in it."

Gilbert said: "Innocence can be just ignorance, or it can be an inclusion of knowledge without experience of it. I mean as long as anyone's human, male or female, the cells keep their ancient wisdom, the glands set up their old demands. But so far Rachel's attention . . . her kind of perception . . . is on the level of emotion, not sensation. Be too bad if Dexter . . . but he wouldn't. He's scrupulous and reflective. And he's all tied up with his family."

It may have been that evening, too, that he spoke of Lawrence Hunter. Lawrence had sent him a note, wouldn't he like to look over Dr. Randall's medical books, there might be some he'd like for his own library, Ellen was going to sell the lot. He'd met Lawrence at the town house one afternoon. The house was forlorn, rugs rolled up, draperies down, covers over everything, a film of gritty dust that stuck to your fingers and filled your nostrils. Lawrence had been staying at his club, the house hadn't been lived in since Dr. Ranny had died and Ellen had gone to the hospital. Ellen was still at the Cape, Lawrence had been down for a fortnight. The servants were coming back in a week or so to put things in order. Dr. Randall's desk was just as he'd left it that morning, when he'd run out for a taxi for Ellen.

"Lawrence hung around, talking, trying to fill up the empty house, I guess. He looks rat-nibbled, for all he's sun-burned. He says the trouble with New York for a summer widower is there's too much to do and none of it any good. Full of gals who can't bear to see a man lonely. He thought his resistance was good for just about the rest of September. Then Ellen would be home. Mostly talk, I think. I never heard him run on so. If he'd let me alone, I might have made a better choice. But once we were inside the house, he just wanted to get out again. I picked out half a dozen or so. I kept seeing things I wished I'd talked with Dr. Ranny about. You remember the way he'd carry around a book he was reading, his long forefinger marking his place? Well, that's that."

"How is Ellen? Did Lawrence say?"

Gilbert's face altered, the Doctor closed his book, his long forefinger marked the place no more. Yes, Lawrence had talked about Ellen, too. She had given up her job at the Agency. They couldn't hold it open for her any longer, and the doctors said she simply could not take on a nine to five work-day. It was a proof of what a sick girl she'd been that she yielded without much fuss. The market was wonderful, according to Lawrence, and that helped, Ellen wouldn't miss her salary.

"Too bad," I said. "She was so keen about her work."

"You don't sound too sorry."

"Of course I'm glad it's not me!" There was a dark chant to which I would not listen, words beating up which I tried to deny before they took clear shape. *It's Ellen's own fault, she thought she was a super-woman, she could have everything, now see! See what happens to women!* "Whatever will Ellen do with herself?" That's it, sound friendly, concerned. "Just spending Lawrence's money. . . ."

"She's got her house and the children," said Gilbert. "And she's still got a job getting well. She won't hang on to poor health for her avocation, I know that. She's got too much character."

"If you call hardness character!"

"Say she's too much of a realist, then."

"Oh, let's not argue about Ellen."

Gilbert looked at me, his eyebrows drawn down in a quick frown, and under them an effect of his thoughts suddenly rearing back, at an unexpected barrier, wheeling, cantering off into diminishing remoteness.

There is one more fragment which belongs to the end of that summer, although I can not for all my trying draw out the whole shape of the scene, only Gilbert's voice, and a few things said. "You're glad to get back to the city, aren't you? You don't care as much about our house here as I do. It's not a steady, deep satisfaction to you."

I tried to explain to him. Now that we really had a house, it seemed less the miracle it had seemed when we planned it, more a possession we had a right to expect. Of course it was a satisfaction. But it was a problem, too. A man wouldn't feel that, but a woman would. The house was a rival, demanding my time, my interest, my energy. "I don't want to be purely domestic, and the house wants me to!"

Gilbert was sympathetic about that; perhaps in another year we could afford a hired girl, I'd had far too much drudgery since our marriage. I said it wasn't drudgery, I liked it, I knew it was my job, at least till we had more money, I just didn't dare let myself care too much about the house or I'd never get anywhere. I admitted that I did like New York, too. All the wonderful things there to see and do and have! Gilbert said he'd like to stay right there on the Ridge the whole year round, if he could manage his work. I jeered at him as a farm boy, and he agreed. He liked to put down roots, he said, and I wanted to spread out in branches. Together we made a fine tree!

"The trouble with a tree is it doesn't get anywhere!"

"It gets bigger and bigger."

"All right, you grow bigger and bigger! What about me? Do you think I want to be just branches, waving in the wind?" Gilbert's chance phrase was a flame turned too high, and whoop! over boiled the whole mixture in the retort! The night of my big blow, he called it afterwards. I was proud of him, the way everything he did led wonderfully into something else; the White Plains institution had invited him to stay on, Bellevue wanted him back, there was a new State Committee on Mental Hygiene . . . oh, everything! And what was happening to me? I could go on forever counting blood cells and detecting malaria and getting sugar content, and never have anything handed to me except a few kind words. Gilbert knew as well as I did that the department never would promote a woman, never would make her a professor, or put her in charge of the work. Women are fine as assistants, they're so conscientious, so careful, and if they get restless and want something more, there are always more eager young things to take their places!

Gilbert said Wheeoo, he'd supposed I liked my work, and I asked how he'd enjoy finding himself caught in a blind alley. It would be the same way at any other university, or any of the good hospitals.

It is difficult and in a way ridiculous to try to reconstruct the intensity of my feeling back there in the twenties about the sad lot of women, about the unfairness of the world. The girls today don't talk about economic independence, they work if they have to, and at anything, but they make no bones about their eagerness to chuck it all for marriage; they'll settle for a man and some children, the best of them. They make careless use of the changes in behavior or custom which to the earlier generation were symbols of defiance and achievement. Well, people always move comfortably into a country which pioneers have cleared and settled.

It was an easy time, too, to believe in causes. The world was almost as small as your own life, and as neat as your own set of beliefs. I find difficulty in trying to reconstruct that feeling, perhaps because I'm not too proud of it. I was young, but that's not the excuse I'd like it to be. In a way everyone had a child's view of the times; America was a fine place, it had holidays, ice cream and cake, toys for good children (automobiles, radios, wonderful new toys!), money to put in the toy bank, everything! But the boys got more than the girls, more of everything —more freedom, more fun, more money, more fame; and the girls had decided, in a phrase which seemed clever enough to settle everything, that women were people, too.

Gilbert always listened to my thories with a kind of skeptical tolerance so that sometimes, perversely, I wished he would have more standard male antagonism, just to give me a spring-board for more argument. "You think being a woman is hard," he

said, once. "I think being a human being is the terrific problem."
My outburst about my future at the University was different,
being particular and personal, and Gilbert's response was different. "You don't have to stay in a blind alley. There's always
a way out or through or around!"

I didn't see how. It was easy to talk, but I had no gun to hold
at their heads to make them do right by me! They'd just say
they could replace me easily enough, I'd be in wrong with
them. A woman had to be a genius of some kind to get ahead,
and I wasn't that good.

"Don't disparage yourself," said Gilbert. "You're pretty
good. You just ask the full chance to prove it." We must have
talked for a long time, for I remember the frenzy into which I
wound myself proving that my alley was inescapable. I couldn't
leave New York (For how could he go away, his work was all
he wished it to be!) to try my luck at some woman's college,
or farther west, at some more liberal, less fossilized institution,
I was doomed, I'd never be anything but an underpaid under-
ling! "What would you do if I agreed with you?" asked Gilbert,
and bent up the corners of his mouth in a grin. "You're awful
convincing!"

"Sometimes you're so exasperating! You won't see anything
but what you want to see!"

"I want to see you having what you want." He balanced his
fingertips together, pumping his hands like a small bellows, as
if he fanned his forming idea from a spark into a steady flame.
"Look, Carey. You want to stay in New York. Point one. You
don't want to stay at the University. Point two. You don't want
to try for a post at some other man-run school or hospital. That's
point three. So what? I don't know why I never thought of it
before. Start your own place. Be your own boss. Collect your
own clients. Dr. Moore's Laboratory, prompt and accurate
service."

"How could I?" The idea was fantastic, had he any notion how much such a place would cost for equipment? Even if there were any clients . . . on and on, my fever of dejection furnishing a hundred obstacles, and the steady flame of Gilbert's notion turning them to no more than charred flakes. We needn't hurry, take our time, talk it over with the doctors I knew, he'd drum up trade for me at Bellevue, or White Plains, or wherever. Figure out the costs, train some good assistants. Keep it strictly professional, none of these commercial affairs.

"I have a feeling this is it." Gilbert said. "It fits. Nothing startling about it, now we've thought of it. One of those things that sits around and waits for the owner to claim it!"

I was frightened. Suppose I tried it and failed? Reputation, money, oh, it was too great a risk!

"You could always get a job as good as the one you have now. There's no risk in looking at it as a possibility, in planning for it."

"That's the biggest risk of all!" Imagination leaping across the barriers of reality, all my energy moving off the solid earth into the dissolving cloud of a day-dream, "I couldn't bear it to be disappointed! If I let myself believe . . . why, just since you spoke, I can see the very shape of the rooms! See myself running my own laboratory, so independent and proud! If I let myself go . . . I won't do it! No money, no experience, no backing . . . no, I won't be hurt that way!"

"What a scared-cat you are!"

"I'm trying to be practical."

"The practical man doesn't get emotional, he gets busy collecting data. You put it out of your head, and I'll report back after I put out feelers."

Of course Gilbert was right about his idea fitting exactly, and he was right, too, about my being something of a coward. The story of my laboratory, the Moore Laboratories, is not the story of the Ridge. I should find it much easier to write, because it is a simple chronicle of development, marked in such obvious ways as moving into larger quarters, taking on more assistants, wiping out the debt. I remember the stages of the growth because they were all I really heeded through most of the intervening years. The story of the Moore laboratories is a success story, which I have told with great pride, and now it is a shell, empty of human feeling.

A little of the history explains why I saw less of the Ridge and its people for the next few years. There was one summer which I spent in Chicago, working in a laboratory which a chemist and his wife had run for several years, another when I made a tour of a dozen cities, having worked first in summer session to earn money for car-fare and hotels, and looked over a dozen laboratories. Gilbert couldn't leave his work to go with me, but I made notes on equipment and policy, and fairly ran along the platform toward the gate where he waited to meet me, eager to tell him all I had learned. Then the actual impact of meeting, the quick, rich tingling of all the senses, sight, hearing, touch, expanding, enlivening the flat wraith figure which seems real enough, vivid enough in separation, would push away everything else. Later, sitting on stools at a lunch counter in the station, we would talk. Sometimes, if I hadn't slept well on the train, the noises, the rushing-rocking onward movement, the cindery warmth of my berth would buffet me into doubt, and my mood would be as unsteady as my legs when I met Gilbert. "They're all very nice to me as soon as I say I'm connected with the University. There's a kind of prestige. . . . If I give that up, I won't be anybody!"

"We started this because if you don't step out, you aren't anybody."

"But they think I am!"

"Well, which do you want?"

Then, as I drank orange juice and coffee, and under the edge
of the counter Gilbert's foot moved along the rung of my stool
to find my foot and push against it, as I heard the warm resonance of his voice and knew its quickened tempo was his quickened heart-beat, I would sit erect, the uncertainty and the
sensation of persisting movement both gone.

The details of the actual settling on quarters, collecting equipment, working out the financial problem, although they absorbed me pretty completely for the next two years, are not, as
I said, the story of the Ridge. By 1928 the name Moore Laboratories, 622-24, was on the address bulletin in the hall of a
building in mid-town, a building of doctors' suites and science,
the large shallow windows on either side of the entrance full of
dusty trusses, braces, and surgical instruments. Rachel Thayer
was chief assistant and partner to the extent of a thousand dollars
of the five Gilbert and I had raised. The other girls in the
laboratory, one at first, more later, are a procession of young
things, some of them clumsy, some clever, most of them earnest,
and most of them temporary.

If we had waited another year or so, I never should have had
my own place. For by 1930 no one was lending money, the
mortgages in which Rachel's small inheritance had been invested
were worthless, and as Gilbert said, although hard times made
more patients for him, they didn't provide for payment of bills.
The difficult years didn't affect my business, except to make me
work harder because I didn't wish to risk the money additional
girls would take. We worked on a cash basis; the patient came,
we took his blood smears and his fee before he went away. We
had patients from the first week; most of the doctors I had
known at the University were willing to give me a trial, and
Gilbert had worked up a good list.

Several of the Ridge neighbors dropped in during that fall
of 1928 to see my establishment. I remember Ellen Hunter,

looking elegant in a bizarre and expensive outfit, her eyes rest-less. "How it smells, Carey!" was her first comment. "Gas and God knows what else! Terrific! How do you stand it?" She stood in the doorway between my own small office and the lab-oratory, her teeth clicking against the stem of a long amber cigarette holder. "Are you really making money at it?" She said hello to Rachel who ducked past just then in her white uniform to answer the bell, and turned to watch Rachel usher a client into the screened room where tests were taken. "You might hire me for office girl! You must come to dinner some-day, Carey, and tell me about everything! I've asked Gilbert, and he always says you're too busy."

I remember Adelaide Burchall, her hair flying under a shabby hat too far back on her head (she never wore a hat except when she rarely came into the city), and her face warming quickly from its stiff waiting expression when I opened the door. "I was afraid I had the wrong place," she said. "All those awful things in the window downstairs! Goodness, I haven't seen you forever and ever, Carey! You look very professional in that rig. No, I don't want to see anything but you. Do you cut up rabbits and things?"

She sat on the corner of my desk, chattering, and Rachel opened the door.

"Hello, Adelaide," said Rachel, and for a moment I thought Adelaide meant not to answer. She stepped down, square on both feet, her plump bosom swelling out the loose tweed coat, her nose and eyes crinkling so that the freckles made little ridges of gold. She did speak, however, just, "Hello, are you working here, too?" and Rachel, picking up a folder from the desk, closed the door. Adelaide looked at the door, swinging her purse. She looked at me with round eyes hard as glass aggies, and then decided to say nothing. Is it still Dick, I wondered, is she still jealous? She had to run along, she said, she had a hundred things to do. She did wish I'd spend more time on the Ridge, they missed me. Was that a hit at Rachel, too? She had lived in our house for a few weeks last summer and the summer before.

I meant to ask Rachel about Adelaide. Rachel hadn't mentioned her when she thanked me for the use of our house during her holiday. She had said, "You'd scarcely recognize the children on the Ridge, they're growing up so fast. Henry Burchall's an adolescent dynamo in long pants, Dick's gangly and self-conscious. He's sweet when you get him by himself, he came over to mow the lawn and to carry in logs for the fireplace. But most of the time he's Henry's shadow. Alicia yearns after them, but they think she's just a girl. She'll catch up with them in a year or two. She's a serious child, you know, the kind that can't escape responsibility. She's always rescuing that spoiled younger brother, Robert, from mishap. He's the kind of boy who's always stepping on nails and sitting on bees and falling out of swings. Then poor Alicia feels to blame. Her mother says, 'But I trusted you to watch out for Bobby!' I'm going to ask Gilbert someday if Bobby's capacity for getting into trouble isn't suggestion. His mother lives with previews of all disasters! And Alicia accepts the blame, just as . . ." Rachel broke off, and I finished, "Just as Dexter does, you mean?"

"They're too vulnerable," said Rachel.

Nothing in that to suggest why Adelaide should be hostile. But Rachel slipped out for luncheon before I asked, and we were so rushed the rest of the day that I forgot my curiosity. I had not reached the stage of a competent secretary and office girl, so that in addition to keeping an eye on the girls in the laboratory and an ear open to their summons if anything obscure or abnormal or elusive showed up in the tests, I made up the medical reports on the printed sheets headed "Moore Laboratories," frequently, since I was working at the desk, I answered the telephone and entered the calls in the appointment book, and tried to keep accounts straight.

Rachel handled the clients, ushering each of them into the cubicle we used then for the examining room, reappearing with her tray of vials and sterilized needles, her manner so deft and pleasant that the patient began to enjoy giving up his drops of blood. She wouldn't help with the reports. "I'd mix them up, Carey," she said. "I'd have nightmares every night, knowing I'd put Miss X's figures down on Mr. F's sheet! Anyway, nobody could read my writing, and I always hit the wrong key on the typewriter!" I suppose I liked doing it myself, looking at the letter-head, folding the sheet into the long envelope, noticing the name of the doctor to whom the report was going, one of the men I had known at the medical school who had promised his work, or a stranger, now how had he heard of me, no doubt about it, our reputation was growing.

At first I even stayed into the evening, to oversee the scrubwoman, lest she disarrange the specimens, or damage some of the apparatus. I pretended to be busy with accounts, but I found her lowering at me as she humped herself along the floor, a square of folded carpet under her knees, scrubbing brush jerking back and forth. "Ten years I've cleaned the offices in this building, and never a complaint," she said. "I'd have you know I've my pride. Snooping."

I pretended not to hear her, and she made a great clatter emptying the metal waste cans, rinsing them at the deep iron sink. It was my laboratory, and I'd stay as late as I pleased! Gilbert laughed when I told him about it. "She wasn't funny," I said. "She was impertinent, and I can't very well fire her, the building furnishes her as part of the rent."

"Why fire her?" asked Gilbert. "She sounds like a well-adjusted scrub-woman, if she has her pride."

"You think it's all right for a woman like that to—why, to

order me out of my own office? She'd never speak to you like that! And you laugh at me!" I didn't know what had started the landslide of words, but I couldn't stop it. "You're always striking that superior, tolerant air! What about *my* pride?"

"What about it?" asked Gilbert. "I didn't know it was involved." His voice was quiet, too quiet!

"When you know it's just that I'm trying to be sure not one detail goes wrong! We've put an awful lot of money in that laboratory, and if people don't respect my authority . . ."

"Who's threatening your authority? You just don't make sense, Carey."

My landslide went crashing downward. I don't remember what I said, except to tell Gilbert that he was impervious to outside opinion, he was self-sufficient—like a rock; he was so sure of himself, the surer he grew the less sympathy he had. He expected me to be the same way, and when I wasn't, he thought me foolish or childish or unreasonable. This wasn't the first time he'd said I didn't make sense. He didn't try to understand what troubled me. Gilbert listened, a harried look under his heavy brows, as if he sidestepped the landslide and waited for it to crumble into silence.

"I don't know what you want, Carey," he said, finally. "You're making me a whipping boy. I don't believe you know why yourself."

"I've told you why!"

"But all this fuss over a trivial incident! By this time you should feel secure enough . . ."

"That's what I mean! It's trivial to you! No matter what it is to me! Even that dreadful time last month when I thought I was pregnant! What did you say?"

"So that's it," said Gilbert, slowly. "You're still angry about that."

"Not angry. Aghast. At proof of how you really feel. In spite of everything."

(Black, whirling consternation, and Gilbert saying, "Would it be so terrible? I'm making plenty of money now." Bondage and pain and an end to all my work. "You're built just like me, Carey," my mother had said. "You never'll be the same if you have children, they'll tear you to bits." And Gilbert, "As long as it's happened, if it has, why don't we celebrate?")

"And even the doctor you sent me to, Dr. Hodges. You'd primed him, hadn't you? You thought I wouldn't guess."

("You're one of these modern young women, Mrs. Carey, driving yourself so hard your whole endocrine system's out of balance. You aren't pregnant. Much better for you if you were. In love with your husband? Have a few children. What are you afraid of?")

"I don't know what Hodges said to you, except that you were not pregnant. Whatever he said, he needed no priming from me. After all, he's a gynecologist, nothing surprising to him if a woman has a child." Anger had dried the resonance out of Gilbert's voice.

"You might have explained to him why it would be a catastrophe right now! So he wouldn't think me just a neurotic, selfish woman. Sitting back in that smug, complacent maleness and giving me advice! And you were just as bad! You didn't care how I felt, you were pleased."

"You would have liked it better, would you, if I'd been outraged."

"It's a shock to discover how you really feel."

"It might be, at that, if you ever did."

For the first time an Arctic bleakness settled around Gilbert and me. How long it lasted I don't remember. We were frozen into the distorted shape we had taken on in the quarrel, unable to move, and for the first time there was no sudden warm wind of love to free us. Gilbert was formal and alien, the ice which encased me thickened until nothing seemed to live at the core except a compulsion to justify myself. There was no reason why Gilbert should be angry. If anything had threatened him, I would have fought it. I was proud of his achievements, I had done everything a wife should. Had he just pretended his concern about my achievement? "You have to give her credit for taking the risk." Years ago, he had said that about Ellen. I had thought he was my shelter, my strength, and all the time he had been my secret foe, biding his time.

There are women, and men, too, who find relief from this kind of personal wretchedness in talk. I remember how my mother would pour out recriminations about my father, building up a triumphant picture of herself. That would have been impossible for me. What I did not recognize then was the cognate impulse which drove me in my work. In the laboratory I made sense enough! The doctors who sent me their patients, who recommended me to their colleagues so that some days half the reports went off to strangers, additions to the small group I had known, those doctors knew me as a woman of intelligence and skill. The test-tubes of blood in the racks along our counters, the smears on the numbered slides were proof. The future welfare of the donors depended upon our findings. The Carey Moore in white smock, leaning over the shoulder of the bacteriology assistant to identify the unexpected parasite, was a useful performer. The girls had a friendly respect for my opinions, my decisions about their problems.

I can see now that Rachel set the tone, with her steady admiration of me, her lack of any need to compete against me for her own prestige. She took for granted that any one of the assistants could see what a wonderful opportunity she had in working under me. Left to myself, I should have been too tense and authoritative, too anxious about details. Of course the major responsibility was mine, as well as the major investment. Not only money, Gilbert's and mine, but all the years of struggle, of preparation, and all the future years. Rachel had less at stake. Easier for her to keep her light touch, her drollery. But she did handle the girls well. Altogether the laboratory in those days was like one of our flasks for culturing microbes, the right temperature and culture-base for pride.

I carried on unspoken dialogues with Gilbert, in which I told him about the new doctors who had telephoned, or quoted, as modestly as possible, something one of the assistants had said to Rachel. But a small crisis in the policy of our laboratory was necessary to crack through the frozen separation.

Shortly after we had opened, just after the Board of Health had certified the place, and I was waking in the thin morning hours to count over the checks I had written for equipment, for labor, for rent, I came in from luncheon to find a representative of a chain drug-store company waiting for me. He understood I was just starting in business, was that right? He had a nice offer to make, a contract, monthly minimum guaranteed, flat rate above the minimum, standard urinalysis, some trouble with present firm, customers yelling about delays and all that, they furnished containers, messengers, report charts, all they asked was promptness, check every month, nice little back-log, good way to pay the rent. I said I'd think it over. He couldn't wait, too many concerns holding out their hands for their business, his stores had good conspicuous signs, right out in the window, none of these fly-specked cardboards hidden in a dark corner. Well, if I'd let him know the next morning. When he had gone, I talked it over with Rachel. Routine work, an easy way to pick up several hundred dollars. Just like a salary coming in regularly.

"It smells," said Rachel. "Maybe it's just that dead cigar he had. You better ask Gilbert."

"Nothing doing," said Gilbert. "You want to drive igno-ramuses to doctoring themselves for Bright's disease or diabetes? Why not advertise and take mail orders! What are you running, a factory or a scientific laboratory?"

"My part of it would be honest," I protested, "and this man said it often averaged a thousand dollars a month."

"How much do they make off it? Did he tell you that? Where's your professional ideal?"

"Scared out of me by the bills," I admitted. But I followed his advice, and never told him how often in the first few months I computed secretly and sadly the way that drug store contract would have kept us out of the red.

That had been at the beginning, and Gilbert had been right, of course. Now, with the ring of the telephone, I found myself in another predicament, one I had heard discussed but hadn't met. Dr. Scott's secretary, Dr. Scott wished to speak to the person in charge. Dr. Scott was a new name on my list, a Park Avenue doctor who had sent several patients the past month. Dr. Scott bellowed at me. I'd been well recommended, he'd sent me patients in good faith, only this morning one of them, an influential woman, too, whom he'd billed at his usual rate for biological tests, stated she had paid at the time of the tests, paid me. Completely out of order, most embarrassing, why, she was a wealthy woman, unless she paid well she put no value on services, did I mean to tell him I'd done that with all his patients? Pray, where did he come in? What about his time? Anger and panic vibrated at the pit of my stomach, made my voice hard to manage, as I tried to explain that I had followed our usual custom, that I didn't understand.

"Can you understand you've made a fool of me? As well as robbing me." His bellow changed into a brisk volley of orders. His secretary told him several more of his patients already had appointments. Instead of cancelling them, he would allow me to rectify the incredible mistake and bill them to him. Possibly my usual clientele was so doubtful that I found it necessary to collect at the door. He could, of course, swing a great deal of desirable business in my direction, through his colleagues.

The click of the telephone as he hung up without even waiting for me to reply was a final stinging slap. Rachel came into the office with a folder of duplicate reports for the files, and I pressed my spine hard against the back of my chair, trying to stop the whirl of confusion which was louder in my ears than the rasp of the cabinet drawer she pulled out.

"Double-you-oo, Ex, Y!" she said. "That's funny. I always thought Y came before Double-you-oo. You sure it doesn't?" She dropped in the folder and turned. "What's the matter, Carey? You sick?"

I told her, not too coherently, what Dr. Scott had said.

"Why, the old so-and-so!" Rachel was pretty when she was indignant, with a glow under her white skin, not color so much as light, and her eyelids, with the soft brush of dark lashes, lifting high over her clear, brilliant eyes. "Wanting to graft on our work!"

"He was the rudest boor! You wouldn't believe anyone could be so rude!"

"I hope you told him where to get off!"

"I didn't have a chance to tell him a thing. He told me."

"Of all the outrageous ideas! That's what they call fee-splitting, isn't it? You must have told him we never did that!"

Suddenly I was cross at Rachel, too, because she couldn't see how complicated the matter was. If fee-splitting was common practice, how on earth could we refuse?

"Just say no!"

I explained with dignity that I had to consider our whole policy, and if certain practices were common with reputable doctors, I couldn't risk antagonizing important men. I was trying to bolster my own uncertainty by proving Rachel was wrong. Rachel never fought back. She seemed to yield to opposing opinion. Perhaps you're right, she would say, with a deprecatory, who am I to argue manner. Only after years of knowing Rachel did I realize that she never yielded a crumb, she simply lacked the need to impose her attitude or belief on the other fellow. What she said this time was that Gilbert would know what we should do. "Where's Gilbert been, anyway? He hasn't dropped in lately. Why, I haven't seen him since—"

"He's been frightfully rushed," I interrupted.

"When wasn't he?" asked Rachel. "Doesn't he love us any more? Call him up, Carey, please! Ask him if we have to put up with this old vulture! I'd like to write a letter that would sizzle the feathers right off his breast-bone! 'Dear Doctor Scott, if you can't make a living without mulcting our laboratories . . .'"

"Very amusing. You offend him, and what happens to the good will we're trying to build up?"

"Ask Gilbert. Let me call him, if you don't want to. I don't think we know enough to settle this."

I pretended to be busy in the rear room, checking over the work of one of the girls, while Rachel telephoned. She came in presently for a tray of sterilized tubes and needles. "Three customers at once," she said. "Who balled up the appointments? He says he'll be here about five." She gave me a satisfied little nod as she scrubbed and dried her hands, and a sigh of relief expanded the tension with which I had waited. Gilbert might have said, Do as you like.

Gilbert was late. The assistants had gone, Rachel had hung away her smock and emerged from the lavatory looking very smart in fresh blouse and tailored blue suit. "You look as if you were going somewhere," I said, as I took her place at the mirror and smoothed my hair.

"Yes," she said. "I hope Gilbert isn't held up too long. Not that you need me, I'd just like to see him."

"You got a date?"

"Oh, sort of." She moved out of sight toward the office, and I called after her.

"You must stay! It was you who insisted on calling in Gilbert! He'll probably laugh at us for babes in the wood, and tell us we're idiots not to know that's the way to get more business."

"I don't believe it," Rachel sang out. "I don't have to go just yet."

Funny of Rachel not to say where she was going, I thought crossly as I tried to scrub a dye stain from my fingers. I wanted her here when Gilbert came, or he'd think I'd used her as a way to call him back when he had been so hostile.

"Here he is right now," Rachel called, and I heard the pleasant, deeper tone of his voice, the light gaiety of Rachel's greeting, although their words were not clear.

As soon as I looked at Gilbert, the uneasiness, like dry fingers fraying the ends of all my nerves, suddenly stopped. Stocky, calm, dark, friendly crows feet at the corners of his eyes as he smiled at me, why, he was glad he'd been summoned! "What's the trouble now, girls?" he asked, and even before we told him, I knew what he would say. Dr. Scott's threatening importance shrunk into a pin-point of annoyance.

"We just tell him to go to hell," said Rachel. "Good. I hate to truckle."

"I didn't intend to truckle," I said. "But I was afraid . . ." Gilbert's eyebrows drew together. "I mean you can't always do things as you like, you have to consider what people expect."

"Not too much," said Gilbert. "Just take a stand, no palm greasing, you may lose a little carriage trade, what of it?"

"That was what I wanted to do," I said. "But I had a vision

of him blacklisting our place." I tried to make a joke of the weight of apprehension I had carried all day.

"Poor Carey! If the brute calls up again, let me at him!" Rachel picked up her purse. "Now that's all settled. . . ."

The doorbell buzzed, interrupting her. Rachel glanced at me, her eyes almost black with the sudden dilation of the pupils, her mouth tucked in at the corners; her hand reached for the doorknob with perceptible reluctance, and she turned it, standing with her arm outstretched to hold back whoever had rung. It was Dexter Willetts.

"I thought I'd missed you," he began, and then saw Gilbert and me. He jerked up his head, the eagerness in his face blanked out. "Hello, there. How are you? The elevator man said you hadn't come down." That to Rachel. "He didn't tell me—"

"I was on my way," said Rachel, serenely. "Gilbert had to settle a moot question for us. Gilbert's wonderful with moots, they vanish at his touch! If ever you have a moot, Gilbert's the boy!"

I have forgotten the rest of Rachel's nonsense, although I remember the quality of her voice, warm, unhurried, and I remember the way Dexter lost the stricken embarrassment of his entrance moment, and laughed at her.

"Sit down," Gilbert urged, "and tell us about the Ridge."

"I can't tonight." Dexter glanced at his watch. "Some other Thursday, I'm in town every Thursday evening. Have a class at eight. Extension. Easy aid to the budget."

"It won't seem so easy if you miss your dinner!" With a casual wave of her purse Rachel strolled into the hall, and Dexter, his "Good-night" just as casual, followed and pulled the door shut.

"Well," I said, "how long has that been going on?"

"Just what is going on?" asked Gilbert.

"Didn't you see Dexter's face when he found us here?"

"You can't tell anything from Dexter's face. He's got a perpetual sense of guilt. Genevieve's seen to that. Rachel wasn't disturbed."

"Couldn't you see how she set to work to put him at ease? Why, it was like—like a blood transfusion!"

"I don't suppose it's any of our business."

"But she's ruining her whole life! How can she? Think what Genevieve will do! And she's bound to find out."

"Rachel was just going to dinner with him, not to bed."

"I'm not going to argue about it, I know. Why, she practically flowed around him and lifted him! I felt I ought not to watch! And we'll be blamed, you see! That's why Rachel wanted our house on the Ridge. Oh, how can she be such a reckless little fool!"

"If you're right, it's certainly their kettle of fish, not ours." Gilbert gave a low whistle. "I didn't think Dexter had the guts. His conscience must be a heavy load for Rachel to carry. I guess she's up to it, though."

"I suppose you admire her!" Unexpectedly all the misunderstanding of that earlier evening, held fixed and cold all this time, pushed turgidly into this new channel. "Throwing everything away for a clandestine affair! Implicating us!"

"Which worries you, the consequences to Rachel, or to yourself?"

"You see! You twist everything against me! To my discredit! Oh, I can't bear it!" I pressed my thumbs against my eyeballs, trying to hold back the hot tears, and rocked away from him, my head down to my knees. I heard him push back his chair, and felt him stand over me, heard his "Why, Carey!"

"You . . . you're so cold . . . you just stand off and . . . and disapprove . . . you don't even like me any more!"

With sudden, welcome violence Gilbert jerked me up to my

feet, plunked himself down in my big desk chair, and pulled me into his lap, his arms hard around me. "Shut up," he said. "You talk too much. You're all fashed up."

Warmth and haven and lovely peace. After a long time I stirred, my cheek tingling from the pressure of his. "Why didn't you do this sooner?"

"You didn't encourage it."

"You're supposed to be smart about what folks want. That's your business, seeing things, isn't it?" I felt light-headed with relief.

"With other people. Not you. You're too close. You breathe on my spectacles and I can't see a thing."

"I thought you were off at the edge of the earth, scowling at me, not liking anything about me any more!"

"I thought you didn't want me—any nearer—any more."

"Oh, it's been awful!" He was looking at me with a patient, questioning compassion, and I hid my face against his shoulder, pushing one hand up along the rough wool of his coat. "I can't be any different," I whispered. "I can't bear it when I feel you comparing me with other women . . . Rachel . . . or Ellen. . . ."

"But I don't." Gilbert's hand moved softly over my head. "I've been clumsy. I want you to be happy, Carey."

"Because I try to look ahead, to forsee consequences. . . ."

"You torment yourself, and I try to stop you! I'll admit that! Don't you know no one is ever fully safe until he's dead? Lie still, I won't let you up!" He reached past me to snap off the desk light. "There, relax. Shut off your mind. Don't worry, I'm not going to make love, not now. That worries you, too! Listen, Carey, you're my girl. I don't want you any different. As is, you're mine. Whatever else this damned world has for us, this is good, you and me, quiet like this, together."

A shaft of light across the floor from the inner room, the impersonal evening traffic sounds of the city, someone's heart beating steadily under my breast, was it mine or Gilbert's? Then, in the quiet, Gilbert's voice. He had never talked about his feelings, and now he spoke slowly, with long intervals between his phrases, as if his reticence kept rolling up in silent waves, and he waited for the wave to curl back before he could pick up the next words.

At first I thought why should he tell me this just now, what is he driving at, and in the intervals my mind shuttled drowsily over what had already been said. Nothing had been resolved; Gilbert had denied none of my reproaches, he had yielded nothing. You torment yourself, he had said. I won't make love, that worries you too. Easy enough for a man to say that! And yet what had been harsh dissonance was altered into concord, as a chord in music is resolved.

"Are you listening, Carey?" asked Gilbert.

"Yes," I said. "You were telling me about when you visited the priest."

It seems extraordinary to me now that what Gilbert tried to tell me had so little meaning for me at the time. I probably remembered it for a few days, and then pushed it away as theorizing which made me uncomfortable. But now, looking down through the transparent years into the clear water of the past, I can see it shining and whole, disentangled from the weedy growth into which my resistance had thrust it.

What Gilbert said, not in his hesitant, reserved speech but in essence, was this. As a young man he had gone once to talk with a Father of some most devout, ascetic order. A friend of Gilbert's, a proselyting friend, had made the appointment. The priest, lean, dark, fiery, had been impatient with Gilbert's lack of belief, and Gilbert's questioning, what do you start from, how do you know, had brought the answer, given with violence, "An act of faith. You know God by an act of faith." The phrase had stayed with Gilbert, although he had made no second visit to the monastery, and his friend had given him up as lost.

"I don't know how religious I am," Gilbert said, "but I've come to see that the basis of life is an act of faith. Hast thou faith? Have it to thyself before God. Love is an act of faith. You accept your lover without question or curiosity, whole, without knowing why. He fits you, that's all. You know. I think that's the way men know God. You offer yourself and you accept the lover. Passion, all the physical pull, is just part of it. Then, later, you begin to see the person you love, you learn his ways, you search for him. But these details aren't why you love, nor do they affect your love. Men lose God, too, when they lose the will to believe, the act of faith. They put their feeble minds on Him, they try to reconcile cruelty and pain and suffering with God. Once they try to figure God out, they are lost. It's like that with love. If a man says I love my wife, but I can't stand her untidiness or her temper, he doesn't love her, he's lost her. Not that love is uncritical. It's inclusive. Not that it's blind. It accepts. But it must renew itself, it must forever repeat the initial act of faith. That's all. I've tried to say it."

He waited, his breathing heavy as if he had been running (beating the thickets to flush the bird of truth), and his expectancy pulled at me uncomfortably.

"If you mean you love me, no matter what," I said, uncertainly, "that's fine ... although it sounds as if you had to put up with a lot!"

Gilbert gave an explosive, nervous laugh, and sat forward, with a sharp contraction of all his muscles, so that I lost my balance and spilled off his knees, scrambling to my feet.

"Anyway, I'm not untidy!"

"I never said you were." Gilbert stood up as I turned on the desk light and the first flash glistened in beads of moisture along his upper lip, before he dragged his knuckles against them; he shook down his trouser legs, jerked down his coat-front. "Anyway, you got the main idea. That's the time I didn't make much sense." He was matter-of-fact now, smiling at me, the mood of the darkness gone, its intensity, its expectancy, its final moment of embarrassment, as he said, "Get your duds, Carey. Let's go find some dinner. That's what ails me, hunger. Did you ever notice, when I'm most profound, it turns out to be lack of food?"

I could run then for my hat and coat, snap off the laboratory lights, relief spiralling up and up. Gilbert set the night lock on the outer door, barred my way for a moment with his arm. "Everything all right now, Dr. Carey Moore?" he asked, and I nodded and kissed him quickly. "That's fine," he said. "That's the way we want it."

That night I did not know that more had happened beyond reconciliation after misunderstanding. But here again I have been drawn back into personal history, when I started to tell the whole story of the Ridge. Enough of my own affairs. The next ten years for me moved as I determined them that evening. Perhaps the others, Ellen, Lawrence, Dexter, Rachel, even the children, Alicia, and Dick Burchall, had as unwittingly set their courses.

Book Four

ADELAIDE, JOHN, AND OTHERS

$\mathcal{A}$DELAIDE held her darning closer to her nose, squinting as she pushed the long needle over and under, over and under. These September evenings were dark so early, and she didn't like to turn on the light till she just had to. She could help John that small way, scraping a penny here and there off the electric bill, off the grocery bill. The boys ought to be home soon. She didn't like to have them riding bicycles after dark, but this was the last week of summer holiday before school opened, and they'd have to stay in week-nights, doing their home work. They'd just gone up to the Willetts', to see Alicia's new puppy. Adelaide wasn't sure Dexter had been wise to bring home another dog, after the way Alicia took on about Mister's death. Alicia was much too intense about such things. Adelaide was sure Genevieve had meant well, sending Mister to the vet's to be put out of his misery, dragging around with his hind legs all paralyzed, but perhaps if she'd talked it over with Alicia first. . . Children were reasonable, if you talked things over.

Adelaide patted down the cross-hatching with which she had filled the heel of the sock, rolled the sock up with its mate, and leaned back in her chair, her eyelids pleasantly drowsy. Hard to keep awake if she sat still in the evening, especially if John and the boys were out. She did hope John would get that job in Yonkers; not that it was much, just some repair work on a factory building, but he worried so! Since the two big contracts for houses had fallen through, he'd just driven himself like mad, trying to run something to earth, as he put it. Adelaide couldn't understand at all why people seemed to have stopped wanting houses built, but John ought not to worry so much, any minute this queer mix-up about stocks and bonds and banks would stop and he'd be as much in demand as he had been two years ago. It was silly to think that what happened down there on Wall Street could make any real difference in a big, prosperous country like this one. Now, if John had been working down there, the way Lawrence Hunter was! Well, then they might be worried. John had explained it to her, but Adelaide always came back triumphantly, "But there must be just as much money! The government makes it, doesn't it? And nobody's torn up all the bills or anything. And there's just as much of everything, wood, I mean, and stone, and what you build houses out of, nails, hardware, and people have to have places to live in. I think people have just lost their heads, that's all!"

Adelaide's head was back against the chair, her hands folded around the little ball of Henry's socks, she thought, when the boys come in they mustn't eat all that cold ham, John will be hungry and I'll make him sandwiches. The dusk was soft and warm with her buoyant forward-look to their coming, and sleep suffused her mind, sweet and dreamless. The telephone startled her, she didn't know she had slept and wondered why the room was so dark. She kicked over her work basket as she jumped up, the bell jangled again, she moved with her hands extended till she touched the doorway, found the button of the switch and blinked at the sharp light.

"Hello! Is that you, Adelaide?" Ellen's voice, a little shrill. "Listen, will you do something for me? I've been trying to get Lawrence, he's out there at the house, something's wrong with the 'phone. Ask John to go over, will you? Tell Lawrence to call me."

"John isn't home yet," said Adelaide. "Is something wrong, Ellen?"

"Why should anything be wrong?" Ellen sounded furious. "I want to speak to Lawrence, that's all. Can't you send one of the boys?"

"They aren't home either. They ought to be along soon, though."

"Operator, don't cut me off!" (No mistake about it, Ellen was in one of her tempers!) "Can't you do something? Must I come all the way out when you're right there?"

"They're at the Willetts," said Adelaide. "I could call them. . . . I suppose they could go around that way . . . although it's dark now."

"It's urgent, or I shouldn't trouble you. Tell Lawrence he must call me!"

"Is someone sick? One of the children?"

"No! Hurry! You might miss the boys! Please hurry!"

"I'll 'phone right away," said Adelaide. "When are you coming out, Ellen? We haven't had a good talk for I don't know when. Ellen! Are you there?"

Ellen wasn't there. She had hung up. Adelaide, calling operator and giving the Willetts' number, thought Ellen might have taken a minute for a personal word or two, she certainly was in a state, probably she'd blown off Lawrence's head and he'd walked out on her. Dexter answered. Funny, when Adelaide saw Dexter or heard his pleasant, restrained voice, she just couldn't believe he'd act the way she knew he did! The boys had already started home, he said, ten minutes or so ago. "They'll be home in a minute, you aren't worried, are you?" Oh, dear, Adelaide didn't know what to do.

"I'm waiting for John," she explained. "He won't have had

a proper dinner. I don't want to go off hunting up Lawrence and I don't want to send the boys back."

"I don't quite understand," said Dexter, politely.

Adelaide passed on Ellen's request, and thus felt free of responsibility. Dexter said he'd stroll up there, nice evening for a walk. Lawrence might be out around his place, not hearing the telephone bell.

"Oh, would you, Dexter? Ellen sounded upset, although I asked her if anyone was sick and she said no. Maybe something came up, I mean business matters, you know."

"I'll see if I can round him up."

"Of course John says there's plenty to be upset about in business today, especially the kind Lawrence is in. . . ." Again Adelaide found herself talking into space, but before she had time for more than a twinge of resentment at this second thwarting of her loquacity, she heard the boys.

John teased her about the way she liked to talk over the telephone. I can never get the house, the line's always busy, he would say. So I know you're there all right, talking your head off. Adelaide did not think she talked very much, but certainly the telephone was a pleasant invention for country life, where people couldn't drop in often, and it didn't matter how you looked nor whether you'd set the house in order yet. Ellen always liked to give the impression that she had no time, she was swept along with dazzling, important engagements. Well, Ellen had kept up a good front this past year, but according to John, Lawrence looked shot to the devil. They hadn't spent any time on the Ridge this summer. Ellen had put the children in camps, as usual, and had gone to a Newport hotel, making a point of the economy in not taking a house for the season. Oh, well! Adelaide moved briskly toward the kitchen. She was fond of Ellen, even if John didn't like her too well, really fond of her, with an old, steady affection. Her one woman friend. She hoped Dexter would find Lawrence all right.

The boys were arguing as they banged up the rear steps. The sound of their voices, and then the first glimpse of them as they came into the kitchen fitted snugly into her mood of waiting. Now, when John came, she would be complete again. Without them, she was like a pool from which the tide has receded, the small sea-animals on rocks and margins contracted, their fullness of life activity suspended until the tide came flooding back. She wasn't going to worry about them, the way Genevieve did, for example, about her Robert, . . . or if she did worry, she could keep it to herself. But their return after absence was a renewed miracle.

"Hi!" Henry grinned at her, his voice had notes just like John's, he spun his cap past her, it dangled on the corner of a chair-back, and flopped off. "Someday I'll get it to stick." He sidled toward the refrigerator, and Adelaide said, "Doughnuts and apples for you. I want that ham in case John hasn't had any dinner."

"You ought to speak to him, the hours he keeps! Where's he hang out till this time of night?"

Adelaide had her mouth open for a spluttering defense of John when just in time she caught the expression around Henry's mouth, lips buttoned over a laugh. She was easy to tease, because she always took words at their face value, as why shouldn't one? But she had at least learned that expression, especially as Henry looked just like John when he thought he'd caught her.

"Oh, you!" she said, and Henry opened his mouth for a doughnut instead of a crow at her. "Dick, don't you want a snack?" Dick had edged across the kitchen, he was so likely to try to escape to his own room instead of being sociable for a few minutes. He didn't turn now, he hunched his thin shoulders forward and swung the door open.

"No," he said, and then, like a reminded child, "no, thank you, I'm not hungry."

"Aw, Jeeps, Dick! I told you Alicia's got to learn to keep her mouth shut! The little damn fool ought to know better."

"Just because she's not a tough baby like that Danieloski girl who hangs around the garage . . ."

"Whatever you're talking about, I don't like it," said Adelaide.

Dick glowered over his shoulder, his throat working, and then stalked out of sight. The tips of Henry's ears were red, as he reached for another doughnut and opened his eyes under the sandy lashes in an ingenuous round stare.

"Just one of those Willett fracases," he said, between bites. He went on quickly with the story, and Adelaide, listening, thought, he's sidetracking the Danieloski girl, I won't pry about her, he's just the age for girls, he has a way with them, he must feel I trust him. Dick was more difficult, they were both good boys. All summer Henry had worked at the village garage, cleaning cars, tending the gas pumps, and Dick, who wanted to earn real money, too, had taken care of the vegetable garden and tended the chickens. Adelaide had said he could have the egg money, but she'd had to use it for the grocery bill, of course part of the bill was chicken feed.

"We were out on the terrace, fooling with the pup, see?" said Henry. "It's kind of a spaniel pup, like a long-eared beetle, wobbly on its pins."

(The Danieloski girl, thought Adelaide. There's a whole raft of them, I didn't know there was a girl old enough. . . .)

"So Robby grabs up the pup and says he's got to teach him tricks and heads for the house."

(Henry would be back in school next week, a Senior, he'd be too busy for girls, he was a natural leader. . . .)

"So there was the pup, smack in the middle of the living room best rug, and Bobby yelling bloody murder, it was nothing but a scratch where the pup bit him."

(They'd have to go in town soon, to pick out a suit and winter coat for Henry, he had saved enough, too bad Dick was taller than Henry, when they were little boys she could make over Henry's clothes for Dick. . . .)

"So there was Mrs. Willett, come a-running to rescue her dolling Robby." Henry pumped his chest vigorously up and down, patting it with a floppy hand, and Adelaide tucked her lips in, not to laugh. That was just like Genevieve!—"The pup lets its rear end spread a little, and piddles all over the rug. Some piddle for a pup that size! Honest, Mother, it was a scream!"

"What were you all doing in the house?" asked Adelaide. "You never go in the house."

"I told you! We chased Robby to get the pup away from him!"

"You always make Genevieve nervous." (Adelaide always meant to follow every word of Henry's stories, and John's, too; if either of them caught her on one of her private detours, she tossed off a small firecracker of admonition before they accused her of inattention.)

"Don't blame me! It wasn't me that bit Robby and piddled on the rug."

"Henry!"

"What Alicia should of done was pick up her pup and sneak off. Mrs. Willett wouldn't of missed her, she was carrying on so about Robby would have rabies and she'd known if they had another dog around, and her favorite rug! But Alicia just stands there, scrouched up, holding the pup, and finally her mother says, 'You're an unnatural girl! You care more for that vicious animal than for your own mother and brother!' "

"You should have come on home!"

"Listen, this is good. Alicia looks at her and says, I suppose now you'll have this one murdered, too! Wow! Her mother's eyes bunged right out. Only just then in comes Uncle Dexter as if he'd been sent for in a hurry, and kinda brushes us out of the room. So we did come home. Dick fell off his bike two-three times. He was so mad he couldn't stay on. He's sore at me, and all I said was Alicia was a fool, making such a fuss about that old Mister in the first place, when he wasn't any good any more, and then talking back that way. Don't you think she was a fool?"

"Well," said Adelaide, "I think dogs should be house-broken."

"Yah." Henry looked reflectively at the last doughnut on the plate, moved his hand toward it, and then shook his head. "Note my restraint! I tell you, Alicia's all right, for a girl. Kinda mushy, that's all. I bet Uncle Dexter got an earful after we beat it."

"Oh!" said Adelaide. "I'd forgotten . . . I called him up. He didn't sound as if anything was wrong. He said you'd gone."

"Were you checking on me?"

"No, of course not. Ellen wanted someone to tell Lawrence the 'phone didn't work. I mean she wants Lawrence to call her. Dexter said he'd go over."

"Glad to clear out, I bet." For a moment Henry's face, with its uncertain, adolescent planes, took on a hard shrewdness. "I saw Lawrence this p.m."

"You did? You didn't tell me."

"How'd I know you wanted to know? I see lots of different people every—"

"Where'd you see him?"

"At the gas station. Checked his car, he gave me half a buck. Fill her up, he says, I may be taking a trip."

"I wish you'd told me!" Adelaide's mind set up a quick whirring. Ellen's over-emphasis. Lawrence filling the gas tank. . . . Should she call Ellen, or wait till Dexter reported?

"Then I saw him again," said Henry, provocatively.

"For goodness' sakes, Henry, if Ellen wants him, can't you tell me what you know?"

"I don't know where he is now," said Henry. "I just know where he was." He grinned at his mother, and added a falsetto, "Hen-ry!" in so good a mimicry of her exasperation that she laughed. "When I was coming home, I saw him. He was riding Suzy, you know, the little black mare, up from the village. Did she put on a show! Acted as if she'd never seen a bike. I had to get right off the road into the ditch. Regular circus horse. I bet she went round ten times! Old Brown doesn't exercise her the way he ought to. I'm going to ask Lawrence if he doesn't want me to take her out. Lawrence sure can handle her, though."

"Lawrence wouldn't let anyone else ride his horse," said Adelaide, dismissing the quick vision of Henry catapulted over Suzy's head. "Well, Dexter will find Lawrence, then." All summer Lawrence had come out occasionally, leaving his car at the Browns', riding Suzy up to his own stable, to have her for an early morning run. This was the first year the Hunters hadn't kept a farmer on the place. "Now don't set your alarm clock," she added, as Henry, with a yawn which he tried to end as a yodel, moved toward the door. "It wakes your father, and he doesn't need to get up so early. . . . I'll call you."

"Okey," said Henry. "Say, what's going to happen to me next year if he doesn't get a job?"

"What nonsense! A whole year!"

"I just wondered." Henry's face, as he peered back at Adelaide, had again the momentary hardening into shrewdness.

"Dick says he could work while I went to college, but then I'd have to help him out and I'd just be getting a start myself."

"Your father will see that you go to college."

"Well, he can always sell apples," said Henry, and dodged for the stairs.

Adelaide picked up a sweater and started toward the front porch, to listen for the sound of John's car, her mind uneasy with the aimless slight motion of many incomplete thoughts, so familiar that they scarcely needed words. Too bad John was kept so late. As if he wanted to avoid the boys. Oh, no, he couldn't feel that way . . . his own sons . . . Henry got on his nerves . . . they were alike.

"Say, Ma!" Henry shrieked down at her as she opened the screen door, "you there? Listen! I thought of a name for Alicia's pup. 'Water Boy.' " He deepened his voice for a line of the spiritual, one of the records John had brought home for Christmas last year. "Water-Boy, Wa—ter—Boy, where are you gooo-ing . . ." His laughter cracked his voice. "Isn't that good? Guess I'll call her up and tell her."

"Leave her alone, you boob!" Dick's voice, a scuffle, and a slammed door.

"Henry! Go on to bed, will you?"

"Gosh, no one appreciates my best cracks."

"You appreciate 'em," came Dick's muffled grumble.

"Please!" Adelaide was imperative. "I hear John's car. Please Henry . . . cut it out!"

"That's him, all right," said Henry, "listen to that motor! I told him to get those valves ground." With that he stamped back into his room.

The light from the car was a glow over the crest of the hill, a brilliance on the under branches of the trees along the road; just as the headlights topped the hill, the telephone rang. Adelaide hurried into the house, fragments of thoughts scattering. Henry wasn't really worried about college or hard times. Maybe he'd overheard something she or John had said. Children were insulated in their own affairs. They took whatever happened at home . . . they took it for granted. . . . They were too young to be worried . . . not that there was anything really to worry about. . . a mortgage on the house if worse came to . . . she'd wanted to meet John at the end of the drive.

It was Dexter on the 'phone. No sign of Lawrence at the Hunter place, windows all shut, doors locked, not a light. No car. No, he hadn't looked in the stables. Adelaide explained about Suzy.

"But I walked past the stables," said Dexter. "I took the short cut. If the horse had been there . . . I'm sure I should have heard something. Lawrence must have come out just to ride. He's gone back to town."

"Perhaps I better call Ellen. John's just come, I'll ask him."

"The boys got home?" Dexter waited; did they tell you anything, his waiting asked.

"Oh, yes. Just after I called you. Thanks, Dexter. Goodnight."

"What's Dexter want?" John stood in the doorway, his portfolio in his hand, a haggard wariness in the glance he sent past her toward the living room. "Do you need every light in the house on? Looks like a Christmas tree."

No luck. "I was out doors," said Adelaide, "I just turned them on as I ran in."

"Upstairs, too."

"I suppose the boys aren't asleep yet." Adelaide broke into chatter about Ellen's call, about Dexter's report, offering Ellen's anxiety, Lawrence's disappearance as a diversion. (John looked so tired, so thin! So chagrined! Oh, she hated the fools who couldn't see how much he offered to them, how remarkable he was!) "Have you had dinner? I saved . . ."

"I had enough," said John. "I had a flat. That inner tube I patched. (Oh, darling! a last straw!) So I got coffee and a hamburger while they put in a new tube. Lucky I counted my money before I ordered pie. Just enough for the tube. Have you called Ellen?" He took off his spectacles, polishing them with his handkerchief; thus exposed, his eyes looked sunken, the rims thickened. "Although why we should pay for a long distance call . . ."

"No," said Adelaide. (Oh, dear! John did feel bad. Ordinarily he would have had a dozen suggestions about where Lawrence was, what to tell Ellen.) "She didn't ask me to call her. You come and have something to eat. A hamburger isn't enough for your inner man."

Food was a tangible comfort, she could offer that as a symbol of all she longed to give him, she could sit opposite him at the kitchen table and watch the hot coffee (weak, not to keep him awake) bring a tone less ashy into his lined face. She told him about the puppy and Genevieve's scene: like the sandwiches, it was a piece of the homely, familiar texture of their life, something to assure him that nothing was lost, the usual still happened, everything would turn out all right. When John said, "That tasted good, I guess I was hungry," her pleasure was an ache so sharp she had to run to the cake-box and clatter the lid to smother her vigorous sniffling back of tears.

"It's funny," said John, finally, and Adelaide hugged her arms under her plump breasts, her flesh warm and content again, "if Lawrence told Henry he was going on a trip, it's funny that he took Suzy out. If Ellen was haired up . . . but a man who's absconding doesn't talk about it. No, he had his ride, just as he's done all summer, tossed off a few (that village apple-jack is potent stuff!) and now he's dead to the world, just didn't hear Dexter."

"Drunk?" Adelaide gave a little squeak of horror.

"I didn't say that. Although Ellen's enough . . . I'd feel a fool, rousing him up just to let Ellen give him what for. Leave him alone, I say. Though at that maybe he's not alone."

"John! Do you really think. . ."

"No. Not out here. Oh, Lawrence is all right. He wouldn't hurt a fly. Trouble with him is he's too easy. Ellen needs a man who beats her every Saturday. Lawrence's never handled her right."

Adelaide gave a sleepy kitten yawn. John was more like himself; with her relief, the end of the day drowsiness submerged her. "Let's go to bed," she said.

John lay in bed staring at the ceiling, his Adam's apple sharp-angled under his extended chin, and Adelaide moved nimbly through her simple preparations, scrubbing her face, her teeth, giving her hair a quick brushing, pattering over to open a window, hurrying to turn off the light and lie beside him, his arm under her shoulders until it prickled, and he drew it out, to roll over on his side and sleep, she hoped. "You know," he said, his fingers touching her soft upper arm. "Maybe I better try something else, just for a stop-gap. I was reading the ads. There seem to be a few for salesmen. Commission basis. You think I could do that?"

"You could *do* anything." Adelaide tried to hold her eyelids open, the ease of his familiar, undemanding embrace, the comfort of his nearness, known in each bone, the hard shell of his chest, the sharp edge of thigh bone, deepened her drowsiness. "Darling. . . ."

The ring of the telephone, startling in the dark and quiet house, scattered sleep, drove her upright in bed.

"I'll go." John was out with the sudden jerk of his body, legs and arms pulled by wires of his nervousness. Adelaide ran out to lean over the stair rail, and almost instantly John's voice was shouting from the lower hall.

"Hello! Oh, hello." (Ellen, by the change in tone.) "No, I'm in bed. At least I was. I didn't see him—Henry did, riding Suzy. Riding Suzy, I said."

Adelaide scampered down the stairs. "Let me talk to her!" she said, but John held the ear-piece firmly against his ear and scowled at her.

"Is it anything that will spoil before morning?" he asked. "Sure, he's all right, why wouldn't he be? No, he left the car at Brown's. Let him have a good night's sleep. Why, he's been doing this all summer, while you've been off . . . I'll send one of the boys over first thing in the morning." John banged up the ear-piece so hard the bells vibrated.

"What'd she say?"

"Getting us out of bed in the middle of the night!" John clumped up the stairs. "She piped down when I reminded her she didn't give a damn all summer what happened to Lawrence."

Adelaide, walking up her night-gown in her haste, pulled the folds up to her knees. "I wonder what she wants. Maybe we ought. . . ."

"It's perfectly obvious." John looked dignified and angry, in spite of the wisps of hair which stood on end away from the thin crown over which he kept them carefully arranged. "Lawrence must have talked back for once, she got to thinking she'd gone too far. Do her good to stew a little."

For several moments Adelaide was restive, trying to fit the pillow under her head, wriggling the toe she had stubbed to see if she had broken it, pulling another blanket up to her shoulders. John wasn't sleepy now, either; she could tell by the degree of rigidity with which he held himself over there at his side of the bed.

"You know," he said, "Ellen's the kind of woman if her goose stopped laying golden eggs, she'd wring its neck."

"But Lawrence'd be a gander, not a goose," said Adelaide.

"Yah!" John grunted, but he didn't add his usual, There you go, being literal again. Instead he rolled over, flinging an arm across Adelaide's body, pulling her nearer. "But you wouldn't. You'd say, oh, he's just moulting, he's off his feed a bit."

"Yes, Johnny. Try to go to sleep." Adelaide relaxed, the weight of his arm was the sweet weight of sleep pressing down upon her.

She woke once, half choking with a nightmare cry which started from such black depth it could not reach the muscles of her throat. Only fringes of the dream were left, and those wavered and were gone in blackness as she heard John stir. She held her breath, had she wakened him? No, he was quiet. She knew what the nightmare had been, for all it had vanished. She hadn't dreamed that way for years, scarcely since the first years of her marriage. Fleeing, ragged figures, their dark and foreign faces lighted awfully by flames from the burning village, the thatched roofs bursting into blaze like great torches, feet torn and bleeding on the rocky trail, the cold wet odor at the mouth of the caves, the dreadful expansion of children's crying into clangor inside the unknown blackness where fear-harried and pursued the figures sought refuge. Her mother had told her that she couldn't possibly remember any such nights, she was too young, she'd made it up out of her mother's stories in lectures for the mission boards. Adelaide wriggled herself closer to John, close enough, not touching him, just knowing in every cell, in warmth, in emanation, that he was there.

The next morning she woke, slipped into house-coat and hurried along the hall to shake Henry, all in a single continuous movement. No slow emergence from the chrysalid of sleep for Adelaide. Rested, sanguine, energetic, her hair curling over temples and ears, damp from her hasty scrub, she ran down stairs,

planning her day. She liked mornings, she liked knowing what
she had to do, nice definite tasks for her hands, hope cometh in
the morning, what was the rest of that? John would surely find
something today. Dick must gather the rest of the tomatoes,
she'd put up another dozen quarts. A lovely September morning, golden and still, with the smell of apples in the air. As she
set the kettle on and measured coffee, she heard John calling
her. She'd better send one of the boys over to the Hunters
before Ellen exploded again.

Dick went, after an argument with Henry which Adelaïde
settled. Of course Dick's work was as important as Henry's, but
Dick kept his own hours and Henry had an eight to five job.
"Just an ole time-clock puncher," muttered Dick.

"Tell Lawrence to use our 'phone," said Adelaide. "Tell him
I'll give him breakfast."

Henry had gone, his lunch-box tied to the carrier on the rear
wheel of his bicycle, a final squawk from the horn (discovered in
the cars junked behind the garage and attached to the handle-
bars) as he coasted off down the hill. Adelaide wished he could
get home for a hot luncheon, but he said it was too far. Of
course in the summer the road was awfully hot and dusty. John
came down, hitching his wrinkled pajama trousers tighter around
his waist. What the devil did the boys do with the hot water,
not a drop left, not warm enough to shave with, did they swim
in it? Adelaide filled a pitcher from the kettle. She'd go down
to look at the heater, she'd forgotten it!

"I'll see to it later." John stalked away. Oh, dear, thought
Adelaide, he's too thin, look at the way the top of his spine
sticks out, he ought to stand up straighter, all that bending over
his draughting work . . . I ought to speak to him . . . Someday
when he felt better.

The little round stove squatting beside the furnace was cold,
her careful shaking sent up fine white ash around the clinkers

and found not a glint of red. Why couldn't she remember it? Now she had to pick out the clinkers and rebuild the fire. It had been John's pet, but now his hours were so irregular. The boys built too hot a fire, so that the boiler thundered and steam burst out of the faucets. She had at first put a note to herself, Fix the pot-stove, in her dressing table mirror, but that had irritated John.

She sat on her heels, waiting till the kindling caught and she could sprinkle on the first coals. Any minute John would finish shaving and come down, she'd like to have it going. . . . But John didn't come, and finally blue flames licked up through the fine black coal, and she shut the door gently. She must be a sight, if she shut one eye she could see a smudge on the tip of her nose, and look at her hands!

No one in the kitchen yet. John might have cut himself. She scrubbed her hands hastily at the sink, rubbed the towel over her nose, and then as she turned to the table under the window, movement outside held her eyes and she stared. John, partly dressed, shirt tail not tucked in, as if he'd come down in a hurry, Dick, and Dexter Willetts, the three of them a curious, close, triangular tableau, Dick's head pivoting slowly from his father to Dexter, and back, John's elbows jerking, (he must be talking very fast) and Dexter hunched forward, the fingers of one hand raking his cheek.

Something had happened! For a moment Adelaide shut her eyes tight, in an involuntary rejection of disaster. Don't see it, don't hear it, pretend it isn't so! Then, reluctantly, she walked down the kitchen steps and along the path.

"Brown hasn't a 'phone," John was saying. "I'll drive down, to make sure Lawrence's car is there."

"He wouldn't have left his horse wandering in the woods while he went off in his car!" Then Dexter saw Adelaide. "Good morning," he said, his glance apprehensive, that of the male dreading female emotional participation.

"Suzy's up there," said Dick, "tramping around the garden. With her saddle half off and her knees all skinned. . . ."

"I'll bring Brown back with me," went on John, "and two-three other men. If we've got to search the whole district. . . ." He was tucking in his shirt, his posture erect, charged for action.

"Ellen called me this morning," said Dexter. "She wanted me to tell Lawrence to wait out here, she was coming out . . . I'd just coaxed Suzy to let me catch her when Dick appeared."

"Whoever put on that saddle didn't fasten the cinch buckle," said Dick. "Golly, she musta thrown him right off!"

"You can't tear off without breakfast!" Adelaide buttoned her fingers tight around John's arm. "Five minutes more won't hurt Lawrence! He's probably broken a leg or something . . . or maybe he's stopped somewhere and they haven't got a telephone. It won't do Lawrence any good if you half kill yourself!" Her last phrase hung for a moment, John and Dexter stared at her, just an instant, and then blinked off the sudden conjecture.

"I could drive the car down to Brown's," said Dick. "Lemme go, Dad. I could get him and—"

"That's it!" cried Adelaide, tugging at John's contrary arm. "He'll drive carefully."

"Now wait a minute!" John had to get things organized. "Tell Brown to get that brother-in-law, Coombs, he knows the woods, he poaches in them enough. Don't go shooting off your mouth, no use raising a stink till we know . . . Lawrence wouldn't like it. He may even show up any minute, you know, not hurt at all, just dumped too far away or lost his road in the dark." Dick was edging away, stretching the string of instructions till distance snapped it and he ran for the garage. "You ought to have heavier shoes," John went on, looking Dexter up and down, "and some kind of jacket, if we're going to. . . Hey, Dick!" He shouted above the noise of the motor as Dick shot backwards out of the garage. "Dick! Ask Henry just where he saw Lawrence yesterday, and what time it was."

Dexter started briskly toward his place, he'd be back as soon as Dick was. Adelaide set out John's breakfast and ran upstairs to find his walking shoes (bring my puttees, too!) and khaki fishing coat. Of course Lawrence was all right, as John said, he'd come walking out of the woods somewhere, but they had to act on a gloomier supposition. She certainly hoped Lawrence would turn up before Ellen arrived, she couldn't make that first train, somewhere toward the end of the morning. It was wonderful, the way John rose to an emergency and just took charge of everything.

The gathering of the men in the road before the house, an hour or so later, had a theatrical effect in the quiet September sunlight. Brown, a stocky, ponderous man whose overalls wouldn't quite fasten around his massive abdomen, was on the defensive. He hadn't seen Mr. Hunter at all, hadn't had any word to expect him, the wife said she'd warned him Suzy hadn't been run lately, he'd harnessed her himself. His brother-in-law, lanky, sallow, chinless, maintained a suspicious silence: just why had he been included? He didn't know as he knew the woods any better than plenty of others. "We'd oughtta look over the mare," he said. "Was she sweaty? Run far?"

"She had mud dried on her knees," said Dick, "and on her hind-quarters, I mean on one quarter . . ."

"Mud?" John was testy. "Where's there any mud? Hasn't rained for weeks."

"Swamp," said the brother-in-law. "That old beaver dam."

They were off, finally, Dexter and Brown to follow the bridle path where it took off from the top of the hill, John and the brother-in-law to drive on ten miles or so to the point where the bridle path emerged to cross the road. Dick begged to go, but John said he should stay with Adelaide, he could keep an eye on the Hunter place in case Lawrence showed up, anyway with Ellen on her way out, his mother needed him. With last minute efficiency from John about signals and meeting, they departed.

"I might as well can those tomatoes," said Adelaide, feeling as if she came fluttering down from a balloon which had soared off and left her. "No use wasting the whole day."

"I'll bet," said Dick, his face twisted in a grimace of baffled desire, "if I got on Suzy, she'd take me right there!"

"Don't you dare touch that horse!" Adelaide tried, quickly, to moderate her tone. "After all, Dicky, if she'd throw Lawrence, and you know what an experienced rider he is! You bring me in a good basket of tomatoes, and then you can run up to the Hunters', just to see. . . ."

As she set out the jars to scald, she pulled in the corners of her mouth in quick, furtive, not fully recognized satisfaction. It was good for John, having a task like this, it brought out . . . Poor Ellen!

Adelaide kept lifting her head from her work, hearing a car which kept turning out to be nothing but her expectation ringing in her ears. She filled a large kettle with water and set it on the burner behind her canning kettle, most inconveniently, but hot water was always useful. She considered going to the station to meet Ellen, but after all she wasn't sure Ellen would come on that noon train, and if John came back, he might need her.

She was lifting the rack with the second batch of six jars from the canning kettle when Ellen spoke, and she was so startled that she all but dropped all six cans.

"You certainly look concerned!" said Ellen.

"Ellen! I didn't hear you!" Adelaide scalded her fingers, running across to the table with the jars. "Where *did* you come from?"

Ellen stood at the entrance to the dining room, erect and elegant in sleek fawn-colored suit, the beady eyes in the small pointed heads of her long fur scarf no harder, no more glass-like than her own. "Don't let me interrupt you," she said, and averted her face as Adelaide rushed to embrace her.

"I couldn't just sit down and fold my hands!" cried Adelaide. "I had to do something! Ellen, darling, I'm sure they'll find him all right! Come in, take off your things."

"Don't pity me!" Ellen's hands were clutched over the top of her brown suéde purse, her cheekbones were prominent, her mouth thin. "Perhaps they have found him! They wouldn't tell me. Brushing me aside! Some state troopers, the village constable, getting up a little party just as I arrived. That dreadful, avid, wolf look, off to the hunt, yoicks! Men only! Oh, I hate them! The constable's the coroner, too! Even Gilbert, they took him right along, in case they needed a doctor." Ellen's teeth clicked in a violence of shivering. "How could he do this to me? How could he?"

"Ellen, darling, come sit down! Is he hurt? He didn't fall off Suzy on purpose! Ellen!"

"You could have prevented it!" Ellen brushed away Adelaide's hands. "If you'd listened to me last night." She swayed, her body rigid, her eyelids shut, and Adelaide, competent and maternal, got her into the living room and flat on the divan. She couldn't find the flask of brandy in the medicine cabinet. John must have taken it with him. She had smelling salts somewhere, a little purple bottle her mother had given her. There it was!

Ellen pushed it away, her nostrils flaring.

"I'm all right," she said. "Leave me alone! I wish I were dead, too. But the children!"

"You mustn't talk like that!" Adelaide was shaking a trifle herself, as she tried to pull out the fur scarf, to smooth up a rug. She heard steps in the kitchen, and ran to the door. "Dick! Have you heard anything?"

"How would I hear anything when you won't let me go?"

"Go down to the village and ask Henry. They might know at the garage."

She envied Dick his quick spurt of action. She made tea for Ellen (she'd known that hot water might be useful!) but Ellen refused it.

"I wanted to help, last night," said Adelaide. "We couldn't do anything, Lawrence just wasn't around."

Ellen stared at her, her hazel eyes almost the pale fawn of her suit, the pupils contracted to points.

"I'll get you a hot water bottle," said Adelaide. "Would you like a hot water bottle? Your hands are so cold. It might wrinkle your suit."

Ellen began to laugh, a high, mirthless crackling sound, and suddenly flung herself over, face hidden on her arm, her shoulders twitching, the laughter choking off. Adelaide's face burned, she had jumpy feelings all over her body, frustrated impulses to do something, anything! She'd like to shake Ellen! She was trying to help her.

"Addie!" Ellen rolled her head just a little, freeing her dry lips from the pressure of fabric. "Are you there?"

"Yes." Adelaide sat down on the edge of the divan, bracing her heels to compensate for the scant space. "Right here."

"It's not my fault, Addie. I didn't ask him to take money that wasn't his, I didn't know. I was so shocked I didn't know what I said to him! Disgracing me . . . and the children! I didn't mean what I said to him. I wanted to kill him! Oh, it's been terrible, this whole year! Wouldn't you try to save your children? That's all I did. It's not my fault! I won't have it!"

"Goodness!" Adelaide gave her plump buttocks a little hitch, she reached one arm around Ellen, just for balance, and Ellen clung to her hand. "Did Lawrence . . . did he steal?"

"He borrowed. They all do, he said. He got caught. He wanted me to pour everything else down the drain! The town house, the farm, everything! I didn't know what I was saying! Is it my fault if he was such a coward?"

"Ellen, you'll make yourself sick! Hush, Ellen dear! It was an accident . . . we all say things we don't mean . . . you'll need all your strength if . . . whatever's happened. . . ." Adelaide squirmed into a firmer position, and patted Ellen's shoulder. "There!"

"Men are such brutes! When I've tried. . . oh, God, how I've tried to make something out of . . . out of him! Even Gilbert . . . I thought he was my friend. It was Lawrence who said that about the insurance! I didn't mention it till he brought it up! But I did try to find him last night. To tell him he could have everything, he could make paupers of us."

"Now, hush, Ellen. It isn't your fault if you couldn't locate him."

"To have Gilbert take Lawrence's side! When I trusted him. That's why I sent for him. I was half crazy, I haven't slept for days! He turned on me."

"My goodness, when he's always been more than half in love with you!" Adelaide floundered, as Ellen's body grew very still under Adelaide's patting hand. "I mean . . . nothing bad, of course . . . but you told me, when he first came to New York . . . don't you remember, you used to laugh about him?" Nothing out of the way in Ellen's asking his advice, that was really his business now. But Ellen was so hushed, as if every cell held its breath to listen that Adelaide hurried on, "Of course you never dreamed he'd get to be so successful, he was such a solemn little country bumpkin, and Lawrence did seem to have wonderful prospects."

Ellen shook into harsh cackling laughter again, which rose sharply into dry sobbing, and Adelaide, after a dismayed moment, laid her hands firmly on the tormented shoulders and pulled Ellen up.

"Stop it," she said. "I'm going to put you right to bed and give you one of John's sleeping pills." That was the thing to do, she shouldn't have sat there letting Ellen talk herself into such a state. She was strong and firm, her arm around Ellen's body was a bulwark of warm affection, she pushed and tugged her toward the stairs, and Ellen, surprisingly, was docile, moving at Adelaide's volition, without resistance.

Adelaide stripped down the spread on one of the guest room twin beds, she brought her best silk night-gown, she helped Ellen's fumbling fingers with hooks and snaps, making little murmurs of there! now this! that's it! Why, they might have been girls in college again, and Ellen with a sick headache, her body was as ivory smooth as ever, a little fuller . . . lovely . . . but so cold! "Now swallow this!" She popped the pill between Ellen's thin, pale lips, she held the glass of water in a steady hand.

"Give me two," said Ellen. "I've taken so much dope."

"One's enough, they're strong. Lie down, I'll get a water bottle."

She drew down the shades, pushing the ruffled organdy curtains out of way, it was a pretty room, not as elegant as Ellen's, of course, but still . . . Her briskness, her efficiency as she hurried down to the kitchen for hot water quite supplanted other emotions; she had established a small space of light in which she moved, with the impending fog of disaster standing outside, waiting to close in. She hurried back, plumping the water bag to squeeze out air, tightening the stopper, and thought at first that Ellen was already asleep. But as Adelaide slipped the bag under the blanket, Ellen's icy fingers shut around her wrist, her eyelids moved into deep creases. "Addie!" she whispered. "Oh, Addie!"

"Now don't worry," said Adelaide, and stroked her forehead gently. "Dear Ellen."

"It's like coming home, Addie."

"There! Don't try to talk."

Ellen's fingers unclasped, and after a moment Adelaide withdrew her hand and tiptoed away. It just went to show how you could misjudge people, she'd thought Ellen was so engrossed in her gay city life, of course it hadn't been very gay lately, but still, a friend was a person you could turn to, and no one had ever taken Ellen's place. John would say, Yeuh, when she's in trouble, she comes running! But I'll just tell him how pitiful she is, thought Adelaide, affection expanding to crowd out any doubt about John's attitude, expanding into assurance that John would share her feeling. No matter what, she would stand by Ellen.

Adelaide busied herself washing and setting away the canning utensils, tightening jar covers, standing the jars on their heads in sunlight, uneasy for a moment at the splotches of color on the white oil-cloth where the light fell through the gules of the fruit. It wasn't like blood, she mustn't be morbid, and anyway, if Lawrence had broken a leg, there wouldn't be any blood. She didn't know just what to do about lunch, and finally settled for a large potato salad; if no one came for lunch, she could use it for dinner. Occasionally she went to the foot of the stairs, to listen, and twice she climbed softly to the door of the guest room to look in at Ellen, finding her motionless, her drugged breathing loud.

"It's the best thing for her," thought Adelaide, soft-stepping down the stairs. "After life's fitful fever . . ." That must have popped into her head from some college course where she and Ellen had sat side by side. Perhaps it wasn't just the best quotation! She wished Dick would come back. She didn't like to call Henry at the garage, he'd been very firm about that when he first took the job. "Listen, Mom," he'd said. "We had this car down, see, doing a valve job, Mike had to drop everything to answer the 'phone, then he had to yell for me, we lost a monkey wrench in the waste pan, took us an hour to catch up. Next time you want a yeast cake, you send Dickie-boy for it, or wait till tomorrow." She walked very slowly past the telephone. Even Mike might consider this important! Still, John would surely come home, why should he go first to the village?

The telephone rang while she lingered, and she jumped for it.

"Mrs. Burchall? This is Alicia."

"Yes!" exclaimed Adelaide. "What is it? Have they come back?"

"Mother asked me to call you, she doesn't feel very well, is Father there?"

"Nobody's here. Except Ellen Hunter."

"He . . . he hasn't come back from his walk yet?"

"Goodness, don't you know?"

"Yes," said Alicia. "He and Mr. Burchall were going for a long tramp." The harried, fluttery tone in the girl's voice caught Adelaide. Of course. Dexter had said, Don't worry your mother, and probably right now Genevieve was lying on the divan in the living room, with the door open into the study, so that she could hear every word.

"No, they have not come back," said Adelaide.

"It's such a nice walk, I mean a nice day," said Alicia. "Tell Father, if he comes that way."

Adelaide buttoned her mouth in disapproval as she went on to the kitchen. It was all very well to try to spare Genevieve, but wasn't it training Alicia in duplicity? And wasn't it queer, when Dexter was so solicitous about things that didn't really matter (of course an accident to Lawrence mattered, she didn't mean that exactly, but it wasn't a personal thing to Genevieve) that he could carry on the way he did with that Rachel Thayer? Not that Adelaide had any proof of how far they'd gone, but she had her intuition, didn't she? For a moment she had a vague feeling, just a ripple among her drifting impressions, that perhaps if Dexter hadn't had to exercise so much solicitude . . . But that was exonerating him! Firmly she smoothed away the ripple, and sat down for a hasty, solitary lunch. If no one was coming, she might as well eat.

She changed her dress, hesitating at the door of her closet, seeing its contents through Ellen's eyes. Milgrim, the label in her suit said, and that lovely satin blouse, the same color. She mustn't be silly, Ellen didn't care what she wore! Like coming home. But for all that she chose her second best summer dress, a rose colored silk shirt-waist frock, and then hung it back as too gay for whatever might come before the day ended. The green and white gingham was better, although it was a little snug. With her face washed, powder dusted over the freckles on her nose, her hair brushed into neatness, she stood at the door of Ellen's room, wondering how long Ellen would sleep, when she woke she'd feel better and they could have a good talk. Half way down the stairs Adelaide heard the car churn into the yard and stop, and she ran, forgetting to be quiet.

John and Dexter emerged from the car, one on either side, with Dick spilling out after his father. They all looked at Adelaide as she hurried toward them, and they all looked alike, their faces shuttered with unwillingness to speak.

"Did you find him? What is it?"

"Yes," said John, and threw back his shoulders, stretched up his head. "Is Ellen here?"

Adelaide shook his arm. "She's asleep upstairs. Tell me!"

"Asleep?" John's lip drew back over his teeth. "Asleep? She would be."

"I gave her a sleeping pill," said Adelaide. "She was in a terrible state. What happened?"

"He was thrown," said John.

"Is he . . ."

"Yes, he is."

"But where is he? What. . ."

"I'll tell you about it."

"I'd better go along," said Dexter. "If you don't need me. . . ."

"Well, we can't break the news till she's awake, can we?"

"Alicia called up," said Adelaide. If Dexter would go on home, she could find out from John; together, the two men seemed bound to silence in a fraternity of shared experience. If Henry were with them, instead of Dick, he would have told her everything in a breath!

"She did?" Dexter barely glanced her way; his face was more than ever like a hawk, with the long, aquiline nose prominent, the cheeks sunken with fatigue.

"I didn't say a word about *anything*," said Adelaide.

John came around the front of the car, and the two men shook hands (Like a pact, thought Adelaide.) "Damn glad you were with me," said John. "Don't you want Dick to run you home?"

"No. I'd rather walk. Let me know if . . ." He set off slowly, the scholar's stoop of his tall body noticeable, his narrow long head almost silver in the light.

"You go on back and wait for Gilbert," said John, and Dick slid into the car. "Tell him Ellen's here and your mother gave her a sleeping pill. She'll probably need a doctor when she comes to." He watched as Dick backed down the drive. "For God's sake, be careful!" he shouted.

"Darling, you must be simply dead!" said Adelaide, her hand reaching for John's arm. "Oh!" She pulled her hand in a smart slap against her mouth. "I mean . . . you must have tramped miles! Aren't you starved? Come in."

"I couldn't eat," said John.

"Hot coffee, then." Adelaide corralled him into the kitchen, she made him sit down (Ellen wouldn't hear them out here!), she brewed fresh coffee, she poured the next morning's cream recklessly into the cup, and set food unobtrusively beside the coffee. As she had hoped, John reached automatically for a roll, and with the second cup of coffee, ate his way through the plateful of salad and scraps of ham.

"No matter what happens," he said, half sheepishly, "a man has to eat."

"Of course." She pushed back the dishes, and leaned against the edge of the table. "You don't look quite so gone," she said. She looked at him, warm tears brimming over her under lids; darling John, breathing, squaring his shoulders, swinging one leg over the other knee (how muddy his boots were!) wriggling his mouth in the funny way he always had when he got ready to tell a long story. "Oh, poor Ellen!"

"Poor Lawrence, you mean. Did Ellen tell you why she was so worried about him? Last night?"

"Um. (Not the quarrel, Adelaide wouldn't betray that.) Business troubles."

"I thought so. Gilbert knows more than he will tell, too."

Then John began his story, and Adelaide slid off the table into a chair, her hands clasped tightly, the tears drying from her round, startled eyes, her face flushed. John's voice was hushed and quick; he was aware of Ellen upstairs, of Gilbert on his way from the village, he wanted to finish before another chapter began.

The brother-in-law, Coombs, had wanted to head in for the

old beaver colony, the place where they'd dammed up the brook and the trees had all died. But the dam there was broken, the brook was practically dry, no sign of hoof marks. Coombs then suggested the duck-pond, about three miles in; Adelaide had never walked that far. Not on the regular bridle path, but an old wood-road cut past it. Some signs of beaver work, trees lying around, sort of hit or miss. Coombs said they'd given up the place, not enough water once the spring thaws were past.

"He was going on about beavers and how smart the little cusses are," said John, "all the time single-footing along like an Indian, his eyes on the ground, when he found the hoof-marks. Going both ways. 'Those are fresh marks,' he said, 'come just this far and go back.' He shut up, then, and the next minute we found Lawrence."

There was a tree, a tall ash, down across the road, at an angle, the top lodged in hemlock branches, and beyond it, at the marshy rim of the pond, in a nasty huddle, was Lawrence. The mare hadn't cleared the tree, you could see where she'd skidded and rolled on him.

It wasn't long before Dexter and Brown showed up from the other direction. But in the meantime Coombs, rooting around, had picked up a revolver, one shot fired. No bullet holes, you understand. But they'd decided they'd better send for official help.

"That's why Ellen saw the police," said Adelaide.

Dexter and John had stayed. "Now this part," said John, "is the hard part. You see, it's an accident, they've put that label on, it's finished. It was dark, Lawrence didn't see the barrier, the mare didn't clear it. So. You know, I . . . I wouldn't have believed Lawrence had it in him." John's face looked withered, his puttees rasped as he twisted his legs together. "He had one hell of a time, that fellow."

They'd been standing around, he and Dexter, waiting for the

return of Coombs and Brown and the rest. Dexter had picked it up, one of those books of matches, shiny coral colored, with HUNTER HILL in gold letters. An empty cover. John had found the cigarette stubs, half a dozen, stuck on end in moss around an old stump, and heel marks flattening the moss.

"He'd sat there that long," said John, "before he got back on Suzy, and rode her at the tree. And Brown said, 'Funny he'd risk a shot, he knew she was the gol-damdest gun-shy mare ever had four legs.' He put a hand into a pocket of his jacket, and held out the bright bit of pasteboard. "We scattered the butts," he said. "The verdict is accident, pure and simple. Pretty smart of poor old Lawrence."

"You mean he just sat there and planned it? But how could he be sure. . . ."

"Maybe he couldn't be positive," John scowled. "Maybe that's why he hung on to the gun, just in case . . . And the saddle. You remember what Dick said, the cinch strap wasn't buckled? That's what upset Brown. He kept saying, 'If I'd been home, I'd of saddled her properly and it never would have happened.' They all liked Lawrence."

"It was a wicked thing for him to do!"

"My God, Adelaide!" John glared, a sudden hostility leaping in his eyes. "Can't you see him, sitting there, going round and round and no way out? I tell you, a man can't stand more than so much!"

"Johnny, don't you talk like that!" Adelaide rushed at John, flinging her arms around him, pulling his head against her throat, clinging to him. "I won't have it!"

"Look out, you'll fall over." John pushed her back into balance. "It's true," he insisted. "They don't all get into the papers. Look at the trouble he went to, just to save her face, the bitch!"

"Sh! Oh, poor Ellen! John, you must try to like her! You

must feel sorry for her, now. She hasn't any one else— She mustn't ever know."

"I'd tell her fast enough," said John. "But Gilbert and Dexter say no, it's the least we can do for Larry. No one is to know. Dexter never tells his wife anything anyway, except what kind of a day it is. And Gilbert hasn't got a wife, he's got a laboratory!"

Adelaide wished that John would go on with his implied comparison but he was pushing himself up from his chair.

"Lord, am I stiff!" He tried his knees, one and then the other. "How far do you suppose we tramped? Got to get off these boots." He limped as he started across the kitchen. "Blisters," he said, and looked around at Adelaide, removing his spectacles. His eyes wandered, not focussing on her, as if they looked at shadows in the morning woods. "Queer," he said, slowly. "Larry was such a big guy, didn't you always think of him as big? He looked so damned little, huddled up there in the ditch."

"Poor John! I don't care what you say, I think it was very inconsiderate of Lawrence to make so much trouble for everybody!"

"You're as bad as Coombs," said John, grimly, "wishing the hell Larry'd pick a place nearer a good auto road the next time. It was some lug."

Before Adelaide could point out that her remark had more sense than what Coombs had said, John flung up his hand.

"Listen! Yes, it's Gilbert." Limp forgotten, he bolted for the front door, Adelaide nimbly at his heels.

The car stood at the entrance to the drive, the engine still running, and Gilbert stepped out and slammed the door.

"Dick!" called Adelaide, "*Where* are you going?" But the car, in a series of convulsive leaps, rushed away, with a blurred impression of a man's head rocking at the rear window.

Gilbert came up the drive, planting his feet doggedly, not lifting his head until he reached the steps. "How are you, Adelaide?" He took off his hat, a gray felt, and turned it between his hands. Goodness, how old he looks, thought Adelaide, and didn't tell him how she was, because he wasn't even looking at her, but at John. His bushy eyebrows made a bar under his creased forehead, his jaw was heavy and dark (perhaps he hadn't had time to shave this morning!), his hair looked quite gray. Of course he never did look genial and Adelaide never did feel quite at ease with him because he always looked as if he kept his thoughts to himself and you couldn't tell what went on (or was that just because she knew he made a business of probing into people?) but this afternoon he looked actually forbidding.

"It's all right," he said, to John. "I signed the certificate. They're satisfied." John drew a quick, deep breath. "Even the coroner. No autopsy." He glanced at Adelaide, dismissing who knew what gruesome details. "Dick's driving Brown on up to . . ." he hesitated . . . "to the Hunters' place."

"But Ellen's here," said Adelaide.

"Brown's after the horse. He says somebody should have rubbed her down this morning." Gilbert's mouth stretched into a grimace, less than a smile. "He's trying to make amends. I told him no one blamed him. And Dick needs something to do. He takes things hard, doesn't he? Too bad he happened along just as he did."

"He ought to have more guts," said John, violently.

"Why? What did he do?" He had looked half sick, Adelaide remembered; she'd been too intent to notice, at the time. That trick of his, running his tongue over his lips, when he was a little boy he'd even throw up. "He's never known anybody before who died!"

"Neither has Henry, but he didn't turn pea-green, he gave us a hand with the stretcher."

"Dick is younger." (Always when John was nervous and tired, Dick annoyed him.) "But they weren't in the woods with you. . . ."

"For God's sake, no!" John burst out in exasperation. "They weren't in the woods, they were in the village, they saw us come, everybody saw us come, we had the body in Brown's truck, we had to get it out, didn't we?"

Gilbert made a sudden violent gesture, looking up past them, his face tightening, some vise drawing skin and flesh hard over the bones of skull and eye sockets and jaw. Adelaide spun around, clapping her hands over a shriek, Ellen stood in the doorway, her features heavy and lax, her hands pressed against the screen, her slow, difficult breathing lifting her breasts under the clinging silk of the gown. Gilbert climbed the steps, and pulled at the handle of the screened door, but Ellen held it.

"I heard you," she said. "He's dead. What did he do?"

"Ellen, darling!" Adelaide tried to brush Gilbert aside. "It's all right. I mean it's terrible, it's an accident. Let me in! You mustn't stand there like that!"

"Tell me!" Ellen didn't look away from Gilbert, under her swollen lids her eyes were almost black. "Go on, I can take it."

"Tell her!" Adelaide shook her fisted hands, she wanted to shake the men, Gilbert and John, to make them speak, quickly! Once they had spoken, the dreadful truth would be forever hidden.

"Lawrence was thrown from his horse. Last night. He must have died instantly." Gilbert's voice was quiet, slow. "Are you listening, Ellen?"

She had moved a step backwards, her arms outstretched, the palms still flattened on the copper screen.

"I told him that mare would kill him someday," she said.

"Unhook the door," said Gilbert.

"I'll go round to the back," cried John, plunging down the steps.

"Tell me," said Ellen. "Just what happened."

"He's dead," repeated Gilbert. "Neck broken, chest crushed."

"You can't blame me—for that!" Ellen's words were like the slowest bubble rising through thick, viscid blackness, breaking at her unmoving lips.

John had his arm around her, he reached for the hook and Gilbert pushed the door open. "I'll put her back to bed," he said. "Come along, Ellen."

As Adelaide said later, talking everything over with John, the way Ellen pulled herself together was just a miracle, no less! You could see her slow inward turning toward her will against the lethargy of her flesh, she seemed to stand taller, to summon her heart to pump more strongly; the struggle, the torment was like the breaking of the pupa case, the painful emergence, ichor-drenched, crumpled, the shaking out of irridescent, brittle-brilliant wings ready for darting flight. Something of the dragonfly about Ellen the next few weeks, too, fragile, swift, incalculable, and unemotional, and every winged movement directed toward survival.

All she said that first moment, as she laid a hand on the stair-rail and glanced up, as if measuring her new strength against the climb, was, "I won't be long. Please wait. There is so much to do."

The telephone bill the next month was a record of the first things that were done before Ellen went back to New York on the evening train. Adelaide looked it over, trying to identify the strange exchanges and numbers. The undertaking establishment in town. They'll see to everything, Ellen had said. It must be a church funeral, it would look queer if we just hid away out here in the country. The law firm. Too late to speak to Mr.

Murray. The Long Island call must have been to his house. "I'll be in town by nine, I must see you tonight!" Obituary notices, read in Gilbert's quiet slow voice. Ellen's house in town, Ellen saying, "Don't scream at me, Libby! there's nothing we can do about it. Don't tell the children, I'll tell them myself." Gilbert had gone down to the little back room of the furniture store, where Lawrence lay, to wait for the sombre car from town.

John had driven Ellen to the train, Adelaide sitting beside her on the rear seat, sniffling a little, partly for Lawrence, partly perhaps because Ellen's hand was so firm and unresponsive. "I'd go in with you," Adelaide had said, "but I can't very well leave. . . ."

"There's nothing you can do," said Ellen. "I don't know how much I can do . . . later . . . when it's all over. . . ."

"Always feel it's the place you can come to," said Adelaide, and if she lowered her voice that was only because she didn't want to bother John, who had maintained a darkling silence during the hours of discussion and telephoning, a silence which felt critical, but which might be just from fatigue. For a moment Ellen's hand turned in Adelaide's, gripping her fingers.

Adelaide had missed the funeral, because John was sick. He had a temperature and a sore throat, and she knew if she left him, he wouldn't stay in bed. He'd overdone, hunting for Lawrence, that was all, on top of the way he felt anyway about not finding work. Genevieve Willetts telephoned in the evening to tell her about the affair. "Most impressive," she said. "Marvellous flowers, a good soloist, and Ellen just swathed in crepe. A great many distinguished looking people. I didn't know they had so many friends."

Adelaide, climbing the stairs with a supper tray for John, thought, they couldn't have had such a nice funeral except for John. Well, Dexter and Gilbert, too, but chiefly John. John didn't want anything to eat. Toast scratched his throat, nothing had any taste. After some urging, he tried the scrambled eggs, and absent-mindedly ate everything on the tray.

"I'd like to know why he did it," John leaned back against the pillows and watched Adelaide brush crumbs off the sheet. "I keep thinking about him sitting on that stump, figuring things out."

"Can't you put it out of your head? He's buried by this time."

"Money, of course. But he wouldn't go to pieces if he lost money. Look at the trouble he went to! He was thinking about his family. A man has to . . . no, it was somebody else's money, it always is when a man jumps out of a twentieth story window . . . or off a horse! And I bet I know whose it was."

Adelaide moved uneasily out of range of John's restless eyes. She knew she looked conscious of secrets, she didn't want to tell what Ellen had let drop about insurance and everything.

"That old Mrs. Puller who died here two-three weeks ago, you remember? I said then she was a widow of a relative of Lawrence's, there was an old Puller in the firm Lawrence got his start with. I'll bet you anything he was her broker, and when they had to settle the estate, blotto! there wasn't any."

"John, you mustn't get so excited, you don't know. . . ."

"Now nothing will come out. That's it!" John jerked himself half out of bed in order to see Adelaide. "I wish you'd leave that curtain alone and listen to me!"

"Lie down, John! I am listening." Adelaide hurried to the side of the bed, and John flopped back, propped on an elbow. "Ellen told you, didn't she?"

"She . . . she didn't mention any names," said Adelaide, swallowing hard. "She was terribly worried."

"Yah! I'll bet she was. Poor old Lawrence, knowing they'd never prosecute a dead man!"

"Well, in a way—" Adelaide groped, bewildered, among the impressions of these past days; they were out-size, they were too harsh and bleak, too disruptive. Ellen, swathed in crepe, a most impressive funeral, so many friends— "In a way," said Adelaide, coming up briskly out of her confusion with a firm grip on her feeling for Ellen—"it was the best thing he could do. You know, just like that character, what was his name? Sidney Carton! 'This is a far, far better thing that I do . . .'"

"My good and beautiful God!" John jerked himself upright, his eyes fever-bright, his thin hair on end. "Would you like it if I popped myself off? Would you?"

"Johnny!"

"Here I am, sick, no work, no prospect of any! Maybe you'd like to collect my insurance! How do I know?"

"You must be delirious!"

"If it was such a fine thing for Lawrence. . ."

"I didn't say that!" Adelaide was crying, her words spilling out. "I didn't say any such thing! I was just trying to make the best of it . . . when everything's just terrible! You mustn't say such things, you scare me so!" She flung herself down beside him, burrowing her wet cheek against his throat, clinging to him, feeling the blessed thump of his heart, the gulp in his wind-pipe, the dry heat of his skin. He was sick, she mustn't pay any attention to him, she mustn't bother him!

"Sometimes you scare me!" But his hand moved up to her hair, pressed her face hard into the bony hollow of his throat and neck. "You get off the damnedest cracks! There, don't cry so hard!"

"It feels good!" Adelaide sniffed up tears, she tasted them on her lips. "I don't mind anything, as long. . ." She pushed herself up, her hands under his shoulders. "You'll get something, darling! You just be patient. Why, everybody knows how smart you are! You'll get something soon."

John brought the palm of his hand down in a good smack on her thigh. "What you'll get is my germ, if you don't watch out!"

From the lower hall came a shout, "Hi, Mom! Where are you?"

"I'm coming, Henry," called Adelaide, as she stood up quickly, dabbing her eyes. "I'll have to get their supper," she said, and her smile had a half shy, half conspiring quality, bidding her lover wait while she turned to serve their sons. "Try to sleep," she said. "I don't think you've got any germ. You're just worn out."

She picked up the tray and started for the door, glancing back to see John settle, an arm bent under his head, his eyes following her.

"I'll tell you one thing, old lady," he said. "If I'd been in Larry's boots, I'd of bumped off Ellen instead of myself!"

"Sh!" said Adelaide. "You go to sleep!"

After a few days John was up, fretful, wobbly. He agreed with Adelaide that he ought to give himself a little time to get his strength back, he'd tackle some of the odd jobs that had been piling up around the place, save the price of a hired man, he wouldn't do any more than he felt up to. The boys, looking shorn and neat in hair-cuts and blue shirts, started in school, and for a week John was in and around the house, moving at an accelerated tempo which kept him convinced that his work was necessary. He took off all the screens and painted them. He got down the storm windows and doors from the loft of the garage, and painted them. He would have put them on in spite of Adelaide's protest that December was early enough (he might not have time by December!) except that the clear, cool days softened over night into hazy warmth. He fussed, as if Adelaide had connived with the weather, but he stacked the windows around the sides of the garage, and then ran into one of them, splintering frame and glass, on his return from a hasty trip to the village for a new axe handle, his next project being wood for the fireplace. Adelaide, who kept track of him by the various noises he made, ran out.

"If I'd put those on, as I wanted to!"

"Oh, goodness! I thought you were hurt!" Adelaide backed away from the brandished axe. "John, you will be careful! You might cut your foot!"

"Someone's moved those windows! Those damn boys!"

"They had to pump up their bicycles. I heard Dick say the pump was over in back, on the wall."

"You see! Everything I try to do!"

Adelaide retreated. John would work off his temper on the black birches he had marked to cut down.

By the middle of the second week the warmth dissolved into a fall rain, with wind. Adelaide, listening at the kitchen door, was troubled by the lack of sound other than that of wind stripping off old wet leaves, and rain falling in a silky monotone. Finally she went in search of John. She wouldn't nag at him for staying out in the rain, for all he might catch cold, but she had to know what he was doing! He didn't hear her approach. He was sitting on the rear bumper of the car, staring down at his hands, up-turned on his knees, and when she spoke his name staunchly, he scarcely lifted his head. She stepped inside, shaking rain drops from her hair, dropping the old coat she had flung around her shoulders.

"Hello," she said. "I didn't hear a thing."

John thrust his hands into the pockets of his khaki trousers; the movement pushed back his shoulders, altered slightly the dejection of his posture.

"No," he said. "I've quit kidding myself." He stared out at the rain. "If I'm nothing but a handy man, the least I can do is to hire out to someone else."

"Goodness! Look at all you've done!"

"Yah. Why haven't you kicked me the hell out? Stalling along . . ."

"It's been nice, having you home." Adelaide perched herself beside him, finding the bar most uncomfortable. "Somebody for lunch, to talk to. . . ."

"First stage of a bum," said John. "It's over, old lady."

"What are you going to do?" Adelaide's voice was matter-of-fact, but she tucked her hands under her thighs, against the metal bar and buttoned her elbows hard into her sides. Of course, someday he had to set out again.

"First, I'm going down to the firm where I got my start. They might need a draughtsman. Sometimes a big concern can get contracts. If too many other fellows thought that up first . . . God, there must be something to do! I've been sticking out for my own work. Aiming too high. Always room at the bottom." He held up his hands, shaking them violently, cuffs sliding back from the prominent wrist bones. "I'm going to get a job, if it's driving a garbage truck."

"But that would smell!" Adelaide lost her balance, grabbing for John as he jumped to his feet, his body arced like an old man's. "Johnny, listen! You mustn't do anything rash . . . it isn't as if we were starving, we can get on for weeks and months."

"I'm not doing anything rash!" John shook off her hand. "You don't mind if I press my gray pants, do you?"

Adelaide trailed him to the house, and the rest of the day was good, a small sealed ampoule in a gray, hostile world, with safety and little domestic tasks, shelter and food and steam from the old pillow case as John laid a knife-edge crease in his trousers (a knight, shining his armor!), pleasant hubbub when the boys came home early to mill about the kitchen, rain-housed and hungry, little cat-naps for Adelaide over her sewing (turning in frayed cuff-edges on the boys' shirts) while the boys were too busy with school work even to spar, and John went early to bed. "I have to catch the early train," he said, and his authoritative tone established him as a man of affairs again.

For a few days Adelaide minded the blank spaces which John had filled with sounds of hammering and sawing, or sudden yelps for iodine and bandages, or inquiries as to where Henry had left his screw-driver. But she had the fall house-cleaning, delayed by John's presence, and it was almost as if he had work again, he kept such regular hours, in to town on the seven-thirty, out again on the six forty-two. When she saw him coming (he walked now, all nonsense to use the car for that drive to the station, leaving it all day for the sun to eat up the tires!) she busied herself with the final stage of preparing dinner, so that not even her first glance at him could betray the slightest pressure of anxiety, how did it go today?

Henry brought home news one evening. Mike, at the garage, where Henry still worked on Saturday, said some men from New York had hired a car to drive out to the Hunter place. Maybe they wanted to buy it. John, who sat in the big chair near the fire, the evening paper unfolded on his knees (Adelaide watched to see if he ever turned its pages) looked out of his concealment behind the deep wing. "Dr. Ranny would rise up from the dead," he said, harshly.

"Who's he?" asked Henry. "You mean Uncle Larry?"

"Naw! You know, that old boy with the walking stick and white hair? Always said, 'Hello, you young savages!' Don't you remember him?" Dick pulled reflectively at a lank fore-lock, and Adelaide thought, goodness, they need another hair-cut so soon, it's always something.

"Oh, him! Vaguely, vaguely. That was a hundred years hence! I was a mere child then."

"A hundred years hence will be your mere second childhood," said Dick.

"If you go hence, you go away, don't you?" Henry was loudly superior. "A hundred years hence—"

"Isn't a hundred years ago! You sound like your Polish friend!"

"Sh!" Adelaide made a little warning gesture toward John, who was crumpling his paper in an irritated fist. "Don't squabble about a word."

"I just wanted him to speak English," muttered Dick, sinking back with his book.

Over the surface of Adelaide's mind, like long-legged water-bugs, little thoughts darted: that Danieloski girl, she hadn't heard a word about her since summer; Ellen might have telephoned to her or something; the boys should be more careful, they got on John's nerves so; funny the way Dick was the one who remembered everything, when he seemed to pay much less attention than Henry did. Just as it was Dick, now, who said, reflectively,

"Dr. Ranny was sort of the founder of our Ridge, wasn't he, Dad?"

"English!" snorted Henry. "How could anybody found a ridge?"

"Oh!" Adelaide gave a pleased little jump in her chair. "I see what you mean, John! You mean he wanted it to stay in the family. . . ."

"That is exactly what I meant." John disappeared behind the flange of the chair.

"Poor Ellen! She must be hard-pressed."

John grunted.

"It's queer, if she's going to sell the place, that she hasn't said anything to us. I thought I'd hear from her."

"You will as soon as she wants something of you."

"Well." Adelaide picked up her sewing. "That's what a friend is, someone you can ask to do things."

The skimming thoughts went faster, Dr. Ranny had thought his grandchildren would live in his house, just as she and John had thought this was home forever, and after them, Henry, perhaps, and now John was afraid . . . Adelaide pricked her finger, as a new thought startled the rest into flight; she stared at the globule of crimson blood, and dabbed at it with her tongue. If Ellen sold, they would be sure to need alterations, no one ever liked anything exactly the way other folks had it, perhaps John could—why, of course he would be exactly the right man for such a job, she'd write to Ellen this very night! A letter would be much better than telephoning, sometimes people said no if you popped something at them, and if they had time to think it over. . . .

John went upstairs early, crossing the room with an artificial sprightliness, and then slowing down on the stairs. Dear God, he tried so hard! Adelaide squeezed her finger tip; it had stopped bleeding, she could go on sewing now and leave no stain on the white shirt, but compassion was like the taste of blood between her lips. She waited, no longer drowsy, until the boys, too, said good-night and went. Then she wrote to Ellen, she'd love to see her, she'd meant to write sooner, she'd been busy, couldn't Ellen come out, the country was lovely now, the fall color would be gone in another week, she thought so often of Ellen, John was sort of in between jobs just at present, if it was true that Ellen was planning changes in the big house he might have time. . . .

For several days Adelaide had a pleasant feeling of accomplishment. She hurried every time the telephone rang, hoping it might be Ellen. She watched the road for half an hour after each of the good trains out from town. She asked Henry if Mike ever said anything else about people looking at the

Hunter place. She wasn't in the least surprised when one morning a week or so later Ellen drove into the yard in the small
roadster which Lawrence had used all last summer. But she
dodged back from the window lest she seem too eager, and
waited until Ellen rang at the front door, and opened it, calling
out "Addie! It's Ellen!"

Adelaide kissed Ellen, her own face growing rosy-warm in
her effort to hold back her shock at Ellen's appearance. Why,
she looks as if someone had squeezed the juice all out of her!
It might be the severe black of her wool dress and coat, of her
small hat with the veil flung back from the strained, colorless
face. Black wasn't good on Ellen. But even her smooth throat
looked dry, almost crinkled. She looks hungry, thought Adelaide. Oh, dear!

"I came out to pick up the car," said Ellen. "It's been there
at Brown's all this time." She stripped off her black gloves, let
Adelaide take her coat and hat. "It's good to see you. I've seen
no one except vultures and buzzards." She was restless, moving
about the living room, picking up magazines, ash trays, talking
in spurts. Adelaide, with an uncharacteristic caution which almost smothered her, asked no questions, made no comments
beyond little ejaculations and murmurs, as Ellen talked. So
much depended upon Ellen, so much for John!

Ellen had disposed of the house in town, practically gave it
away, but she couldn't swing it. Her lawyer had protected the
small insurance Lawrence had left, scarcely enough for young
Larry's school. "They expected I'd turn that over, too," she
said. "If I'd stripped myself to the bone, it wouldn't have been
a drop ... so why should I?" Now she didn't know what to
do. She had to have a place to live, she supposed, although why
she bothered ... except for the children. Libby was staying
on till she was settled, on Linda's account. Linda should
be in school, of course. Yes, she'd sold the place out here,

too, all but a few acres. She wanted to talk with John. Those small sheds . . . greenhouse, the study her father had built, Adelaide knew the lay-out. If they could be moved, thrown together, into some kind of shack. . . . Only where would she stay until the work was done?

"Here, Ellen! You could say here, and John could build you a darling little house. There's the guest room . . . oh, it would be lovely to have you here!" (John couldn't object, not if it meant work!)

"It wouldn't be a great while." Ellen stood very still, looking at Adelaide, but her quiet was that of the dragon fly, poised on the swift invisible movement of wings. "Just till John had made a shelter for me." She laughed, a gay, malicious laugh, and for a moment her youth came back to her gaunt, colorless face. "It would be a way to make him work fast, wouldn't it?" She made a darting flight toward Adelaide, seizing her hands. "Oh, I know he hates me. We don't have to pretend, thank God! You're the one person in the world I could stand to be with now, Addie. Your letter was the first human sound I had heard! You could manage John, couldn't you?"

"He doesn't hate you, Ellen! If you knew each other, I'm sure . . . anyway, he knows what a terrible . . ."

"Never mind! As long as you'll manage him. I should insist on paying him, even if he is your husband."

Adelaide swallowed hard. She could hear herself saying, "Why, he wouldn't take a penny!" She hurried into other words before that magnanimous offer leaked out. "He couldn't spend his time out here, unless . . ."

Ellen gave Adelaide's arm a sharp nip as she dropped her hands. "How you cover up for that man! How long since he's had a good house to build? Lawrence told me last summer. He held you up as a glittering example of how a devoted wife acts when her husband is heading for the bread line."

"You mustn't say anything like that to John! He'd think I'd been talking."

"Don't worry. I want to stay here. With you. Tell John I've got some money, a few thousand." Ellen was in motion again, pausing a moment at a window, flinging out her hand in a brittle gesture. "Addie, if Lawrence had broken his neck a year ago, I would have had all I needed!" She pinned her fingers against her temples. "Ten months ago!"

"Ellen, darling! You mustn't . . ."

"Oh, I know! He's dead, I must be a gentle, heart-broken widow. There's more nonsense about death than I can stand! I mustn't blame him for being a fool! How can I help it? Oh, I'm sorry he's dead! Because I can't make him hear what he's done to me. He's the lucky one! He's well out of the terrible mess he made, and I have to pick up the scraps and struggle on."

Oh, dear! Adelaide pressed her lips tight together. If Ellen *knew*, she wouldn't talk that way! But always, from the beginning of their friendship, Adelaide had admired the way Ellen always knew what she felt and dared speak out, instead of pretending to have the expected feelings. Sometimes it was more comfortable if people weren't quite so honest, she supposed.

"You must look ahead and not backwards now," said Adelaide, with relief as the platitude floated off the top of her other thoughts. After all, John and Dexter had only made up a theory about Lawrence, quite as if they were in a detective story, and how did she know they were right? "You've been very brave, and you've picked up quite a few scraps. And all the trouble . . . I mean what you spoke of before . . . none of it came out at all."

Ellen sent her a glance of swift, harsh inquiry, her nostrils flaring, eyes narrowed. Just for an instant. Then she shrugged.

"Not in the papers, if that's what you mean. It was a beautiful sight, the way family feeling raised its head, the minute they finished picking the bones. It's incredible, Addie, the way relatives act if they smell money. But the name, the wonderful Puller-Hunter name . . . Don't get me started on them! You're quite right, I must look ahead. But it's all so unjust, so unfair! Why should such things happen to me? Maybe God's in your world, you always thought so, but he's certainly not running mine!"

"Sh!" said Adelaide. Too much like tempting the Fates, this noisy resentment. "Things will work out for the best, you must be—"

"Not patient! You know me better than that! But don't you worry, I won't talk this way when John's around, I'll be sweet and clinging. Only you're special, Addie. You can persuade John, can't you? Tell him I'll put in a word for him about the big house, too." Ellen settled herself on the divan, and for a half hour was practical, informative.

A group of doctors had purchased the big house, "Father would approve of that, wouldn't he, since I have to sell?" Ellen asked. For a small, exclusive, very expensive sanitarium. Ellen hadn't met the doctors, her lawyer had dealt with their lawyer, but Gilbert Moore had vouched for them. He'd really steered them Ellen's way, and that was something to be grateful for in these times, when a large place in the country was nothing but a very large white elephant.

"Oh, dear!" exclaimed Adelaide. "You mean crazy people? Walking around our nice Ridge?"

"You sound just like Genevieve Willetts," said Ellen, drily. "Gilbert said Dexter had rushed into his office, he thought something should be done to stop me, he didn't dare let Genevieve know because she'd be so nervous. How Dexter heard I don't know."

"Rachel Thayer!" Adelaide was so pleased with her deduction that she forgot for the moment the impending disaster.

"You know, that girl in Carey Moore's laboratory. Carey told her, and she told Dexter."

"Oh, oh! Are they that way?" But Ellen was too intent on her own plan to linger, even for a spicy bit. "Gilbert had suggested that I consult the Ridge dwellers. I said the one argument I could hear would be a better offer from one of them . . . of you . . . than the one and only offer I had."

"But, Ellen!" Adelaide swung in a long arc, from lunatics on the Ridge to work for John.

"I said a sanitarium, not an insane asylum. Why, you'll never know anyone's there, nice refined nervous breakdowns, convalescents . . . you know. And of course it means a tremendous remodelling job."

Ellen didn't know when work would start, but of course she'd put John in touch with the right people. "I don't know who they are. Gilbert's so close-mouthed he must have a constant toothache. They're incorporated, they're bound to have lots of money, people pay simply enormous sums to psychiatrists and analysts to listen to their troubles."

"It's much cheaper, really, to be a Catholic, isn't it? I mean, then you just go to confession."

"Adelaide, you're priceless!" Ellen laughed, and stopped, startled, the sound of her own laugh unfamiliar.

Adelaide's pleasure at approval was stimulating; her mind scurried busily, seeing John engaged in a vast transformation of the sprawling white house into something between a hospital and a prison (bars for the most serious cases, perhaps?), seeing John and Ellen in the evening bent over blue-prints for a darling little house in which Ellen would live, seeing Genevieve Willetts, agonized about the prospect, and Adelaide explaining to her that she needn't be afraid of escaped lunatics.

"Ellen!" she exclaimed. "Maybe Gilbert's the company himself, and that's why he doesn't object! Right near his own house. Then he wouldn't care if it was bad for the rest of us.'"

"That's funny, too," said Ellen, but she did not smile. "Gilbert should hear that! Why, he acts as if wanting money was a kind of loathsome disease! He could have a marvellous practice, and what does he do? Spends all his time at clinics or on commissions about mental hygiene for wayward girls or incorrigible boys! Gilbert in one of these plush-lined rest-cures?"

"Of course," said Adelaide, hastily, "his wife isn't really interested in his career, is she? I mean, starting that queer place of her own, and not coming out here in the summer any more."

"She's not the right woman for him. But she knows how to get what she wants for herself!"

"I don't see what she ever got married for!" (Oh, it was wonderful, having Ellen to speak her mind to about all these people they both knew. What was the French word? Confidante. Men were funny, they weren't interested in speculations about people. If she said that to John, he'd brush it off with a "She fell for the guy, that's all!" and then read her something from the paper about how President Hoover said we have now passed the worst, and with continued unity of effort will soon recover. Of course lately John had stopped quoting Hoover, and Adelaide had to be very careful what she said about anything.)

"She got married," Ellen was saying, "for a ticket to New York and a boost up in her career. She picked better than we did, you and I."

Adelaide's face flushed, her whole body felt suddenly too warm. "I wouldn't be married to anyone except John in all the world!"

"We didn't want tickets to New York. I wanted a good marriage, I wanted my work. I've lost them both. I've lost everything I wanted, except two children to support and educate. You wanted . . . this." She held out her hands, a gesture which seemed to balance on her palms the very house in which they stood. "And you're scared you're going to lose it."

"It's not John's fault if there's a terrible depression."

"That's what Lawrence kept saying. But who goes under? You know as well as I do that it's the weak ones. I admit it, and you won't. Not yet. Lawrence was a fool. John's no fool. I told you before you married him he'd never get on, he can't get along with people, he knows too damned much. But he's yours, and you'll go on pretending everything's fine." Ellen looked at Adelaide, and suddenly made a rush at her, holding her in a feverish grasp. "Never mind what I say! If you weren't a loyal, romantic little idiot you might not stick to me! Oh, Addie, I've been half mad, I've been so lonely!"

"Of course I'll stick to you. But you mustn't talk that way about John."

"I promise!" Ellen veered into a last minute discussion of practical details. She'd pay board, of course, she could help Adelaide around the house, Linda was a problem. Ellen had had to let the governess go last spring, she simply would not send the child to the village school with all that riffraff, there were good day schools scattered around Connecticut, but transportation was so difficult in the winter, twice a day, and Ellen hated to send the child away during this period of adjustment, on her own account as well as Linda's.

Adelaide's mind scrambled with a rearrangement of her household, she couldn't put the two boys together, they would bend the walls right out!

"I have just that one spare bedroom," she said, doubtfully.

"Ah, but two beds!" Ellen had picked up her small hat with its banneret of crêpe, her fingers, adjusting it slowly, made it emblem of her state. "If you think she'd be too much trouble . . . she's a clever little thing . . . your boys have never had a sister, sometimes a little girl has a charming influence."

"She's so much younger, they wouldn't pay any attention to her," said Adelaide. "If you don't mind sharing your room."

"Beggars can't be choosers," said Ellen. Then, before Adelaide had time to catch the implication, "Linda was crazy about her father. It's just pitiful. . . . It would help her, Addie, to be here, in a normal, happy home."

"I just hadn't thought of it," said Adelaide. "I'm sure John wouldn't mind."

"If it doesn't work out well, we can always go away." Ellen stood at the mirror in the hall, shaking the veil into place, sombre hint of two wanderers in waste places in her tone.

"Of course!" Adelaide brightened. "And it's just till John gets your house built!"

Then Ellen was in haste to be off. She didn't want John to find her here today, not till Addie had a chance to talk him into the scheme. He'd say no at first, but she'd trust Addie to handle him. She left her new address and telephone number. She had another week of dismal work ahead of her, sorting out personal effects, shipping out a few pieces she'd salvaged, her father's desk, her mother's silver.

"It must be terrible, Ellen, giving up your lovely things!"

Ellen stood in the doorway, her long straight coat depersonalizing her soft feminine body, the noon sunlight harsh on her face. The mobility and vividness were gone, she had again that harsh, drained, almost withered pallor. "I suppose it is," she said. "But I can't afford any luxury, not even that of knowing how I feel! Call me, won't you? 'Bye!"

Adelaide spent the rest of the day contriving conversations with John, trying out different opening lines. Usually her household tasks took the place of thought very pleasantly, so that she didn't even worry about Henry and his possible girls, or John and his lack of work. Today her mind kept interfering with her hands, until she was afraid she wouldn't have dinner

ready on time. She wanted a good dinner, too. She wouldn't
say a word to John until the boys had gone upstairs. But she
stopped stockstill, the egg-beater falling out of the bowl and
smearing egg yolks all over the table, to wonder whether John
did antagonize people. He meant well, and he really was
usually right, but perhaps, just perhaps, if he had a little more
. . . well, say *tact*. . . . Her hands, as she tried to scrape up
some of the spilled yolk, trembled, and she was ashamed, as if
she had spoken disloyalty aloud. And it hadn't been nice of
Ellen to talk about handling John, as if Adelaide were one
of these managing women. Sometimes it was the way you put
things, of course.

The boys, fortunately, wanted to go back to the school that
evening, for a basket-ball game. John thought they might stay
at home once in a while, but Adelaide whisked them on their
way. Then, after all her scheming, she just spilled it all out,
much like the egg yolks. Ellen's visit, the sanitarium, the house,
the wonderful chance for John, the house was just a little job,
but the remodelling for the sanitarium! See, her breathless in-
coherence said, see, here is a gift for you! Work, for which you
have so longed and suffered! Please, please!

John, after a violent muscular twitching of rejection when
he first disentangled the main thread, hid himself in the big
chair, nothing visible except one foot beating time on the air.
When, finally, Adelaide ran down, there was silence, and his
foot was still, held at a stiff upward bend. Adelaide wanted to
go around the chair, to look at him, and didn't dare move.
"Johnny," she said, "Johnny, say something!"

"How did that damned bitch know she had me on the hip?"
asked John. "Did you tell her?"

Adelaide tried to say no, she made the shape of the word
and couldn't say it. "When I heard the big house was sold—"
she said.

"I'd as soon have Jezebel in my house! Why, you . . . you even smell different after you've been with her!"

"John!"

"Let me alone."

"But it's . . . it's a good job!"

"And I have to do it. She's got me right where she wants me. I have to do it." He plunged to his feet and across the room, flinging back one sentence, "If it were just myself, I'd starve before I'd have any truck with that harpy!"

Adelaide waited, to give John time to get through in the bathroom and pretend he was sound asleep. It would be complicated, having two more persons for that one bathroom. She'd have to work out a careful schedule. She put out the lights and went slowly upstairs, assuring herself stoutly that in the morning John would be glad he had a job, and when he and Ellen had a good chance to know each other better, they just would have to like each other. I like them both, so. . . It was as simple as one of Dick's geometry problems, something about the angles of a triangle equalling each other. Only of course it wasn't a triangle. Not that kind.

Later Adelaide looked back on that winter as a curious empty place in the flow of her life, for all it seemed so crowded and busy at the time. It was a dead-center where movement ceases, the down-stroke not yet begun; it was a pleasant lull after the bitter strain of the months just past, and Adelaide did not know that hurricanes had that deceptive pause.

She thought Ellen and John were getting along very well, Ellen suave and businesslike, John very restrained for him, not a bit truculent, careful in his explanation of his blue-prints, interested (in spite of himself) in the demands on his ingenuity. Adelaide knew she wasn't seeing much of John. At first he worked under pressure of the season, intent on getting the foundation done, the shell of walls up, the roof on, before the

winter interfered. Then they could work on the interior, losing
no time. He never came home for luncheon, he seldom came
for dinner until so late that he ate alone, from a tray at the
kitchen table. He liked that better, he said; didn't have to clean
up and change from his work clothes. "I don't see what you can
do so late," said Adelaide. "It's been dark for at least two
hours." Oh, he shopped around for hardware, or fixtures, he
went to see about a new mason, he'd fired that damned Italian,
one thing, he could have his choice of workmen these hard
times. Adelaide looked anxiously toward the living room, she
didn't want Ellen to think John couldn't get along with the
men. "Don't tell me shhh! again!" said John, explosively,
and hunched over his plate.

"I just said that because you hollered!" Adelaide whispered
at his ear, and after a period of ostentatious silence from John,
whispered again, "You don't have to act as if you were dumb!"

"You're hard to suit."

"You're as bad as the boys, sulking if I ask them not to
squabble!"

Even when Ellen went up to her room early, with an, "I'll
leave you two," John went right on working with his sheets of
figures, bills, lists of material, until Adelaide would decide she
might as well go to bed as to sleep uncomfortably in a chair.

The day-time hours, with the boys in school and John at
work, were the pleasant time. Ellen took care of her own room,
and then sat down with Linda for an hour or two of arithmetic
or reading, but even then she didn't mind if Adelaide ran in
to talk over what she'd better order for dinner. In fact, she
seemed relieved, and so did Linda, who was what Adelaide
called a contrary little piece. She was small, with shrewd, long-
lashed eyes darker than Ellen's which stared disconcertingly
under the fair straight bangs. She had an engaging smile, and
on the days Ellen went in town she followed Adelaide about

the house, asking, "Why do you do that?" and frequently saying, "Before my father died, we had a big house, didn't we?"

She never had a tantrum when she was alone with Adelaide, but she did have a temper. Perhaps Ellen wasn't patient enough with her, but a child whose first response to any suggestion or command was a loud "No, I don't want to," was annoying. Since her tantrums always ended with an abrupt, expeditious upchucking of her most recent meal, after which she looked pitifully white and pinched, sending her to the room she shared with her mother, shutting her into a closet (kicking and flailing on the way) or spanking her were hazardous. "You don't have to vomit!" Ellen would cry at her, while Adelaide ran for cloths and water, and Linda looked like a sick kitten. Except for these outbursts, when you had no doubt where she was, she had a queer elusiveness, turning up without a sound just when you wished no observer, trying the bathroom door if it was closed, peering in at Henry experimenting with his father's razor, sliding into the kitchen just as Henry was asking how much longer they had to put up with all those people under foot. The boys didn't like the arrangement. Ellen did not pay much attention to them, and Linda was sly.

"She's not sly," Adelaide insisted. "She's just lonesome. You must be good to her."

"I don't know what's got into her," said Ellen. "She needs discipline. Lawrence spoiled her. If I had the money, I'd send her to a strict school. She never even speaks of her father, it's not that . . . a child that age doesn't have any memory anyway. Nor any heart."

"It's just strange people, I guess," said Adelaide. "She's good as gold when she's here alone with me."

"Well, so am I! That's the effect you have. Oh, Addie, whatever would I have done without you!"

Adelaide's little glow contracted with a sharp twinge as she glanced into the hall. Peering between the spindles of the balustrade was Linda's pointed face. It withdrew instantly, and when Adelaide stepped to the foot of the stairs, she found the child bent over a large picture book, talking busily to herself about the animals on the opened pages.

Sometimes on pleasant afternoons the three of them walked over to the site of the building, an acre just where the road curved for the final climb to the original old house. Ellen had at first an apathy toward the work, she didn't care which way the new house faced, how long the living room should be, all she wanted was a hole to crawl into. She refused to watch the engineering project of moving the two-roomed study which had been her father's, and which was to serve as nucleus for her house. She couldn't bear it, she said. Linda went over with the boys, and was so excited at the novel spectacle of a house taking a walk on the road, that for the first time John dropped his tacit resentment toward the child as Ellen's daughter and part of the heavy bonus he had to pay for his escape from idleness and lifted her up to ride part of the way inside the small building, her rapt face looking from a window. Sunday he built a small house for her, out of shingles and a box, fitting it with the rear wheels of a velocipede and for weeks Linda trundled it about the yard, playing house-mover.

As cold weather came on, Ellen refused to take the long walk and stand around in the cold building. The walls were up, the roof on, but doors and windows had to wait for the casings to be finished. "She acts as if it was beneath her notice," John complained to Adelaide. "She'll wait till I have the plastering done and then come horsing around, wanting this changed and that changed!"

"It's hard for Ellen to take any interest in anything," Adelaide defended her.

"Yah! You tell her for me if she wants as much as a nail changed after it's in, it'll cost her money."

At Christmas Ellen went away for a week, taking Linda, to the Inn patronized by parents of the boys in the Academy. She couldn't afford it, she said, but she couldn't leave young Larry alone this first Christmas, and since the house wasn't finished . . .

"Good God," said John, "I told her four months at the shortest!"

"She didn't mean that," said Adelaide. "But Christmas ought to be happy, and I wanted her to stay, only where could I put Larry?"

"All I need for Christmas is to find Ellen in my sock."

Adelaide buttoned her lips tight together. It was too bad for John to be so unreasonable, just when she was trying to work up a real Christmas spirit. She didn't say a word, but John glowered as if she had spoken her reproach, his Adam's apple jumping, that queer twitching of his eyelids beginning again.

They might have enjoyed the week, but John was first crotchety and then really sick. He had worked too hard driving the snow-plow he had made to clear their drive and the approach to Ellen's new place, he had to break the road, they'd promised to deliver the flooring and some of the inside trim the day after Christmas. He got up for Christmas dinner, but he was sneezing too hard to eat, and spent the next four days in bed, with Henry and Dick alternating on errands of instructions to the workmen. Adelaide was glad when the holidays were over, John was out of the house, and Ellen was back.

In January John began spending nights at the new house. He had to keep an eye on the heating apparatus, he said, until he was sure of it. "Why not a watchman?" asked Ellen. "I never knew architects did all the manual labor themselves."

"This one does," said John, curtly.

"Well, I suppose you pocket whatever you save."

"In case you want that, too," said John, "let me remind you this is a contract job."

Ellen's face was a mask of forbearance; on Adelaide's account she would keep silence. When John had gone, she said, "He meant that he blamed me for keeping anything out of the wreck, didn't he?"

"He just lets off steam," said Adelaide, trying not to sound apologetic. "He's working awfully hard."

"Um." Ellen reflected. "Well, it makes a grand alibi. Better than a late conference at the office."

Adelaide laughed. "That's one thing I never have to worry about!"

"I hope he's not using my house for a rendevous. I shouldn't care for that!"

"Ellen!"

"Oh, well, maybe, maybe not. How do you know? How does any wife ever know? I'll give you one tip. Whenever Lawrence was especially amorous, I knew he'd been having luck, and I don't mean in the market!"

"But John hasn't been amorous at all lately," Adelaide burst out, and then flushed with her effort to swallow the rest of her candor. Not since Ellen had moved into the next room! It was so easy to say things to Ellen, but somehow that remark seemed better unsaid.

"Not that that proves anything, either," said Ellen. "He's a different type. But you aren't naïve enough to believe any man is faithful, are you? Goodness, look at your neighbor, Dexter Willetts. Certainly if any man ever looked like a priest, he does!"

"I'm not excusing him at all," said Adelaide. "But that girl made a dead set at him. There's something about her men like. Why, she even had my Dick crazy about her. I don't mean that way, he was just a little boy, but he still . . . Why, two or three summers ago, let's see, he was just thirteen, that's three summers back, she had the Moore's house, and I was terribly upset, I found he was going there, he said he was cutting grass for her, but how did I know? He was just an innocent little boy, but suppose he found out about Dexter!" She stopped, with the obvious warning glance of one adult to another. Linda was, unmistakably, in her favorite ambush on the stairs. But Ellen missed the glance.

"Thirteen's old enough," said Ellen. "why, young Larry .. ." she looked up at Adelaide's gesticulation, and interpreted it as maternal horror. "I'll tell you that story someday. You're the only real innocent I know, Addie! It's sort of sweet. But I think Dexter's got some excuse. Can you imagine Genevieve in the throes of passion? Well, try! I'll bet all she ever clasps to her bosom is a hot water bag!"

"Linda!" Adelaide went briskly to the hall, she had to put an end to the talk! "You're in plain sight behind that newel post!"

"I wasn't hiding," said Linda. "I was just coming down stairs." She ducked under Adelaide's arm and scampered out of doors.

"She couldn't have made sense out of anything I said." Ellen settled back with her needle-point; she had to do something, she said, and there was a pleasant anesthetic effect in the fine, repetitious stitching. "She's too egoistic to listen, anyway!"

Adelaide wasn't sure about that. But as she went about her housework, instead of the old pleasant absorption (a kind of anesthetic, perhaps!) her thoughts slowed down her hands. Of course Ellen was wrong about John. Absolutely. How did she know? That deep, unfaltering certainty of flesh and spirit . . . why, it was almost as if Linda slipped past, hearing what she thought, and Ellen lifted those fine, light brows of hers. . . . Perhaps, as Ellen said, she was too naïve, taking for granted that John felt just as she did, that some people thought too much about sex. They overrated it. It was such a small part of your living together. Nice once in a while, like a holiday, or something special for dinner. But as you grew older and had two boys growing up, you just belonged together in a thousand ways. Adelaide looked around her kitchen, her brown eyes soft with bewilderment. She wasn't very good at finding words for her feelings, she didn't often bother to try, she just went along. Why, she had to take John for granted, just as she took herself for granted! That was what being married meant, an acceptance, an inclusive affection, tenderness, concern, she could feel it, the matrix in which her whole life had its existence.

She must be nervous herself, perhaps she had caught it from John or Ellen, having such notions! She flung herself down the stairs to collect jars of vegetables for dinner, so recklessly that she stumbled and wrenched an ankle. Hobbling up from the cellar she was glad of the pain, slight, definitely located. Poor Ellen! Lawrence had seemed so devoted to her at first, too. And even if Genevieve was what the boys called a wet smack, Dexter had married her and he had no right to forget his vows.

Adelaide set her jars upside down in a pan of hot water to loosen the caps, and seated herself beside the table, rubbing her ankle. John might have his faults, who didn't? But *that* wasn't one of them. She mustn't allow herself to be nervous, after all the strain was really over now, and if John only got the sanitarium to work on. . . . Funny Ellen hadn't said anything about that lately. But she wouldn't worry! Only yesterday Ellen had said, "You're wonderful, Addie, the way you keep so calm no matter what! Why, those boys of yours would simply drive me mad, and you're so patient with them."

"Goodness, I'm used to them!" (Ellen must have caught the reverberations of the squabble last night; it had been too bad

of Henry to read that poem of Dick's, but Dick shouldn't have
been so fighting-mad, and anyway, Dick was much too young to
write that kind of poetry, even if it was just for Alicia and he'd
known her all his life!)

"Ah, but John's used to them, too!"

"It's harder for a man to realize they're just little boys," said
Adelaide, defensively. "He sees how long their legs are and ex-
pects them to act grown-up. A mother knows."

"It's jealousy." Ellen's hard, clear voice had the incisiveness
of enjoyment in pursuit of an idea. "The older male resents the
young males always! And John's a regular Othello anyway."

"Oh, Ellen!" Adelaide gave a delighted shriek. "Why,
Othello was that black man who killed his wife! Oh, the things
you think of!"

"Perfectly obvious. John can't endure your liking anyone.
Why, look at the way he hates me! Men don't, as a rule. Just
because we've been close friends . . . why, longer than he's
known you! Hush, don't try to save my feelings. I don't mind,
as long as he doesn't turn you against me."

There was a queer spicy taste of forbidden fruit in such talk.
There was knowledge of John's fury, if he had any inkling of
it. There was a troubling need to defend and justify John's
slightest mood, a feeling of disloyalty in the mere knowing
that Ellen noticed his moods. And there was a fascination, almost a romantic quality, in hearing herself thus talked about.

Adelaide put her foot squarely on the floor and tested it.
The pain was better, she hadn't really sprained anything. Of
course she was nervous. She might as well face it. She was just
being pulled apart! Perhaps she was seeing things more clearly
now. Having an outsider, even an old friend like Ellen, made
her look at things. Like the big circle of darker gray on the
broadloom rug, where she'd tried to clean up the lemonade the
boys had spilled, or the thin, sleazy look of some of her bath

towels when she hung them on Ellen's rack. The way when someone knocked at the door, she ran around the room picking up scattered papers, pushing chairs into place.... And now John's sulkiness, his stubborn fits ... why, he didn't need to stay away nights!

Adelaide stood up in the middle of her kitchen, irresoluteness in her eyes, in her half lifted hands. Here she was, with a hundred things to do, right here in the house she loved, and she didn't know herself! Her compact, rounded, deeply contented body felt as if it would fly into a million loose ends, and panic churned inside. The back door creaked open a small space, and Linda peered in.

"Come in," said Adelaide, sharply. "Don't let all outdoors in, it's hard enough to keep the house warm." She whirled on the jars, turned them up on the table and wrestled with the stiff bails over the glass tops.

Linda sidled in and closed the door. "Outdoors can't come in, it wouldn't be outdoors if it was indoors. Are you cross, too?"

Adelaide drew a long breath. "No. Why should I be cross?"

"Johnny was cross. My papa was cross before he went away, too. Is Johnny ever coming back?"

Ellen was at the inner door of the kitchen, the crisp canvas of her needle point crumpled between her hands, her face ravaged.

"You're a vulgar little eavesdropper," she said. "Go up to your room."

"I don't want to," began Linda.

"Listen to me, Linda!" Linda, poised for a lusty stomp, paused, her hand clapped over her mouth. "If you have one of your fits, do you know what I'll do? I'll take an axe and smash your house! I'll put it in the furnace! I mean it."

Linda listened, and the very shape of her face seemed to

change, a stricken, helpless look tautening her brow, darkening her eyes.

"Not my house, my darling little moving house?"

"See that you behave yourself, then. Go on upstairs."

Linda went, reluctantly, holding her head and shoulders askew as she passed her mother.

"I'm sorry." Ellen smoothed out her embroidery. "But it worked."

Adelaide pried at the cover; the rubber ring was just frozen inside. Oh, dear, oh, dear! Everything was just too much! Linda had heard that quarrel, that last quarrel before. . .

"That's the only way to manage such a child." Ellen was trying to cover her violence, to pretend nothing had been revealed. "Hit her through what she cares about."

"But you wouldn't really smash her house," protested Adelaide. (How explain that to John?)

"Oh, I won't have to. She'll behave for a while, as long as she's crazy about the little house. One of these days she'll smash it herself, she's like that."

Then Ellen went in town for a fortnight, for sessions with the dentist. She ought to take Linda, but what would she do with her all those suffering hours? She'd be wrecked anyway, without a child to worry about. Adelaide assured her again that Linda would be no trouble. "Maybe the old man will move back," said Henry, "and we'll have old home week." But John did not. He was too busy, he was comfortable where he was.

Adelaide flew around the house, in a frenzy of spring housecleaning, her head full of little waspish buzzings. John was simply too obstinate, he didn't care how she felt, he expected clean shirts and good food, she certainly had done nothing to deserve such treatment. She was so tired by nightfall that she slept, and then, her fatigue eased by the first hours of deep sleep, she might wake choking, stifled with the panic of her old nightmare of flight, feeling almost that she was caught in a black and airless cave, that no creeping, groping around its rough and horrid walls would ever lead her to escape. Then she would sit up, thump her pillow into plumpness, turn away from the untenanted space at her side, and coax sleep back again. After all, John was at work, presently Ellen's house would be finished, she would move in, all this would be over.

The way in which it all ended not even Adelaide's nightmares had forecast. She didn't like to remember that final scene, although later she comforted herself with the thought that sometimes a good hard thunder storm did clear the air. Ellen drove into the yard in the late afternoon, and Adelaide ran out to greet her, Linda dashing past her to climb into the car beside her mother. Ellen was tired, she'd had an awful time, had they missed her? Adelaide lifted out the suitcase, Linda carried the basket of fruit, a gift for Adelaide, and the three of them were at the door when John swung his car up the drive and stopped, brakes squealing, bumper clashing against the rear of Ellen's car.

Ellen gave a startled, "Good Lord, can't he see?" and Adelaide thought, oh, dear, now he's put out because her car's in the way. She set down the suitcase. He wouldn't like that, either, if he noticed that she was carrying it. He got out of the car and came after them, not hurrying, but stepping along with care, almost gingerly.

"Ellen just came back," said Adelaide.

"So I see."

"See the lovely basket of fruit she brought."

John's eyelids twitched, as if he squinted for clearer vision, and his voice had a queer twang, although he kept it low, as he spoke to Linda.

"There's something for you on the back seat of my car," he said. "Will you stay there and look at it until I come out?"

Linda looked up at him, a droll and ageless cunning in her eyes.

"Couldn't I stick around, Johnny?"

"If you close the car door, you'll be warm enough. When you've opened the last one, put them back just as you found them."

"Johnny! Is it the little nest of boxes? Did you finish them?" Linda clasped her hands under her chin, her conflict made a small pendulum of her body. "You aren't going to tell about me?"

"No more than I promised," said John, and Linda scudded to the car.

"What's she been up to now?" asked Ellen, as John opened the door, picked up the suitcase, and stood aside with an effect of effrontery in his courtesy.

"She's been as good as gold," said Adelaide, hurrying into the house.

"You didn't know she came over to see me." John closed the hall door. "Saturday, when you went shopping and left her with the boys. They didn't know it. I drove her back. But she came all the way by the road, dragging her house. She seemed to think it was threatened. She gave it back to me, to keep it safe."

"Oh, dear!" cried Adelaide. "They said they'd watch out for her . . . I had to go for supplies!" That was Saturday, days ago! Why should John act like this?

"But nothing happened to her." Ellen had one foot on the first step of the stairs, her black gloved hand on the post. "Why all the shouting? I certainly would never blame you, Addie, for anything Linda did."

"Would you ever blame yourself, Ellen, for anything you did? Like frightening a child?"

"I've got a bad headache." Ellen's sidelong glance entreated

Adelaide. "I'm sorry Linda's so difficult. I do the best I can."
She moved up a step, her head drooping, the lifting of her
body up the flight of stairs a sad burden.

"Wait a minute," said John, and shook off the hand Adelaide
laid on his arm. "Would you blame yourself for lying to a
man?"

Ellen swung around, her veil floating. "What has that child
said to you? What fantastic . . ."

"Linda?" John gave a little whinny. "Why, she's so loyal
it hurts. No, it wasn't Linda. It was Gilbert Moore. He drove
out today." John was deliberate, his usual spate of excited talk
held by some unusual single intention. Adelaide was frightened,
panic like froth in her swift jumping blood. John couldn't mean
to tell about Lawrence . . . what else could Gilbert have talked
about? "You played me for a sucker, didn't you? If I'd build
your house, nice little cheap friend job, then you'd get me a
real job, a wonderful job! You'd butter up my wife, you'd
have a good place to hide till things blew over."

"John, please!" Adelaide shook his stiff arm. "Don't say
such things!"

"Shut up," said John. "Maybe you knew it, too. How would
I know? They aren't going to build any sanitarium, not for
years. They never had any notion of it! I asked Gilbert who to
write to, I wanted to start the plans. He'd been talking about
his own house, opening it up for Easter, I just asked him . . . off
hand. . . . He said, 'You must have misunderstood. Ellen knew
the scheme had to be postponed. . . . Waller went broke. . . .' "

Ellen drew a quick, deep breath. Adelaide doubled her fist
against her mouth, hard.

"And you told Gilbert I was a liar, did you?" asked Ellen.

"No. I don't need to tell Gilbert about you. He knows you
. . . better than I do, perhaps."

"You certainly are disagreeable." Ellen shrugged. "It's only in self defense that I . . . well, I think Adelaide might speak up, after all, she wrote to me. Otherwise I should scarcely have picked you! I never said anything about the sanitarium, except that I'd be glad to introduce you."

John stared at Ellen for a long moment, and then turned to Adelaide, with a curious gesture of concealment, pushing together the edges of his overcoat, pinning them across his body, and all the dark misery of his idle months gaped in his twitching face.

"I just wrote a little note," said Adelaide. "I said you might have time. . . ." But all the subtle and insidious ways in which her complete loyalty had faltered, the tacit acquiescence in Ellen's implied criticisms and extolling of Adelaide's patience and wisdom, rose up like flaming swords to cut her off from John. "Oh, John! It was work! I only wanted to help you."

"So you told Ellen. When you knew I'd rather starve to death!" He flung his head back, his gaunt neck throbbing grotesquely. "That's an idea!" He laid a hand on the newel post, and Ellen retreated a further step up the stairway. "I'm surprised you didn't suggest that! After all, I carry insurance, too. Or didn't you know?"

"John, don't!"

"Why not? We've been living on poor Larry's blood money too."

"But Ellen didn't mean it! She didn't want him to kill himself, she tried to stop him!" Adelaide heard her frightened, despairing words roll off endlessly until there was nothing but heavy silence in the little hallway, on the stairs. Oh, what had she done now? What had she said? In another minute she'd begin to scream, what else was there to do when everything was so terrible?

"But it was an accident, wasn't it?" Ellen's voice was light as vapor.

Adelaide dug her knuckles into her eyes, trying to clear them of tears, she couldn't see how John looked, she wasn't sure whether he spoke or not.

"They called it an accident." Ellen spoke more clearly.

Adelaide collapsed on the chest between the doors, the hasp of the brass lock biting into her leg, and John said, sharply, "Stop squalling that way! You haven't given anything away this time! She isn't even surprised!"

"Did you all know?" Ellen leaned down the stairway, her hand gripping the rail. "Even if you hate me, that isn't much to ask! You found him . . . you and Gilbert and Dexter. . . . You all know."

"Is that all you care about?" shouted John, his hands flying up, raking his head, the control he had held so taut exploding at last. "Who knows? Oh, Christ, let me out of this house, I can't breathe the same air!" His pocket caught on the doorknob as he whirled, and the harsh rip of stout wool and stitching before the door slammed was like another oath. Adelaide pressed her fingers against her ears and tried to stop her crying.

She'd just tried to help John, and now he'd never forgive her, and what had she done to have to be forgiven for, anyway? And Ellen had known all the time about Lawrence but it was much worse for her with John telling her they all knew, he shouldn't have said that. But Ellen *had* let her think the sanitarium would be started any day. Where had John gone? How did he think she could breathe when he'd piled wreckage on top of her like this? The boys would be banging in from school any minute, they mustn't find her like this.

"Addie, snap out of it!" Ellen's caustic tone so close to her head made Adelaide jump. She hadn't heard Ellen come down the stairs, but there she stood, right beside her, the long veil thrown forward over her face, not a fold stirring, and her face like a submerged ash-bleached bit of smooth driftwood. "Stop feeling so sorry for yourself and think of someone else for a second, will you?" She turned to the door, so rigid and so quiet that even the veil was sculptured. "They're all alike, men. You try to help them, and they scream at you." She opened the door, and the cold March air moved into the house with its smell of the old year rotted and fermenting under the thawing sun of midday. "Then they slam out of the house and get good and drunk . . . John's on his way now . . . if he doesn't leave a fender on the gate post. . . . Then they come back . . . hang-dog hangover. . . . You lock your bedroom door for a week or so . . . by the time you let him in he's forgotten what the riot was about!"

Adelaide leaned back against the wall, the sound of the receding car terrifying in its finality. What was Ellen talking about? "John never drinks!"

"Linda's coming," said Ellen. She pulled the door to and held it. "You might have told me, Adelaide. When I think of them . . . mouthing it over . . . hiding it . . . gloating. . . ."

"Ellen!" Adelaide got to her feet, earnestness drying her tears. "Oh, not like that! They . . . they wanted to spare you."

"I noticed that."

"Even John did. Only he. . ."

The door-handle squeaked.

"What did Gilbert say?"

"I don't know. I didn't talk to anybody . . . except John. Ellen, where are you going?"

Ellen opened the door, and Linda came in, her hands enclosing her treasure, her eyes sliding quickly from her mother to Adelaide.

"To see Gilbert. If I can find him."

"See, Mother, isn't it beautiful?"

"Yes," said Ellen. "Mother's in a hurry now." And she closed the door.

Adelaide pulled out a handkerchief and blew her nose, turning her face away from Linda's inquiry. The child's nose crinkled, the very air must have the odor of disaster. But the kitchen door opened, Dick called, "Hi, I'm home," and Linda ran to exhibit her boxes to him.

Adelaide patted her hair into place, pulled down the edge of her girdle, tucked away her handkerchief. She had to go right ahead getting dinner as if the whole world hadn't crashed around her. No matter what, the show must go on, she thought.

"Henry went to the station with Dad." Dick stood in the doorway, tugging at the zipper on his wind-breaker. "To drive the bus home. Where's Dad going?"

Adelaide opened her mouth, but it was too dry to make words.

"He said to tell you he'd write. Golly, he drove off like a Jehu, he'll make that five fifteen or else!"

"See, Dick, here's the littlest teeniest inside one of all." Linda joggled his elbow, and he disappeared into the kitchen.

Book Five

CAREY CLOSES THE BOOK

"The spirit walks of every day deceased."

I FOUND that line last night in one of Gilbert's books, the *Journals of Gilbert White,* and wrote it at the top of this sheet. The spirits of all these past days have walked for me these weeks of solitude that I have spent here on the Ridge.

Old men and women, nodding in the sun or in the corner by the fire, give heed to these spirits. We say the senile live over their past. But what they do is only to ravel out the fabric they have spun so industriously since birth, and then to wind the thin fine yarn tighter and tighter in a diminishing ball of consciousness. They are getting ready to die, and I suppose I am trying to get ready to pick up living again. Perhaps what we each wish, the dotard and I, is absolution.

Word must have gone round among the spirits of days deceased that here was a human being who had pushed away the noisy, demanding present and cleared a space, had halted the forever onward movement of time, to look at them, to listen to their voices, to ask them what they carried in their hearts and hands. For they come thronging and marching now, one leading in another and another, until I no longer have to coax them out of obscurity and wait for them to take shape in images and words, but I am bewildered by the need to choose among them. And now I must choose quickly. I have been writing these pages as if I could stay forever, sitting at this desk all day, slipping out at night to walk. But I can't.

This morning someone knocked at the door, and I went reluctantly to answer. A tall fair girl in dungarees rolled to her knees and a white cotton sweat shirt snug over firm pointed breasts stood waiting, a smooth and young indifference on her face. "Why, it's Alicia, isn't it? Alicia Willetts."

"Alicia Burchall," she answered. "How do you do, Dr. Moore? I didn't know you were out here. They thought you were, at Jones's store." She fished in a pocket, tight over her flat little stomach, and handed me a folded paper. "They asked me to stop with this, Western Union didn't know how to reach you."

I glanced at the message, scribbled in pencil on one of R. C. Jones's bill-heads. "Bill's off to the wars on Monday and I mean to trail him till I see the whites of their eyes or something. I can go as far as the Coast. Sorry. If you don't feel up to taking charge, Becky Young can do, call her up and bully her. Love. Rachel."

"Can you read it?" asked Alicia. "I took it over the 'phone, Jones couldn't get it straight."

"Oh, yes. It's clear." Clear as the sharp clatter of an alarm clock. Monday. Two days away. "Rachel came back for a few weeks," I explained, "to run my laboratory." The old discomfiture which I had felt, first with Alicia's mother, and then as the girl grew up, with her, almost a sharing of Rachel's obloquy, my knowledge making me an accomplice, just a faint pin-prick now, made me talkative. "Bill is her husband, Dr. William Price, he's in the navy, a lieutenant or something. Rachel has been expecting that he'd be shipped somewhere."

"Oh," said Alicia, indifferently. She stepped backwards down to the walk, and looked up at me with youthful awkwardness, wishing to be off and not quite knowing the password. "If you have time, come over. Mother'd be glad to see you." She had the same look I had seen on the girls who turned up for a brief period as assistants, a look which refused communication. You are the older generation, it said. You don't know what's happening to us, to our lovers, to our world! We keep our secrets, we'll have no truck with you! Her face was charming in its delicacy of planes and color, but it was a guarding shell.

"It was Dick Burchall you married, wasn't it?" She stood up taller, her fair hair swinging against her throat. "Didn't I hear he was in the service?"

"He enlisted," said Alicia, patient with me for my dullness. "In the Air Force. He wanted to be a Flying Tiger, you know, in China, but he's so good they won't let him go. He's teaching . . . something about . . . not radio, it's something quite hush-hush."

"That sounds better than China," I said, fatuously. "Wasn't his mother born in China?"

"That's not it! Dick believes somebody ought to do something! He's wonderful. He wants to help free India and everything!" Her narrow face shone with defiance, expecting attack. "You probably agree with Mother. She's an isolationist. But I promised my father I wouldn't start any more arguments."

I folded the little paper with Rachel's message into a small square. What was India to me, or China, or this girl? I had been housed with the past so completely that this sudden intrusion of the present was too violent.

"I'll tell Mother I saw you." For an instant, before Alicia hurried away, her long-legged lope reminiscent of Dexter's stride, she looked at me with . . . not curiosity and not compassion . . . just a sudden remembering why I was here alone.

No, China was nothing to me, nor Alicia. And Rachel was nothing to Alicia. And yet, because of Alicia, Rachel was Mrs.

Dr. William Price . . . only now you called him Lieutenant
Price, and I had to pull myself out of fragments into Dr. Carey
Moore, by Monday morning.

This gives me little time to finish the task I had set for myself, and yet without some sharp demand from outside I might
never have had the courage to follow my own story to its end.
I might have stayed at a safe comfortable distance from the
revelation for which I set out, under the pretext of unwinding
the stories of these others, seeming to be in mad pursuit but
really static. A good deal like the lover on Keat's Grecian Urn,
never, never can'st thou kiss, though winning near the goal.

My first thought, as I came back into the library, was that I
didn't care much for modern young people, they seemed to
have no . . . respect wasn't the word I wanted . . . *recognition*,
that was it, appreciation for achievement. They were completely self-absorbed. The girls who turned up fresh from
college in my laboratories were the same hard little pieces,
taking for granted everything they found, including my success
and reputation. Then one of those spirits of days deceased spoke
in Gilbert's quiet voice, with the curious lack of inflection or
emphasis which had become its characteristic, as if he withheld
all emotional color from what he said: "It's like the drug habit,
isn't it? The more you take, the more you need, steadily increased doses."

"What are you talking about?" I had asked. "Something
disparaging, I know."

"Human nature," said Gilbert. "And its hunger for homage."

"Homage?" I scoffed. "You ought to have to handle some
of these brash youngsters. You get homage enough, I notice.
Your patients fall flat on their faces in front of you!"

"That's my human nature," said Gilbert.

I stood by his desk in the library, smoothing out the bit of
paper on which Alicia had written Rachel's message, and

my next thought was that I could take a sudden lurch out of all this mulling over the past, wasn't it morbid of me, anyway, a symptom of my physical exhaustion? I had been sleeping better, eating more, I could fling a few things into a hand-bag, telephone for a taxi, and catch the noon train to town, see Rachel, check over the recent work with her, have a good start for the coming week. Why torment myself with what was gone? Let the dead bury their dead. The thing to do was just to get busy, all that important work on tropical diseases, extraordinary micro-organisms turning up in blood specimens, why, even Gilbert had said that what I was doing might be of terrific importance in the future the way things looked in the East.

I reached for the volume of Gilbert White's *Journals* to return it to its place in the bookcase, moving in a spasm of haste to be gone out of the house, out of the past, and knocked it to the floor. It opened at the fly-leaf, and there was Gilbert Moore, in his hand-writing, and the date, Easter, 1931. Nine years ago. And I must, no matter how frantically I longed to escape, come down through those nine years to the present, even as I had made the grim agreement with myself. It needn't take long. The last act is often the shortest.

Gilbert had brought the book out when we came for that Easter holiday, having picked it up because the old Selbourne naturalist had his name. He tried to read snatches from it to us, I remember, but we wanted to play bridge. Genevieve and Dexter Willetts had come in for the evening, and we had house guests, a young married couple, new friends of mine who were pleasantly impressed with an invitation for a weekend in the country. Genevieve never played bridge, cards gave her a headache, Dexter, rather tentatively, offered himself as fourth, and Gilbert coaxed Genevieve into the library to look over his new book. "Come along," he said. "You can help me compare his dates with those on the Ridge, you know when crows and crocuses first lift their heads."

Dexter was uneasy at first, nibbling at his long upper lip, wondering whether Genevieve would mind his playing, but the talk from the library reassured him, Genevieve sounded almost animated, and we had a good evening. At the end of it, Genevieve carried off the book, she was going to look it over more carefully, she might really start one of her own as Gilbert suggested, after all, she did notice just such details, and if he thought it would be interesting— She never could recall from one year to the next actually just when the first dog-tooth violet opened, she always looked for blood-roots too early.

After our guests had gone upstairs, and Gilbert was clacking down the legs of the card table, I said, "You certainly got Genevieve all pepped up. Dexter must have been grateful to you."

"We had a good time," said Gilbert, standing the table in the closet. "She really has an unusual knowledge of this place. She ought to make a record of it."

"She needs something to do," I said. "But imagine caring whether the crocus blooms a day earlier this year than last! It must be the farmer in your blood cropping out!"

"You don't have time for such trivial concerns, do you, Carey?"

"I certainly don't."

"You planned a garden when we bought this place. Remember? You even crawled around setting out crocus bulbs. 'I must arise now and dibble night and day,' you used to say."

"And the moles ate them, most of them."

"And you made soup of the fancy gladioli bulbs that Genevieve sent over. It wasn't very good."

"Those days are gone forever," I said, impatiently. "I've learned to eliminate what's unimportant. Cooking, gardening, doing the same thing over and over, never getting anywhere."

"As, for example, trumping your partner or whatever you call it." Gilbert's smile had no malice in it, and I laughed.

"Give me bridge instead of crocuses," I said.

"You can have it." Gilbert settled himself at his desk, and I wandered across the living room, emptying an ash tray or two, thinking how pleasant it was that I didn't have to straighten up the house, there were maids to do it in the early morning. I just didn't want dead ash odor in the room.

I reached the doorway to the hall, and glanced back with a "Good-night." Gilbert was watching me, leaning back in his chair, his face in the shadow of his hooded desk lamp, the dark stroke of his heavy eyebrows the only distinct feature. What was he thinking, what did he want? Behind him, the door stood open to his own sleeping quarters, a small wing built on beyond the study a year ago. I picked at random from the evening for a casual farewell sentence. "Dexter says John Burchall has gone west, did you know? I thought you saw him just the other day."

Gilbert tipped forward suddenly, the light catching the gray at the crest of his dark head, catching the alert tightening of his mouth.

"Good Lord!" he said.

"Some fantastic scheme, sheep-raising, I think. I suppose, being John, he knows all about sheep. He's left that house he was building for Ellen, the workmen don't know what he's ordered so they've quit, too. He probably got fed up with having Ellen in the home. Dexter says the Burchall boys just can't endure her, he gets that from Alicia."

"Dexter sounds like a sewing circle," said Gilbert.

The old antagonism for Ellen darted a forked tongue. They don't any of them think as highly of Ellen as you do, I wanted to say. What had set me suddenly on edge? The evening had been pleasant, our brief exchange of words light enough. Just that sombre, watchful look?

"Oh, you know the people out here," I said. "Original members of the grape-vine press."

"They might have a little mercy on Ellen. She's been pretty gallant." Gilbert looked at his watch. "Too late to call them tonight. I don't like it, Carey. John may have counted on a good contract for that confounded sanitarium, though why he should think anyone could finance anything right now . . . He had that bread-line look. And Ellen tried to see me last week."

"I don't see why you should feel responsible if people manage so badly that they get into trouble," I said. "The Burchalls should have made some provision for a rainy day. John's such a pretentious little wind-bag!"

"Oh, Carey, Carey! I hope it never rains too hard for your little umbrella!"

"Don't be patronizing, just because I'm not sentimental," I said, starting up the stairs. "We never do agree if Ellen's mixed up in it, anyway, and I'm not hard-hearted, I'm just sensible."

I fumed to myself as I undressed. Certainly people reaped what they sowed. Ellen's rapacious ambition, John's conceit. . . . What Gilbert knew, and what I have had to try to learn, is this: they reap what they sow, but they don't know their seeds! The labels are wrong, they sow in darkness.

The rest of the holiday was a tranquil, relaxed week. I suspected that Gilbert had seen Adelaide before he went back to the city on Monday, but he said nothing, and I thought it might be well, since I had my young friends the Thompsons with me, not to stop at her house on our drives and walks. If Adelaide was in some kind of scrape with John because of Ellen, she wouldn't care to see strangers, I told myself. We called at the Willetts' one afternoon and Genevieve fretted because Gilbert wasn't with us, she wanted to show him notes she had been making. She was trying to strike a style of her own not too like the book. The Thompsons were very courteous, listening while she read excerpts first from White and then from her own sheets. It's queer that I remember so distinctly some of the lines, when I felt only impatience at the time.

" 'The little laughing yellow wren whistles,' she read, with her crisp, slightly different intonation. "Isn't that delightful?" She repeated it several times, for all the world like a wren herself. "It's perfect, isn't it? And yet so effortless. He doesn't mention hylas, you know, the peepers. Did you hear them last night? I'm trying to do a line for them. They may be actually indicative . . . what is the word? . . . in—just here, not in Selbourne at all."

"Indigenous," said Mr. Thompson.

"But so many of the same birds, only earlier. I have always had the feeling that spring should begin earlier here!"

Dexter was in town at some kind of meeting of economists; for a moment the plaintive note of one bereft returned to Genevieve's voice. Then it was gone, as she suggested Friday evening for bridge. "Dexter will be here, for your fourth, and Gilbert and I can go off in a corner." Her protuberant dark eyes, with the sallow underlids, were a warmer velvet-brown, and her coiled vivid hair sparkled.

"She's quite a nature-lover, isn't she?" remarked Mr. Thompson, as we escaped, and his wife said, "Mr. Willetts . . . or is he doctor or professor? . . . is much more attractive, isn't he?"

I should have given the volume to Alicia this morning, to take back to her mother. Genevieve may have forgotten what started her off on what she no doubt considers a career. No, she remembers! Of course. That's the reason for the dedication in that little book of hers which was published a year or so ago, *Connecticut Calendar*. To G. M. from G. W. I do remember how amused I was at the first letters she sent to the small weekly newspaper out here. Has anyone heard the mourning dove this year? Please communicate. Has anyone seen the black squirrel reported near Danbury? People did communicate, apparently, and after a year or so Genevieve had a small box on an inside page, with Nutmeg Almanac as title. We had not been at the house on the Ridge for several years when Genevieve wrote Gilbert that her Almanac was now syndicated, newspapers all through the east were using it.

"Isn't it extraordinary!" I said. "I certainly thought Genevieve Willetts meant to spend her whole life enjoying being an invalid!"

Gilbert slipped the letter into its envelope and held it on his hand, weighing it gently. "The human personality is like a mole," he said, in his slow, dispassionate way. "Burrowing in the underground, tireless, blind, searching endlessly for its full satisfaction. It knows instinctively what its true food should be, what its full cycle of life should be. If it comes up in a mole-trap, that's too bad."

"I haven't seen her lately," I said. "I can't imagine her changed."

"She's happier, that's all," said Gilbert, and went off abruptly.

I thought, it has been lucky the way things have worked out for Genevieve, but I don't see what the mole has to do with it! It wasn't luck at all, it was Gilbert's gentle wisdom. I'll take the book to Genevieve tonight, when I go out for my last walk along the Ridge roads.

Now I must go on with that spring, and the years that followed. The Thompsons were enthusiastic about the country, and when we looked at the house John had built for Ellen, they stood on tiptoe to peek in the windows, past the little mothlike stickers on the panes. It was lovely, why weren't the workmen there, here it was all locked up and not really finished. When Gilbert came out again on Friday, they asked him about it. They'd like one just like it, they'd like to live on the Ridge, too.

"You can have that one, if you really mean it," said Gilbert. "It's for sale." He glanced at me, a secretive, worn look about his eyes. "Ellen's gone abroad. She's putting Linda in a school. She's going to live in France, she thinks."

The Thompsons were excited about the house. Adelaide had the key, she was to sell the house, collect John's payment . . . after all, his work was practically done . . . and send the rest to Ellen's bank. I went with them, my curiosity about Ellen dangling through my pleasure at the prospect of the Thompsons as neighbors in place of Ellen. Later, when I asked Gilbert why she had gone, what she meant to live on, he was not expansive.

"I saw her for only a few moments," he said. "It's Lawrence, of course. She wants to get away from the Ridge. We talk too much."

"But what made her decide so suddenly? After she had her plans all made? Something John said, of course."

"No. She says she can live more cheaply abroad."

"I should think she might be more comfortable," I said. "People haven't gossiped, they were all fond of Lawrence. But of course that accident was just too opportune. In a way you can't blame Ellen if he went off and got so drunk he couldn't sit on a horse. I know you've always stood up for Ellen. . . ." I hesitated; Gilbert looked sick, not bereft. "But he never would have got involved in all that money trouble without Ellen's pushing him."

"He wasn't drunk," said Gilbert. "He never was so sober in his life. I've made a wretched botch of everything, trying to tinker up the Lord's schemes. I've driven Ellen out of the country."

Gilbert told me briefly what Lawrence had done. "He'd tried so carefully to build a good farewell scene for Ellen. I felt it was a final behest. Ellen says I lied to her and treated her like a child."

I pitched my voice to sound like the friendliest chaffing. "But you probably did, my dear. Most of your patients want just that."

"I believe you are pleased! Ellen hiding in some third-rate pension. . . . Is that the way you are now? First you'd have no sympathy for anyone, now you rather enjoy their trouble?"

"You do have a way of preaching at folks. That's what they pay you for, isn't it? Only this time Ellen didn't like it."

"You don't even lose your temper any more, do you?"

"Not about Ellen. It's rather funny, the way flaws in my character always crop up when you've been having too much Ellen."

We may have been interrupted then: I remember nothing more, except a feeling that I had shown restraint. Perhaps the Thompsons came in, from further inspection of Ellen's house. One advantage of house-guests, I thought, was just this curtailing of unpleasant scenes. After all, Gilbert had no responsibility about them, and if he was bored, he always had the subterfuge of a report to write.

Not until last winter did I hear the story of Ellen's flight, and then from Ellen herself, when she had yielded to young Larry's insistence that France was no place for a girl like Linda, nor for his mother. Larry was travelling in Europe that summer with a wealthy family, tutoring the backward young son, earning money for his first year at college, and when the family put its plans into reverse and went scampering home on confidential news through the father's banking connections, Larry pried Ellen out of her small villa in Southern France. That must have been several years ago, before Hitler marched into

Poland. Queer, how those dates of world catastrophe all run together in my head. I did not see Ellen until last winter, when she came to New York, having heard of Gilbert's illness. But I shall put that aside until I reach it in proper chronological order.

These spirits of days deceased refuse to keep their order in time. They mass together, transparent as ghosts, who ever thought that we came one after another in sequence they ask, who thought that time was the tick of a clock or a list of numbers on a calendar, time is now, look through us, now is then, it is all here, coeval, coexistent. You thought you had so little time, why, you have it all! Only as I say a name to myself, like a spell, will images press forward through the transparency, forming a darker nucleus at which I may look. Instantly, if I loosen my intention to hold the images, the nucleus has merged into the vague pressure of all the past.

If I say Thompson, I have a moment's impression of the delight when they bought Ellen's house and settled on the Ridge. But they did not turn out to be the pleasant companions I had anticipated. They were pleasant enough, but the rate at which they produced a family, four children,—or is it five?—in seven or eight years, meant that they were engrossed in domesticity. Their house is amusing now, when I stroll past it in the evening, if I am not too late, with the light which streams from the dormer windows upstairs and the long bay window of the living room seeming vocal itself, so many sounds of talk and laughter and occasional bickering float out. I haven't seen either of the parent Thompsons during my stay here except as a figure hurrying past one of the windows. Adelaide Burchall has found them what she calls chummy.

Adelaide's name brings the quick picture of her call at my office, that first week after Gilbert's death, before I had been forced to accept what Dr. Allyn had told me. I thought that if I stepped back into the routine of my laboratories, I should find

myself, my ordinary, old, busy, eager self. He warned me I'd
crack up. Perhaps my condition made me more highly sensitized
to impressions. At all events, there is Adelaide, more vivid than
reality, so plump that her round legs, with the stubby, flat-
heeled shoes, seemed attached curiously to her bosom as she sat
opposite me, her white hair like dandelion fluff around her
plump, unwrinkled face, her brown eyes a trifle smaller in some
way, the lids thicker, and her freckles darker. She wanted to
talk about Gilbert, she was bringing what Gilbert had done for
her as a final wreath after the casket was closed, the grave
sealed.

"I didn't know he was sick," she said, reproachfully. "Not till
I saw the long obituary piece about him in the paper. I told
John we hadn't ever appreciated how distinguished Gilbert
really was. He was so quiet. I never told him how much he did
for me, and now it's too late. So I thought I'd come to see you
and tell you. I didn't suppose you'd be back at work, but I suppose that's the best way to bear it."

I set myself grimly to endure her garrulity, her insensitive
assurance that I wished to listen to her, thinking irritably how
unchanged she was under the added padding her small bones
now wore, still compact of the same smug certainty. Then, un-
willingly, I began to listen, to let her words have meaning.

She knew I wouldn't care to hear about her troubles, and she
didn't mean to go into that, she said. But things were just as bad
as they could be, and she wasn't very clever, herself, at thinking
out what was wrong. Gilbert had come to see her, he'd put two
and two together from what Ellen had let drop. "He told me
I'd been unfaithful to John. I simply spluttered, I was so
furious. But he went right on, I'd been unfaithful in a nice,
refined way, so I didn't even feel ashamed. Just when John had
most need of me. He wasn't being disloyal to Ellen, he'd told
her the same thing." Ellen was a subtle and devious woman,

he'd said, unscrupulous, perhaps. She tried to bend people her way. "She wanted your affection, Adelaide, at any cost, and she tainted your relation to John. So much static, interfering with proper reception. The boys have a radio, haven't they? You know what static is?"

Adelaide went chattering on about how confused she had felt, how she tried to defend herself, and I was conscious of dull pain, scarcely more than numbness, that Gilbert, always the champion of Ellen, would condemn her for Adelaide. Perhaps Adelaide was making it up, putting words into his mouth, wanting perversely to add to my burden. But she looked ingenuous enough, and suddenly her eyes filled with tears.

"It's strange," she said, "how some little thing can be the most important thing anybody ever says, isn't it?" She went on, her chatter softened, the tears brimming against her lids but not falling. Gilbert had walked about the room, not answering her confusion, and had picked up an old toy which the boys had found in the attic the night before when they were searching for baseball mitts and bats, spring being in the air. A stereoscope, one Adelaide had had in her own childhood, with a pile of yellowed cards.

"You know, each one has two pictures, side by side?" He had fitted the cards into the wire holders and held the wooden frame to his eyes, and Adelaide had stopped her voluble protests to watch, puzzled and indignant. Then he had set it down and turned, a red mark above his heavy eyebrows where he had pressed the wood so hard against his forehead.

"He made me listen to him," Adelaide said, "he was gentle, but it was like . . . oh, like a wind you didn't hear coming up, and it pushes you and you move faster and farther . . . I can't explain it. He said he'd just discovered something, he'd found out what marriage was. It was a stereoscope. It sounds silly to you, Carey, but he made me see it. You know, two ordinary photographs, quite flat, and then you peek through the glass and something happens, you get one picture, only it isn't flat, you look right into it, it's like a real street with real people. Nothing looks the same to any two people, he said. Mostly one of them tries to make the other look through his eyehole. If they work to see things together, each from his own angle, they make this deeper vision. I've never forgotten the way he said it. Then he joked about it. Maybe what the world needed was more and better stereoscopes, he said. An increasing range of blended vision until whole groups of men will see their lives with this new depth, this reality, instead of each man and his flat little picture. 'An intense and honorable attempt to reach this common vision, instead of a terrible struggle to impose one's own vision on the others.' I wrote that down after he went, and put it under the pictures in the box, and this morning I looked it up, so I'd remember his very words. John asks me sometimes what I keep that old thing on the bookcase for, but I never told anyone before. I didn't want John... well, he might feel embarrassed when he meets Gilbert if he thought ... you see?" Adelaide sucked in her breath, her lips folding in tight like an old woman. "Oh, goodness, I forgot Gilbert is dead! It's hard to remember, everything is just the same, I mean you're just sitting there in your white jacket and all those ... do you call them patients? ... waiting outside, and I never saw Gilbert any more, not for quite a long time."

"There are responsibilities in an establishment like this," I said.

"I'm sure Gilbert would want you to carry on," said Adelaide, primly, and suddenly her mood had changed. She had paid her tribute, she had found no mourning widow to console, our old attitude toward each other was in the air, a faint and inconsequential echo of all our encounters, my feeling of inadequacy, her calm censoriousness.

"It was good of you to take the trouble to come in," I said. "I appreciate it."

"It wasn't really any trouble." Adelaide blew her nose vigorously, leaving its tip pink. "I drove in with John, he took the nine o'clock to Washington. He hopes to land something in connection with all the camps for soldiers the government is building. He has connections through his W.P.A. work, you know, all those schools in the South? Isn't it funny the way things work out? If he hadn't gone off to Arkansas that time . . . or was it in Montana he met the senator? Anyway, I was telling him as we drove in this morning that hard times were exactly like labor pains, you thought you couldn't bear it, and afterwards you couldn't remember how it felt! But I mustn't run on like this, I suppose you have lots to do." She heaved her plump bosom in a preparatory exercise for getting to her feet.

"Nothing urgent. Don't go." A moment back I had wanted only to be rid of her, and now I wanted her to stay, to go on talking and talking, defeating the numbing silence which would rise up around me as soon as she had gone.

"If John stays in Washington, what will you do?" (How are you better off than I am, for all you have that pitying disapproval of me?)

"That's it! I could close the house and join him, if he could find some place for us to live. With both the boys gone . . . I had a letter from Henry's wife yesterday, Henry's too busy to write, he has a position in the Ford plant near Detroit, they want me to come out and see the new baby. Of course I'm not lonely on the Ridge, with Alicia just a stone's throw away. I've been doing a little Red Cross work in the village."

My secretary knocked and came in with a wire basket of letters. Adelaide inspected her and listened as Mary gave me several telephone messages. "There's a Miss Wills asking to see you, Dr. Moore. She had an appointment last week. (Cancelled, by unfortunate necessity, implied Mary's soft, quick voice.) She has a good background, she might work in very well."

"I'll see her presently," I said. When Mary had closed the door, Adelaide got to her feet in a sprightly little leap.

"I suppose you must miss Rachel," she said. "The only other time I ever visited your laboratory . . . it wasn't this place, it was just a little couple of rooms. . . ."

"Oh, I remember! Just after I started."

"Rachel came in." Adelaide laughed. "You could have knocked me over with a feather when I heard she was married at last! She was lucky, after . . . I couldn't help wondering how much he knew, I mean the man she married. Did you know she was getting married? It was to a doctor, wasn't it?"

"Dr. Price. Lieutenant Price. He's been trying to get Rachel for ten years."

"Well, then he must know," said Adelaide, vaguely. "Everybody knew. It's funny, when a . . . an affair . . . is as old as that one, it gets to be almost respectable. I suppose you just know they can't be having as much fun as they did at first. They have all the disadvantages of marriage and none of the advantages. They get used to each other, or they have tiffs, or one of them is sick, and yet they haven't anything to hang on to."

Rachel had said almost the same thing when she told me, one Monday morning, over a year earlier, that she and Bill had gone down to City Hall one noon and got married. "I've tried everything else," she said, "I might as well try legal matrimony. Seems to be something in it, the wives always win."

"I was surprised that I felt sorry for Dexter, of course I'd always blamed him, any wife would! But coming right then, when Bobby had run away and enlisted, and Genevieve had that relapse after she'd been so well, it was certainly one more thing for Dexter. I heard about it because that was when Dick wanted Alicia to marry him before he was sent away, and then he wasn't sent overseas but to that camp in Florida, but of course Alicia can't join him there, they discourage that, and it's impossible to find even a room. I always thought Dick knew more than he would say about what happened, about Rachel and Dexter, I mean. But he had that stubborn childhood attachment to Rachel, ever since the time he stayed at your house when we were having . . . let me see, was that the measles or the scarlet fever? Anyway, he'd never listen to a word against Rachel, and anyway it wasn't a thing a mother could discuss with her son. Oh, dear, I didn't mean to run on like this, one thing suggests another, after all, we have a lot in common, haven't we? I wish you'd come out to Connecticut oftener, Carey. Only now. . . . " Adelaide moved toward the door, a buoyant agitation about her. "All I came to say was just . . . we all miss Gilbert. If there is anything I can do . . . but there, you'll carry on."

When she had gone, I sat at my desk, shaken in curious, icy tremors that I couldn't control. She talked too much! Words like stones, bruising me.

My secretary opened the door from the inner office. "Will you see Miss Wills now, Dr. Moore?"

"No. I can't see her."

"She says she can't wait longer. She came up from Philadelphia last week, too. I'm afraid we may lose her, and she's really excellent."

Mary's voice was considerate but firmly challenging. I braced my knees together, and the chill was a spasm of nausea. "Send her in," I began, and then I screamed at her. "I can't see her! Didn't you hear what I said!"

Mary shut the door hastily, and I suppose managed the next hour or so with efficiency. A young doctor in the next suite pumped a sedative into me, Mary and one of the assistants took me home, and for more than a week my own doctor, Dr. Allyn, and a nurse kept me in a blessed twilight. At the end of that respite, Dr. Allyn sent me away. Unless I wanted to be a dope fiend, he said, I'd have to take hold and get well. Go off and have a good rest. He arranged for me to enter some kind of convalescents' home, and at the last moment I refused. I'd come back to my own house, I'd be better off with some activity, I could do as I pleased, eat as I pleased, there were neighbors on every hand, I hadn't been there with Gilbert for years. He listened, and surprisingly, agreed. "You know what you need," he said. "You have to get back to running under your own power." So I came. And now in a day I must go back. Rachel, who had come on for Gilbert's funeral, had taken charge at the laboratories. She was on the loose, she said, while Bill was in the final stages of indoctrination for his active service. If she hadn't stepped in, I should have turned the key in the door. Now I shall find my harness with its buckles shined, ready to drop over me.

I wish that Rachel were staying on. For all that I have been out of patience with her so often in the years of our association, . . . sixteen, seventeen, how long has it been? . . . just thinking of her has an effect I have never noticed before. But it feels familiar, and I know it belongs to Rachel. I feel relaxed, all need to assert myself, to impress myself, to defend myself, all competition, all suspicion gone. It is that single note on a tuning fork of which I spoke when I began this long search. Not just a passive relaxation, though, but anticipation. Rachel will like me, she will render back to me my fullest self, she will even make me laugh. I know it, just as I know that if I extend my hands toward a log burning in the fireplace, I shall feel warmth.

But I shouldn't wish that Rachel were staying, she is already a happier woman, whatever happens to Bill Price. She says I've given her such good boot training as technician, in spite of herself, that she can sell herself to some naval hospital.

Adelaide's comment on the long affair between Rachel and

Dexter had under its incoherent babbling a clear note of wisdom. I remember that Gilbert told me once, when I had set Adelaide down as tiresome, that if I listened through what she said, I should find that she rang a bell more often than she won any credit for. "She's so normal," he said, "that she shares the accumulated wisdom of all females."

Rachel never talked about Dexter, although imperceptibly as the years went along she accepted the general knowledge of the relationship. She would say she couldn't go off to Atlantic City for Easter because Dexter might possibly get a day off and she'd rather be where he could reach her. I was relieved that in spite of our easy, friendly association in work she did not make a confidante of me. She knows how thoroughly I disapprove, I told myself. Just on the grounds of such wasted time, if nothing more. If she had used that time for some original research, if she'd worked for a higher degree in science, she might have had a brilliant career. But after the first year or so I stopped urging her; if she preferred to stay in her modest rut as general factotum and smoother-out of difficulties, she was certainly useful to me. Not until that last evening in town before I came out to the Ridge did she talk of herself. Dr. Allyn had told her I was well enough to discuss business matters, if she wished to see me before I left, and she came in to tell me all was well at the laboratories and I was to stay away without concern about them just as long as I wished, with the one proviso that if Bill got his sailing orders, she might suddenly vanish.

We were in my sitting room, upstairs in the duplex apartment where Gilbert and I had lived for several years, little gusts of snowy wind rattling at the terrace doors, distant whistles from East River tugs, a coal fire glowing in the basket in the small fireplace. Rachel had strolled about the room, looking at the few paintings, American primitives which I had started to collect.

"Funny old things, aren't they?" She came back to a low chair by the fire. "Do you like them or is it just fun to run them down?"

I leaned forward, trying to focus my eyes on the painting opposite me, and I didn't know why I had bought it. Here I sat, dressed, no longer shaken by dreadful fits of shivering, the furry after taste of sedatives cleared out of my mouth, my mind apparently rid of their blurred after effects, and I didn't know why I had wanted the pictures, nor why I had insisted on this apartment, they were messages to which I had lost the code. What was enjoyment, how did you feel it anyway? I may have looked befuddled, for Rachel spoke quickly.

"It's such a pleasant apartment, Carey. Maybe someday Bill and I can have one. Not all this elegance, he'll have to pick up practice from scratch when he gets back. But it will be fun. I've lived in bureau drawers too long." She went on talking, in her droll, casual way, and I listened, aware of her voice, indifferent to what she said. If she would go away, perhaps I could find that code. If the salt hath lost its savor. . . .

She was trying to divert me, she was offering me her story as something to consider for a little while, in place of the blankness which of course, being Rachel, she recognized. "I'd like to tell you about why I pulled out," she began, and for all I had no capacity for interest that night, what she said plays itself out in my head now like a recording.

"You've been a great comfort," she said, "you were so con- sistently disapproving and uncurious. I knew how I'd find you no matter how upsidaisy I was. I was pretty droopy sometimes."

Sometimes, for a week or so, Rachel would be quiet, intent on small jobs about the laboratory, her face expressionless and plain; and then she would come in with her gay nonsense, a kind of bloom over her clear pallor, her eyes bright under the long lashes, her hair freshly waved, her lipstick remembered. That night she looked almost beautiful, her delicate throat a warmer white than the satin of her blouse, a repose in the soft contours of her face.

Rachel is not an analytic person. She told me bits of talk, small incidents, and now as I let the record play itself over, I begin to understand her, and Dexter, too, a little. "It was Dick, of all people," she said, "who told me I ought to get married. I'd had my fun, now I ought to give him and Alicia a break. Funny, isn't it? Back when it began, Dexter couldn't make a clean break because of Alicia. He did want to make an honest woman of me, you know. And now Alicia wouldn't desert her mother, because then Dexter would never be free. 'He'd be relieved if you did get married,' Dick told me, 'so he could stop wobbling.' I just pulled my head out of the sand where I'd had it all these years and didn't even ask how he and Alicia got to be so damned smart."

Rachel wanted Dick and Alicia to marry. She had been afraid that Alicia would bruise herself against Henry's indifferent egoism, and had been delighted when suddenly the girl turned to Dick. Not because of Henry's marriage, he'd had other girls for years; something about the war, Dick's fiery young idealism and Henry's shrewd foresight in assuring himself a safe berth. Rachel couldn't do a thing but get out of their way! And Dick was right, Dexter needed to stop wobbling. For a long time he had been much happier during the periods when he had broken off forever than he had when he came back.

"I'm sure," said Rachel, "that at the beginning it was good for Dexter. My loving him. I chased him till he gave in! We had such fun . . . we never had time enough together . . . he didn't want to hurt his wife . . . and I thought just my loving him couldn't hurt anyone."

Rachel made a quick downward gesture with her hand, a bidding the past to lie down and keep quiet.

"That's not true," she said. "I didn't think anything, except how could I see Dexter, where would he be at such an hour, what was he doing now, when would he call me. How can you think ahead, when you're twenty and in love? You're just plain crazy mad. Anyway, I was. Later. . . I did tell myself I wasn't harming anyone, I could keep it all separate. But nothing stays separate, does it? All mixed up together in a jolly little hellish mess. Still, if you always thought of consequences, you'd be paralyzed. So what?"

Consequences. I had always tried to look ahead, to have foresight.

"You know, Carey, men, fairly civilized men, are more bound by contracts than women. They have more sense of obligation. They're supposed to be the wanderers and women the good little faithful numbers. Look at the way we act, the minute we don't have to hang on to a meal ticket! Why, I could name you a dozen girls . . ." She held up one hand, bending back the thumb with the forefinger of the other hand, beginning to tally, and then stopped. "One's enough. Just me."

I can fill in the gaps in Rachel's tale. Those early years, when Genevieve had no interest except in her own health and her desire to possess Dexter, a desire she expressed in tormenting him. If he winced, then she proved the bond between them. Rachel may have saved the man from complete distrust of himself. He couldn't believe himself quite so selfish, quite so clumsy, if Rachel found him otherwise. But he never could free himself completely. When Genevieve had substituted nature notes for notes on her pulse beat or blood pressure, when she had been too busy writing her diaries and calendars to track down Dexter's every move, Dexter still was not free, instead he fashioned chains of self-torment. Honor? Weakness?

"There were other men," said Rachel. "Two . . . Bill and one other. I thought if Dexter didn't need me, and they did . . . No, I mean I just liked having somebody. You wouldn't understand that, Carey, you're very self-sufficient, you're much more intelligent, of course, or do I mean intellectual? But as soon as Dexter found out, he'd come back. Oh, Lord, I did seem to make a mess of everything! Bill wanted us to get married, but I couldn't, on account of maybe Dexter would finally make up his mind. Dick put me straight. If I married, that would be an end for Dexter."

I didn't know the second lover. Rachel always had friends, which of them?

"You never knew the other man," said Rachel. "It wasn't Gilbert," she added, softly. "I might have loved him, he was pretty wonderful, but he never wanted any woman except you. He was a swell friend. You don't mind my saying that, Carey? I wanted to say it. I keep thinking of things I want to tell him." Her face softened, blurred, in a suffusion of tenderness. I was afraid she was going to cry, but she stood up quickly, pulling her fur jacket over her shoulders. "Now I'll run along to my lonely cot. I don't mind being alone, now I've really got Bill, isn't that funny? Oh, Carey, you're marvellous, so staunch! Get well, darling! I'll hold the fort for you." Her swaying toward me was like a caress, and then she was gone, running lightly down the curved stairway.

I sat immobile, feeling my hands heavy as stones, my whole body heavy, weighted. I would not cry. Rachel had no business washing me over with the flood of her easy emotionalism, just when I was struggling to regain some sane control. Presently it was safe to move, and I went slowly down the stairway to my bedroom on the floor below. My bags were packed, the nurse had gone, in the morning I would go. I couldn't remember why I had decided to go back to the Ridge, but the heaviness of stone was in my head now, I would lie down like a carved figure (on a tomb) and in the morning I would go as I had planned.

Now it is almost midnight of my final day on the Ridge, and tomorrow, another morning, I shall go back to the city, to the laboratories. I had intended to take a final walk along the roads, with the moon not yet half full slanting gold through the blossomy young leaves before its early setting. But the spring rain which started at twilight has fallen steadily, straight silver sheets of it when I open the door and let the light shine out against it, the sound like rivers in the ditches along the road. I can make the circling walk in my mind, past the Burchalls' house, shut and dark, Adelaide having joined John in Washington; past the Willetts' house, with lights in a pyramid, one upstairs where Alicia sits, writing to Dick, a row of lighted windows downstairs, the living room, the study, where Dexter and Genevieve sit, Dexter with copies of English newspapers, periodicals, American papers, making notes for his new course on current affairs (a terrible flood gullying all the roads, tearing along all the ditches!) and Genevieve looks back to see what day in April last year or the year before the first heavy spring rain fell; past the Thompsons', the walls bulging with light and voices; past the looming hulk of the house that had been Dr. Randall's and then Ellen's, darker, emptier than the others, the windows boarded against stones tossed by small boys, the roof line sagging, (what happened to the sanitarium scheme? or to the threat which was rumored about for a year or so that it had been sold again and would be turned into a school for delinquent boys, problem children?) and back at last to sit here at Gilbert's desk in the Moore's house, lighted now, aired, cobwebs brushed down after the years when the Moores never came. I can take the walk a dozen times in a breath and keep my feet dry.

Gilbert must have come out at some time in those years to clear out his desk. He was always orderly, nothing of the squirrel about him, but here are none of the casual things any man leaves if he thinks he is coming back, letters to answer, receipted bills, half used match books. Even the filing cabinets where he kept his case histories have been emptied. I don't know just when he did it, perhaps before one of his trips to serve as advisor in some distant state on commissions about the criminally insane, or youthful criminals, or, lately, the combing out of mentally unfit among drafted men. Any time you'd like to come along for the trip, just sing out, he always said, when he announced his departure. But I never went, I couldn't leave my work, what could I find to do in Syracuse or Chicago or Los Angeles while he was so pleasantly in demand?

Surely he had no premonition of his death. A sudden fatal embolism after a minor unalarming operation is nothing a man can know beforehand! Except that Gilbert had a knowledge of the shape of life, he was conscious that he moved along an inevitable arc, he had always the wise acceptance of that arc which most of us fight down right up to the instant when the gravel slithers over our closed coffins. Not that he went around morbidly brooding about the end of life. Quite the opposite. He valued being alive more highly as he moved up and down its arc. He had tried once to draw me within his knowledge . . . oh, more than once, but once he made a desperate effort, and now I can hear his words as he meant them, life is an act of faith, love is an act of faith, it must renew itself.

Now I can't even clear out his desk for him, tear up his personal papers, burn what he would not wish alien eyes to see. Like everything else, he took care of it himself.

There's just one scrap of paper, a sheet torn from a desk

calendar, which must have fallen out of the volume of Gilbert White's *Journals*. It has two notations, Jer. 45, 5, and Rom. 13, 11, and after some search I've located a little worn Bible with my own name written inside the mildewed cover. I must have carried it to Sunday School when I was a child, and brought it with my few belongings when I first came East. Perhaps the verse is like the sign men used to look for, opening the good book at random and thrusting in a finger blindly, to see what God would say.

"And seekest thou great things for thyself? seek them not: for behold, I will bring evil upon all flesh, saith the Lord: but thy life will I give unto thee for a prey in all places whither thou goest."

The second is short. "And that, knowing the time, that now it is high time to awake out of sleep."

I remember Gilbert's saying once that the men who wrote the Bible were damned good psychiatrists.

"It would be interesting. I might do it when I have to retire from active practice, to make a manual, a modern psychiatric manual, out of Bible phrases. I'll bet I could find a match for every scrap of knowledge we think we worked out just yesterday or tomorrow! We have new Latin names, they hit the nail with the gold hammer of God!"

"That might be interesting," I said. "Of course there are lots of books about the Bible already. I should think a real handbook out of your experience would be more in demand."

"Oh, but think of the fun I'd have doing it! Maybe by that time you'll relax. You could help hunt up the verses."

"That's a long time off," I said.

I wonder whether he was thinking of that when he set down these two references? He couldn't have intended them for me, how could he have thought that I should ever look at that particular book? I am not in the least superstitious, but the silence in which I exist is so profound that I strain my ears for the faintest sound . . . and then, of course, hear only my own blood. But suppose he did mean them for me . . . not that he did, of course . . . what then? The second is easy, a warning, that, knowing the time, that now it is high time to awake out of sleep. Gilbert may have been thinking of anything when he jotted that down. He might very well have meant the nation, or France, or some stupid patient. Knowing the time, the time is late, the time is now.

The first stirs an old antagonism, so that I want, instantly, to contradict and disprove it. What's wrong about seeking great things? Any intelligent person has ambition, doesn't he? Thy life will I give thee for a prey. Your own life will be your quarry, you will hunt it down, you will hold it as booty, you will feed upon it. You will have no fear of it. That was Gilbert. And the opposite, the reverse . . . life hunts you down, you are the prey, the victim. I wish I could ask Gilbert if he meant me to read that verse. I can't, and the grief which I have refused is now a physical pain, an aching in my breasts. I did not know grief hurt like this.

"I doubt that you are capable of real feeling," Ellen had said, and so I come back to the day which I had meant to blank out forever as if it had never happened, to forget, to obliterate. It's there, with all the other days, it is in fact the reason I am sitting here tonight, at the end of my journey through the past.

Gilbert had been complaining mildly that he was off his feed, perhaps he should have a check-up, some small thing out of kilter, when you get along toward fifty all sorts of small defects might crop out. He had always been very well, and I hoped he wasn't going to develop the kind of petty concern about little fluctuations which a good many of the men I met enjoyed. Doctors, especially, seemed unable to resist taking their own pulses! I told him he'd no doubt eaten too many vitamins, and he always was careless about lunch, forgetting to eat it half the time. If he would go home at noon, I'd see that the cook had a good luncheon for him. Of course it would do no harm to have a check-up unless it gave him new symptoms to worry about. If he'd come down to the laboratory, we'd give him blood tests.

"I'll try soda mints," he said.

That afternoon I suddenly realized that I hadn't reminded him I was taking the evening train for a meeting of a medical association at Cincinnati the next day at which I had been asked to read a paper, the only woman on the program. My secretary called his office at intervals and at last, after she had said, "If I don't get him this time, you'll have to let me give the message, or you'll miss your train," she found him in. I told him, and he was silent, until I said, "I have to rush, Gilbert. I'll take the evening train tomorrow, but I might as well come directly here, I can have breakfast on the train. Are you there? Did you hear? You're all right?"

"Oh, yes. I was about to call you. Dr. Allyn suggests Medical Center. I might as well go and get it over with."

"Does Dr. Allyn think anything's wrong?" Mary, the secretary, was just clipping the typed sheets of my talk into a folder, opening the portfolio to insert it. "Gilbert, if you'd like me to stay . . . should I go up there with you?"

"No, thanks. I just swallow barium and give them a look-see. You know."

"Did you feel worse. Why did you go to Dr. Allyn? I didn't know you . . ."

"Oh, I had a stomach ache. Don't give it another thought. Have yourself a fine time. Carey . . . remember to look at your audience! Don't keep your nose down on your manuscript. Good-bye."

I did offer to stay. I didn't want to.

I was in fine fettle when I opened the door of my office the morning of the second day. My talk had gone over well, I had several stimulating suggestions from specialists in leucocythemia, on which I meant to work, I had slept well (I always enjoy a bedroom on one of the good trains, it makes such a pleasant interlude in which you are safe and sheltered and well served and need make no effort of any kind) and I was eager to tell some of my force about the trip.

Ellen Hunter was sitting with her back to the window, her face not distinct against the brilliant sky. I thought how chic she looked in her cossack hat and coat of black Persian, and then as she turned her head, her harsh, stark face with livid crescents under her light eyes frightened me. Mary, looking hastily out of the little room where she worked, her face puffy and crimson, her lips sucked between her teeth, puffed her cheeks fuller and banged the door. I set down my overnight case and portfolio and said, "Why, good-morning, Ellen. I didn't know you were in town."

"I am, though. You'd better sit down."

She told me. She had just come from the hospital, Gilbert was dead. An emergency operation, just a simple appendectomy. "Gilbert refused to allow them to notify you, he said he'd be sitting up when you came back." The operation was all right, Ellen had seen him for a moment last night. This morning he was dead. An embolism in the brain. Nobody's fault. "They didn't know how to reach you. I said I'd tell you. You'll have to go out to Medical Center."

I sat down at my desk and waited for the walls to stop pitching around me.

"They should have wired me, telephoned! They had no right!" My thickened tongue caught between my teeth.

"Gilbert arranged it," said Ellen. "I was in his office when you called. He told you he was going."

"For a check-up . . . tests."

"He said the meeting was very important to you."

I ground my fist against my mouth and hated her. "Did he send for you? What were you doing with him?"

"Instead of his wife, Carey? Doesn't look too good, does it? Oh, I can't go on! I meant to torment you! I can't. Gilbert wouldn't have it that way."

How dreadful! All those doctors, friends of Gilbert's, some of them dinner guests at our apartment occasionally, and Ellen on hand with her officious solicitude, and I, his wife, not there! They wouldn't ever understand! No one could blame me if he knew how it had happened, Gilbert himself had said it was nothing . . . he had sent me away!

I pulled myself together, feeling the toxic stimulus which so often, for me, has followed any shock, my body battening down at threat of disaster, boarding the windows of the senses against winds of peril, urging its hidden forces to stand by. I am acting very well, I thought, controlled, mature. (Do you think you can sidetrack all pain? When had Gilbert asked me that, at another time when he had preferred Ellen to me?)

"Did you see Dr. Allyn?" I asked abruptly.

"For an instant. He came into the reception room where I waited."

"Did he ask where I was?" Dr. Allyn had never liked me, I could tell by the way he never sent any patients to me, and whenever we met he looked at me with a bored, heavy-lidded patience. And now. . .

"No," said Ellen. "He knew."

"If you will pardon me," I said, pressing the buzzer. Mary almost fell into the room. "Please get Dr. Allyn on the wire for me." She nodded, and left the door ajar as she went to the telephone.

"Let me tell you how it was," began Ellen.

"In a moment, please." I was dignified, I had more serious matters than Ellen to attend to, she would see how I could meet tragedy. The metallic jingle as Mary dialled the number was noisy in the room, and then Mary's choked voice, asking for Dr. Allyn. A pause, and she came again to the door.

"Dr. Allyn's in the operating room, Dr. Moore. He left word for you, he'll call at the apartment at twelve today, there's no need for you to go to the hospital, he's gone ahead with the instructions your husband left."

"Thank you," I said. "Please close the door."

That was when Ellen said that I was incapable of feeling. She hurled words against me in her light, imperative voice, knowing that I was sealed and guarded, insistent that I listen to her. She didn't know whether I was jealous, or merely annoyed that the picture hadn't been quite right, loving wife was not on hand. She wished Gilbert had sent for her because he wanted her. But he hadn't.

It had been the children, Larry and Linda. Ellen's money, what there was of it, was tied up in France, French investments, and you know what they're worth today, and the villa, supposed to be rented, but of course no rents coming through, not even any news. Gilbert had been helping Larry, who was a pre-med student at Cornell, and he'd coaxed Linda out of her wild scheme to train as a nurse so that she could get back to France and find a young aviator she had been crazy about at fifteen, into good stiff work at a preparatory school, making up missing credits. She might go on to college, she was marvellous in languages. "She's much better, away from me," said Ellen, sombrely. "Gilbert saw to that." Ellen herself had a small job, translating foreign news for a small weekly. Enough to subsist on.

She looked prosperous enough. She had thrown back her Persian coat, she wore a sleek, saffron-colored wool frock, with heavy metallic embroidery at the throat, her restless hands looked younger than her ravaged face, the wrists delicately veined under the smooth pale skin.

"I know," she said, surprisingly. "I still look smart. I will as long as my French duds last. Gilbert hadn't told you about the children? No, he wouldn't."

He had arranged a trust fund for them, in case. . . . (No! Hold yourself steady, admit nothing!) When they were past need of it, it would become a fellowship fund, the George Randall fellowship. "He loved my father," said Ellen. "Gilbert was very tenacious about his loving."

I glanced at my wrist watch. Twelve o'clock. A summons. I couldn't even send word, I prefer to stay here, in my office, better insulated.

"That's why he sent for me," said Ellen, getting to her feet. "You'd have known anyway, it's in the will."

"It's quite all right."

"It's far more than that. And it's not as if you needed . . . anything."

"No." I spread my hands along the polished wood of the desk, gripping the edge. That was solid, part of my achievement, that at least I had.

"We've always hated each other, haven't we?" Ellen walked across to the window, a stiff black silhouette against the shining glass. "You had what I wanted . . . but you were uncomfortable with me . . . you couldn't make me admit you had anything. You did well to be jealous of me. I'd have taken Gilbert if I could. Not at the beginning. I was a fool then. I thought I had to have . . . oh, a man smoother, more urbane, one who knew his way around, for the kind of life I planned.

"Then you turned up, such a funny little timid hen. You've learned how to preen your feathers. But Gilbert never changed.

Later, before I went off to France, I was mad for him. I couldn't see him, hear his voice, why, even see a man with heavy dark eyebrows like his . . . I told him, that night at the hospital, even cartoons of John L. Lewis would start me off. I told him just to hear his laugh. . . . I'd go off like a Jew's harp inside, the wildest thrumming. Oh, dear God, why did he have to die? I don't know why I say all this to you. I thought I'd lived down that kind of longing for him. The other day, in his office, I just felt peaceful. Gentled. That's the word. Glad Gilbert thought better of me at last."

Ellen turned toward the door, her dark lidded eyes heavy with an inward groping look, and I knew she didn't see me, and if I spoke, Gilbert's voice would be louder in her ears.

"He didn't blame me for Lawrence's death. I always thought he did, he had told me I must go find him, and I was too late. But he said, only two days ago, that each of us has to bear his own full responsibility for himself, he can be pushed only to his own limits. Then he laughed, and said that was a hard saying, and he wouldn't explain it, and I was much nicer now I knew how remorse tasted, but I needn't eat too much of it. I'm telling you, Carey, because I had a feeling he was talking about himself. Well, this is good-bye, isn't it?"

He was talking about himself, and about me. I stared at the door through which Ellen had gone, thinking only that his last words had been for her, his last concern about her children. I went through the next days without feeling, nothing but a dry kernel inside my battened house. Dr. Allyn and other doctor friends of Gilbert's managed decisions, Mary signed checks, and I moved automatically through the necessary formalities. I didn't believe Dr. Allyn when he warned me, I meant to stay hidden.

Now I have reached the end of my exploring. Each of us

must bear his own full responsibility. Then life will be your prey! Gilbert meant me to find that. If he were here now, I would ask him to show me how not to be afraid. It is almost morning, the rain has stopped, the air is sweet with its clean wetness. In a few hours I shall start back to the city.